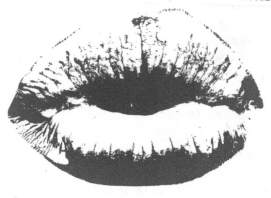

ABOUT A KISS FOR A KISS

I'm Jake Masterson, single dad, and the General Manager of Seattle's NHL team. I walked away from a career as a player so I could raise my daughter. For the last twenty-plus years, Queenie has been my main priority, but now she's getting married.

And there's a small complication.

A beautiful, sexy complication named Hanna.

She's my son-in-law's older sister. Or at least that's how they were raised. The truth is a little more scandalous than that.

I've been drawn to her from the moment I laid eyes on her. And I spent months trying to keep a lid on that attraction.

Until we finally give in.

It starts with one searing kiss, but quickly ends with us between the sheets—and in the shower, and the hot tub, you get the picture—and turns into months of sneaking around.

Here's the problem: we live on opposite ends of the country. It can't be anything but casual. And as I've already said…it's complicated.

But when Hanna finds out she's pregnant…suddenly things get real serious.

PRAISE FOR HELENA HUNTING'S NOVELS

"Nothing hits me in the feels like a Helena Hunting romance!"
—*USA Today* bestselling author Melanie Harlow on *A Lie for a Lie*

"Helena Hunting delivers a smart, funny, emotional story that grabs you from page one."
—*Wall Street Journal* bestselling author Ilsa Madden-Mills on *A Lie for a Lie*

"A sexy, heartwarming read!"
—*New York Times* bestselling author Elle Kennedy on *A Lie for a Lie*

"*A Favor for a Favor* is now my favorite hockey book of Helena's! I loved how real the characters were. I loved the build of their friendship. It's my favorite trope, and Helena did it superbly! A huge recommend from me. Also, it was really funny too. *wink wink*"
—*New York Times* bestselling author Tijan

"Stevie and Bishop are just as funny and hot as you've come to expect from Helena Hunting! Grab a pizza and crack it open because you will not want to miss the steamy shenanigans."
—*USA Today* bestselling author Sarina Bowen on *A Favor for a Favor*

"A thoroughly delicious read."
—*USA Today* bestselling author L. J. Shen on *Kiss My Cupcake*

"An absolute delight from start to finish, this delicious enemies-to-lovers romance sees an independent and driven heroine and an equally ambitious hero take a journey to love that is unpredictable and filled with hilarity, a dash of sweetness, and a touch of steam."
—*Library Journal*, starred review, on *Kiss My Cupcake*

"Perfect for fans of Helen Hoang's *The Kiss Quotient*. A fun and steamy love story with high stakes and plenty of emotion."
—*Kirkus Reviews* on *Meet Cute*

Published by Helena Hunting
Cover Image by Michelle Lancaster @lanefotograf
Cover Model: Tommy Pearce @tommyfierce
Cover Design by Eileen Carey
Developmental Edit by Lindsey Faber
Editing by Paige Maroney Smith
Proofing by Julia Griffis
Proofing by Amanda Rash of Draft House Editorial Services
Formatting by CP Smith

A KISS FOR A KISS

NEW YORK TIMES BESTSELLING AUTHOR
HELENA HUNTING

A Note to the Reader,

When I decided to write Jake and Hanna's story it was intended to be a fun, light romance. But as I peeled back the layers of these two, complex characters, with very different but parallel histories, I realized that I was going to go much deeper than I originally thought.

A Kiss for a Kiss deals with a later-in-life pregnancy and with that comes very real discussions about the potential challenges and complications that come with being over forty and expecting, including Hanna's pregnancy history and a previous miscarriage.

As a mother and someone who understands that loss and has joined friends as they experienced similar trauma, I want to give you, as my reader, that insight into the story before you start this journey with Hanna and Jake. These two hold a special place in my heart, and they deserve their happily ever after.

Xo
Helena

For the mothers who lost before they had a chance to love.

A KISS FOR A KISS

PROLOGUE

We Can Do Anything

Jake

"TEXT WHEN YOU get home so I know the two of you made it in the door, okay?"

"Sure, Dad." Queenie pushes up on her tiptoes and kisses me on the cheek, then she turns to her fiancé, Ryan Kingston. "Okay, Boy Scout, let's get you home."

King pushes away from the wall he's been leaning against. He sways unsteadily, eyes slow to track, but when they land on my daughter, a smile pulls up the corners of his mouth. "I'm gonna be your Boy Scout for the rest of my life. And you're gonna be my Queen. Just a few more months and you're mine forever."

Queenie laughs. "I've been yours since the day I met you. Come on, before you say embarrassing things in front of my dad and Hanna." She slips her arm through his and helps him down the front steps to the Uber waiting at the end of the driveway.

Hanna, King's older "sister", or at least that's how most people know her, steps up beside me, her shoulder brushing my arm. "I hope he's not too much of a mess tonight."

"I'm thinking all those shooters Queenie kept making for him are probably going to result in a serious hangover tomorrow." I wait until the Uber pulls away from the curb before I shut and lock the door.

Tonight was my daughter's engagement party. She's marrying the goalie for the NHL team I manage. Throw a bunch of hockey players and their significant others together for a laid-back barbeque and an open bar and the result is a lot of happy stumbling down the driveway into Ubers.

"I definitely feel like Ryan is going to have some regrets come morning." She pats my shoulder and her fingers drag along my biceps. "You tired or do you want to jump in the hot tub for a bit and unwind?"

Hanna's definitely on the tipsy side. I can tell by the glassiness of her eyes and the flush in her cheeks. It isn't often she lets loose like this. At least not that I've seen so far, and we've had enough family get-togethers and events over the past several months. With more to come since the wedding isn't that far off. Truth be told, I'm feeling the scotch I've been drinking tonight, too.

"Hot tub sounds good." Our gazes meet and lock for several beats, enough for me to wonder how good of an idea this actually is.

We've been dancing around each other for months. Ever since the first time we met, actually. The attraction has been clear from day one, and the more time I spend with her, the harder it becomes to ignore.

Planning the engagement party for Queenie and King means we've spent a lot of time trading text messages, emails, phone calls, and more recently, Zoom chats that often have little to do with tonight.

Her grin widens and her chocolate brown eyes sparkle with a hint of mischief. "I'll change then."

"You bring that red bikini?"

"Are you keeping track of my swimwear?"

I lift a shoulder in what I hope is a nonchalant shrug. "You look good in red." I skim her cheek with a knuckle. "And this blush you're wearing is particularly sexy."

"You're trouble tonight, aren't you?" Her fingertips dance along my traps as she brushes past me. "And yes, to answer your question, I did, in fact, bring the red bikini."

She disappears down the hall to the spare bedroom, where she's sleeping tonight. Because I invited her to stay at my place this weekend rather than at King's. It's not that she isn't welcome there. It's more that she wants them to have their privacy. It also means I get more time with Hanna, so it's a win all the way around. And I'd be lying if I said I hadn't been thinking a lot about time alone with her this weekend.

I change into my swim trunks, pour myself a scotch, heavy on the rocks, and her a glass of wine before I make my way outside. I set the drinks on the outdoor dining table, remove the hot tub cover and check the temperature, making sure it's not too hot.

Once I carry the drinks over and set them in the cup holders, I sink into the hot, bubbly water, stretch my arms out, let my head fall back and my eyes close. All the time I've been spending with Hanna is starting to get to me.

Reminding me that I'm in my forties, and very much still a bachelor. There are a lot of reasons why getting involved with Hanna on a romantic level would *not* be a good idea. Queenie and King's relationship being at the forefront.

But she's fun. And sexy. And we get each other.

A minute later, the sound of the sliding door opening and closing and the slap of flip-flops against the deck have me cracking a lid.

"You better not be sleeping already!" she calls out.

"Not sleeping, just waiting on you."

I watch as she pulls the tie on her robe and the terry fabric slips over her shoulders, revealing that red bikini I'm such a fan of. Hanna is all curves. Amazing curves. The kind I've fantasized about putting my hands on plenty of times over the past several months. And with us spending a lot more time together, it's been hard not to give in to the constant draw.

I rise from the water and hold out a hand as she climbs the steps. Her fingers slip into my palm, sending a jolt down my spine and a stirring inside my swim trunks. "Could you try to be a little less beautiful all the time?" I tease as I help her into the tub.

"Could you try to have more of a dad bod?" She drags her fingers down my abs, brows waggling, a smile on her gorgeous face. "You are definitely good for my ego, Jake." She pats me on the chest and sinks into the water on the opposite side of the tub from me.

Which is probably a good thing since I feel like we're playing with fire tonight. The kind I wouldn't mind pouring a gallon of gasoline on just to watch it burn brighter.

"That was a great engagement party. I think the kids had fun, don't you?" She stretches her legs out. Her toes skim the outside of my thigh and I barely resist the urge to run my hand up her calf.

I don't know what's in the air tonight, but things seem... different. Heightened.

"Yeah. It was good," I agree.

She pokes me with her toe. "Then why are you frowning? You've been off all night. What's going on?" With all the planning and talks we've been having, Hanna and I have gotten to know each other better. And she can read me pretty easily.

"I don't know. On one hand, I'm happy for King and Queenie and I know he's going to be a great husband to my daughter, but I spent all these years raising her, and being there for her. They've been living together for months, but for some reason, it's all kind of hitting me. It's real now." I take a sip of my scotch. "It's different from when she went away to college, and even when she moved out of the pool house and in with King. There's this hole I didn't expect."

"It sounds like empty nester's syndrome." She moves to the spot beside to me, where the glass of wine I poured her sits.

"Is that what this is? I'm all morose and shit."

She chuckles and props her elbow on the edge of the tub. "You need to look at it with a fresh perspective, that's all. You're not losing your daughter. It's different with girls. Sure, she's found her partner in life, but she's always going to be your baby girl. And the two of you are so close."

"I don't know what to do with all of this freedom," I admit. "My entire life up to this point has been revolved around raising Queenie and my career."

"Which means you did your job. And that's a good thing. Think about it, Jake. This is the great part about having a kid young. Sure, you lost out on the freedom of your twenties, but in some ways, this is even better. You're in your forties. You have a great job, you're in incredible shape." She twists and pulls her knee up so it rests against my thigh, her arm extending along the back of the tub, fingertips skimming my shoulder. "You have all of your hair."

"I'm definitely grateful for the last one," I joke.

"You have great hair." She runs her fingers through it. "It's sexy." She bites her lip and then shakes her head. "Anyway, what I'm saying is, you're in the prime of your life. Most people in their forties are raising teens, or maybe their kids are getting ready to go to college. You've done all that. Now you can just live. You can date. Have fun. Do whatever you want."

"Fun would be good." My gaze drops to her lips. "And I'd like to do whatever I want."

"Me, too." Her bottom lip slides through her teeth. "Like right now I could kiss you."

"You definitely could." I skim her thigh under the water with my fingertips.

She nods. "There's nothing stopping us."

"So why aren't your lips on mine yet?" I ask.

Hanna shifts again, her wet palms come to rest on either side of my jaw, and she presses her soft lips to mine.

I slip my hand under her hair and wrap it around the back of her neck. For a moment, I question whether this is a good idea. But when our lips part and our tongues meet, I forget all the reasons why it might not be.

I groan as I sink into the kiss and our tongues tangle. She tastes fruity, like the wine she's been drinking. She straddles me and settles in my lap, her breasts pressing against my chest.

She breaks the kiss for a moment and our eyes meet. "I've

5

been thinking about this for months."

"I've wanted to know what your lips taste like since the first day I met you," I confess.

She runs her fingers through my hair again and I grip her hip and pull her closer. Our mouths collide, tongues stroking, teeth clashing.

"I knew it would be like this," she murmurs and rolls her hips.

"Like what?" I pull the tie on her bikini top.

"Explosive. Intense." She bites the edge of my jaw, hands smoothing down the sides of my neck. "I want to spend the rest of the weekend in your bed."

"I've wanted you to spend every weekend you've been in town in my bed."

"Me, too." Her lips drag across my cheek. "We'll keep this between us."

"No one needs to know what we do behind closed doors," I agree.

"Or in hot tubs."

What's left of the weekend is spent trading orgasms all over my house.

And in the months that follow, my appetite for Hanna never wanes.

Instead, it grows. And changes.

And starts to become something I want more of, even though I know eventually it has to end.

CHAPTER ONE

A Beautiful Complication

Jake

Queenie's wedding day

KEEP IT TOGETHER, *man. Just keep it together.*

I do a couple of rounds of those breathing exercises that my daughter is so damn fond of to help calm me down some. She does them often with the kids she works with. I reach for the glass of scotch sitting on my dresser and take a sip. Between the deep breathing and the scotch, I should be able to find some "chill", as Queenie likes to say.

A gentle knock comes from the other side of my slightly ajar bedroom door.

"Come in," I call out.

Hanna's head appears, and that calm I found a second ago disappears. Her chocolate brown eyes scan the room until they land on me.

"Hey." She steps inside, closing the door behind her with a quiet click.

I let my gaze drop, taking her in. Hanna is wearing a floor-length lavender dress with a slit that runs up the right side, stopping halfway up her thigh. It hugs her curvy figure in all the right places. Curves I've had my hands on countless times over the last several months. "You look stunning in that dress."

A single spiral of her long dark hair skims her cheek, the right side pinned up with a tiny purple jeweled flower. I want to brush it back, so I have a reason to caress the graceful slope of her neck.

"Thank you. You look pretty damn good in that suit." She crosses the room, her smile coy as she arches an eyebrow. "But even better out of it."

I chuckle. "Have I told you lately how good you are for my ego?" As soon as she's close enough, I wrap an arm around her waist and pull her against me. "And this dress is going to look even better when it's decorating my bedroom floor at the end of the night."

She tips her chin up and I drop mine, our lips meet and part, tongues sweeping out. Even though I know now is not the time for this, I allow myself to sink into the kiss, if only for a minute. It's been like this since the engagement party.

In the beginning, I tried not to notice how much I liked the sound of her laugh or the way her face lit up when she smiled. But what started as lingering glances and harmless flirting quickly evolved into something not so innocent the more time we spent together.

Every time she's come to visit from Tennessee, which has been at least once a month since the engagement party, we've ended up in bed together.

And now here we are, making out. Again.

Hanna breaks the kiss and covers my mouth with her palm. "We need to put a pin in this for another twelve hours."

"Agreed." I kiss her palm before I pull it away from my mouth. "But you started it with the suit comment."

"I know. Sorry. I actually came in to see how you were holding up, not make out with you like a horny teenager." She blows out a breath and backs up a step. "How are you doing?"

"Nervous as hell, to be honest."

She gives me an understanding smile. "Nervous is normal. It's a big day for all of us, and giving away your little girl is no small thing."

"It feels like only yesterday I was changing her diapers. All those years gone in a flash." I snap my fingers. "And now here we are."

"Here we are," she agrees.

"Am I good?" I motion to my tie. As the general manager of Seattle's NHL team, I'm used to wearing a suit and tie. I'm also used to large crowds and public events. What I'm not used to is walking my only daughter down the aisle.

She smooths her hands over my lapels, adjusting them before moving on to my tie. She makes sure the knot is tight before she slides her hand over the purple silk. "There. Now you're perfect."

"I'm far from perfect, but as long as I don't look like a hot mess, I'll take it."

"You never look like a hot mess, Jake." Her gaze lifts and a smirk tips the corner of her mouth. "Take comfort in the fact you're the eye candy for everyone over forty, and the real showstopper is Queenie." She winks and her fingertips drag along the side of my neck as she adjusts the collar of my dress shirt.

"How is she doing?" Queenie seemed excited this morning when she and her bridal party took over the pool house to get their hair and makeup done.

"She's great. No jitters and all excitement," Hanna assures me.

"That's good. I'm glad to hear it. I want today to be perfect for her." Or as perfect as it can be.

At twenty, I became a single father after Queenie's mom decided she couldn't deal with the demands of raising a child and bailed on us when Queenie was a few months old. With the support of my parents, I raised Queenie on my own. I walked away from a career as a professional hockey player so I could be a present parent. I adjusted my career path in order to be a father first. I think I did a pretty decent job, all things considered.

And Queenie is marrying the nicest, most stable guy in the

universe, which is exactly what my princess deserves.

"Today will be perfect. Ryan loves Queenie more than hockey and milk, which is saying a lot."

We both chuckle. King takes a lot of good-natured ribbing over the fact he orders pints of milk at the bar rather than beer.

"He's going to take great care of her heart," I tell her.

"And she's going to be a fantastic partner for Ryan." Her eyes turn glassy for a moment.

I can't even begin to imagine how hard this is for her. Her relationship with Kingston is anything but conventional, and this wedding has proven challenging at times. I place my hand over the one still resting on my chest. "He's an incredible man. And the only one I would ever deem worthy of my baby girl."

She smiles warmly. "They're going to make a wonderful team."

"They really are." I give her hand a squeeze. "How are *you* doing?"

"Oh, I'm fine." She fiddles with my collar again, like she can't figure out what to do with her hands. "I need to get the girls in place. I'll meet you out there in a few?"

She's about to pull her hand away, but I squeeze it, keeping her close. "Thank you for being such a huge part of this day, and for being so good to Queenie."

"She's easy to love. You've raised a wonderful, kind woman."

She picks up the glass of scotch sitting on my dresser and folds my hands around it. "Take a deep breath and drink this. I'll see you in the kitchen." She winks again and slips out the door, leaving me to finish getting ready.

A handful of minutes later, I join the wedding party, who is assembled in the kitchen—apart from the groom, who's preparing to walk his parents down the aisle.

Hanna is calmly giving directions, checking on the boys the same way she did with me, making sure ties are straight, before she moves on to the bridesmaids, adjusting bobby pins and smoothing out dress straps.

No one has noticed me yet, so I take a moment to observe

my daughter's friends. They're a great group of kids—adults really—and some of them only a decade my junior.

Stevie, one of the bridesmaids whose hair is nearly the same color as her lavender dress, steps up beside me. "How's it going, Jake? You ready to get this party started?"

"About as ready as I'll ever be. Where's Queenie?" I glance around the kitchen. She should be easy to spot, but all I see are her friends and several of my players. Since Kingston is the goalie for the NHL team I manage, most of the groomsmen are also his teammates, which technically makes me their boss.

"I just saw her. Hanna, have you seen Queenie?" Stevie calls out.

Hanna pauses in her mission to pin a boutonniere to the best man, Bishop's, lapel. "She was here a second ago." Hanna glances around the room. "Where in the world did she go?"

"I think she's with Lavender and Kody? Do you want me to check?" Lainey, another one of the bridesmaids and wife to my team captain, Rook Bowman, asks.

"That's okay. Stevie, can you make sure this is straight on your husband?" Hanna pats Bishop's chest, then crosses the room and threads her arm through mine. "Let's find the bride and make sure she hasn't started an arts and crafts project."

"I wouldn't be surprised if that was actually the case." Stevie grins and then points at the guys. "Hey, you two need to cool it or you're both going to be shitfaced before the ceremony is even over."

I glance over to see Gerald, Kingston and Hanna's brother, and Bishop with their flasks halfway to their mouths.

"Mine is full of grape juice," Bishop says in an effort to lie.

Stevie strides across the room and holds out her hand. "If you're lying, you're sleeping on the couch."

Hanna shakes her head. "I really hope Gerald makes it through dinner without passing out." She guides me around the corner and puts her finger to her lips before pointing to the living room. "Look," she whispers.

And there she is, my baby girl. All grown up and looking

more beautiful than I have words for. As is her way, she's not focused on herself, or the fact she's about to marry the man of her dreams. Instead, she's crouched in front of the flower girl and ring bearer—Lavender and Kody.

They're not family, but they might as well be with how close Queenie has become with them. Lavender is the team coach's daughter, and Kody is Rook and Lainey's son. She's been working with both kids in art therapy.

"What is she doing?" I murmur, trying to eavesdrop on their conversation.

"Being her amazing, selfless self." Hanna hugs my arm. "God. Just look at her. She really is extraordinary."

I nod, unable to tear my eyes away from my daughter. Her dress pools around her slight frame, the skirt an oasis of gauzy layers sparkling with intricate beading in the form of tiny purple flowers. I can feel myself choking up. All the time she and I have spent together, the good and the bad, we've been through it all and here she is, on her special day, making sure that everyone, even these two, feel included.

Lavender's vibrant blue eyes are wide and she has two fingers in her mouth.

"Are you nervous?" Queenie asks.

Lavender ducks her head.

"Want me to tell you a secret?"

Lavender peeks up from under her lashes and nods.

"I'm nervous, too. But you know what's awesome?"

She shakes her head.

"Your mom and dad are going to be waiting for you at the front, and Kody is going to be right beside you, all the way down the aisle. And if it helps, you can focus on Kingston, because he's going to be waiting at the end of the aisle, too."

"I can hold your hand if you get scared, Lavender." Kody holds out his hand, and Lavender wipes hers on her dress before taking it.

"You two are the best flower girl and ring bearer in the entire universe." Queenie claps her hands. "And I have something super special for both of you as a thank you for being part of mine and King's special day. It's sitting at your table, and you can go get it right after the ceremony is over. Does that sound good?"

The kids smile and murmur something I don't catch, and Queenie gives them both a hug. "We should get ready. We'll be walking down the aisle soon."

"I'll give you two a minute together." Hanna steps up and takes the kids back to the kitchen.

"My baby girl." I take Queenie's hands in mine. "Let me look at you." I shake my head. "When did this happen?"

"When did what happen?" She smiles up at me, looking absolutely radiant.

"When did you grow up and become this beautiful young woman? I swear it was just last week when you were drawing murals on your bedroom walls in Sharpie."

She throws her head back and laughs. "I hope the people who bought that house never took the wallpaper off."

"I hope they did. That was your first of many masterpieces." I squeeze her hands. "How are you feeling? You ready for this?"

She squeezes my hands in return. "Nervous. Excited. But so ready. It feels really good to be so sure."

"You two are meant for each other. I could see it right from the beginning." I bend and press a kiss to her cheek. "You look stunning, exactly like the queen you are. You know, when I named you Queenie, it was because the moment you arrived in the world, I knew that you would forever be the ruler of my heart." And in some ways, I wonder if that love I have for her—how it trumps everything and everyone else—is part of the reason her mother wasn't able to handle being a mom. Because everyone would always come second to my little girl.

"You know I never get tired of hearing that story." Her eyes soften.

"Good, because I never get tired of telling it." I wink. "And now you get to rule over Kingston's heart."

"Okay, now you're getting cheesy."

We both laugh and then she blows out a breath. "I love you so much, Dad. Thank you for letting us take over your entire house for this. I know it's been a lot."

"I'm glad I've had the chance to be part of it. You have such a great group of friends. And honestly, Hanna has been the one organizing everything. I just got the emails and phone calls and messages telling me what was happening and when."

"She's been a godsend, hasn't she?" Queenie glances over my shoulder, the sound of laughter coming from the kitchen. "I don't think I can thank her enough for all she's done, especially with the number of trips she's made from Tennessee to ensure everything runs smoothly. I'm going to miss having her around."

I shove down the brief pang of guilt. Hanna has been adamant that what's going on between us stays a secret. And I get it. Her family situation is already complicated. "She's been pretty incredible."

And she has. Queenie's mother has never earned the title. To the point that, after a lengthy discussion, Queenie decided not to invite her to the wedding. She didn't want the disappointment, and frankly, she doesn't deserve to have her day overshadowed by the woman who hasn't shown up for any of her important milestones.

When Queenie asked Hanna to be part of her bridal party, Hanna graciously accepted the role. And in the time between then and now, Hanna has inadvertently stepped in and taken on the maternal role that was missing in Queenie's life. It happened naturally, a slow evolution, where Queenie would go to her about the things I couldn't help with. It's been good for both of them.

I bought Hanna a gift as a thank you, and of course, this morning has been so busy that I forgot to give it to her. I should have done it when she stopped by my room, but I'd been distracted.

The grandfather clock tolls, signaling the top of the hour. Queenie's eyes go wide. "It's time."

"We should get in line, shouldn't we?"

"We should." She wraps me up in a tight hug. "I love you,

Daddy."

I don't know if it's possible for a heart to swell and break at the same time, but that's how it feels. "I love you, too. More than anything."

We head back to the kitchen where the girls fawn over Queenie and express their excitement in high-pitched squeals.

Stevie takes Queenie by the shoulders. "In less than half an hour, you're going to be Queenie Kingston, which is a seriously badass name. And you couldn't have picked a better, milk-drinking-rule-following-yet-dirty Boy Scout to marry."

Lainey elbows her. "Censor, Stevie, there are kids around."

"And me." I raise my hand.

"Right." Stevie cringes. "Sorry, Jake."

Hanna raises a hand to get everyone's attention. "We all need to take our places."

"Right. Yes. Places." Stevie moves to the front and Queenie takes her place beside me at the back of the line.

Stevie and Bishop lead the way, and each pair walks down the aisle with Lavender and Kodiak going right before us. They hold hands and Lavender tries to hide behind him and shakes the basket, leaving a trail of petal clumps in her wake.

From my position, I can see all the way to the end of the aisle. King, dressed in a black tux, stands with his hands clasped, gaze shifting from Lavender and Kody to the doorway where I am, waiting for the wedding march to start.

Lavender begins to struggle with all the attention about halfway down the aisle, which is when King leaves his post at the altar and comes to meet Lavender and Kody. He crouches down and says something to the two of them.

There's a rustle in the crowd and lots of clicking of cameras when King scoops Lavender up and gives Kody a fist bump.

"What's going on?" Queenie asks.

I shift to the right. "Stay behind me so King can't see you," I whisper.

She does as I ask and makes a little noise, somewhere between a shriek, a giggle, and a sigh when she sees King carrying

Lavender down the aisle to a chorus of cheers and clapping.

"He really is awesome, isn't he? He's going to be such a good dad."

"You're both going to be great parents, but maybe let's get through the ceremony before you start planning your family?"

She laughs again and then the music changes. "Oh, it's really time, Dad." Her eyes take on that glassy quality and she tips her chin up, as though she's fighting back tears.

I pull a tissue out of my pocket and dab under her eyes. "You got this. Now take a deep breath, because we're about to walk down that aisle."

I place her hand on my forearm and cover it with mine as the strains of the wedding march filter through the backyard. We step out into the sun, the light refracting against the beading on her dress, making a million tiny rainbows appear on the fabric. Her smile widens when King comes into view, and I have to force her to slow her steps so she doesn't run down the aisle and launch herself at him like I sense she wants to.

His face lights up when she finally rounds the corner. His eyes move over her, darkening with lust. It briefly, and irrationally, makes me want to punch him in the face. Except he's her fiancé and about to become her husband. And I'm already well aware that these two are madly in love with each other. So, I tamp down that fatherly protectiveness and remind myself that she's no longer the little girl whose boo-boos I used to kiss better.

I give her a kiss and a hug, and she takes her place at the altar. I sniff once and clear my throat, trying to keep my emotions in check. I'm not much of a crier, and never have been. But she's my baby girl, and it doesn't matter that she's an adult. I'll always remember the first time I held her in my arms, so tiny and new, and how she seemed like an impossible miracle.

I blink a few times and fish a tissue out of my pocket, just in case. My gaze catches on Hanna, standing with her bouquet of flowers in front of her, ducking her head every so often to dab at her eyes.

She meets my gaze and I quirk a brow, a silent, "*Are you*

okay?"

She tips her chin down and gives me a quick wink, signaling that she is indeed okay, before she refocuses on King and Queenie. And I do the same.

Watching my daughter and her son join their lives together.

CHAPTER TWO

A Little Too Real

Hanna

I'M ONLY HALF-tuned into the conversation happening to my right. Soon, I'll have to get up and give a speech. I feel like a bit of a fraud. Not because I don't believe I belong at the head table as one of Queenie's bridesmaids. She and I have grown close. At first when she asked me to be part of the wedding party, I thought she was being nice by trying to include me, to give me a role in the wedding, when the one I truly wanted to be able to claim wasn't mine to take. But I quickly realized that wasn't the case. That the request had been genuine.

I accepted regardless of motive, but in the months leading up to the wedding, I found myself taking on a new role in her life. Not just as a friend, but as a sort of maternal figure. Queenie came to me for wedding advice, and my unique relationship with Ryan gave me a special kind of insight.

Ryan and I were raised as siblings, but the truth is, he's not my brother. An accidental teen pregnancy threw my life into upheaval. When my parents found out, they were upset at first, but they weren't about to leave me to fend for myself. I wouldn't consider terminating the pregnancy, so that meant I could either raise him on my own—the father was in college and not interested in being involved in Ryan's life—give him up for adoption, or the third option my parents presented. They would adopt him and raise him as their own. I'd been young and scared, and allowing my parents to adopt Ryan had seemed like the best choice.

But today has tested my emotional limits in ways I didn't expect. And maybe I should have. It's an odd position to be in—sitting up here as one of the bridesmaids. Being part of the wedding party for Queenie and Ryan, who most people here believe is my much younger brother, when in reality, he's my son.

That's been the most difficult part of today—the realization that I'll always experience the landmarks in Ryan's life from the vantage point of his sister, even though in my heart I'm more than that. I'll forever be in this strange middle ground between sibling and parent. I thought I'd come to terms with that long ago, and for the most part I have, but today hasn't been easy. When I was younger, I didn't have the same perspective I do now. I couldn't see, in the same way, all the things I would have to take a back seat on.

I sip my wine, doing my best to keep a smile on my face and stay engaged in the conversation. I haven't been able to stomach much for dinner, which is a pity since what little I've managed to eat has been delicious.

My mother approaches the head table. She pauses to talk to Queenie and Ryan before she makes her way down the table to me. "Sweetheart, can I talk to you for a moment?"

"Of course, Mom." I set my napkin on the table and push my chair back, meeting my mother on the other side of the table.

She threads her arm through mine and leads me away from all the guests. When we're a safe distance away, she puts her hands on my arms and gives me a warm smile. "You were fabulous today. I'm so glad you and Queenie get along so well. She seems like a good fit for Ryan, doesn't she?" It sounds like she's asking for confirmation more than anything.

"They're perfect for each other," I assure her. And they are. Queenie is full of life, effervescent, and willing to take risks and

19

think outside the box, which is exactly what Ryan needs in a partner.

"Good, good. That's good. You look so lovely in this dress. Such a perfect fit for the bridal party."

"Thanks, Mom. Is there something you need or..." I let it hang.

"Oh. Right. Yes." She adjusts my hair and the strap of my dress. "I wanted to tell you that you're not obligated to give a speech tonight if you don't feel comfortable. I know it's awkward for you, so if you don't think it's something you can handle, don't push yourself, dear. I know today is emotional for you."

That's mom speak for *don't embarrass yourself*. She continues to talk around my relationship with Ryan, and the fact he's not actually her son. It's been a real challenge. And one I really don't need shoved in my face today. "Thanks, Mom. I'll keep that under advisement."

The master of ceremonies for the evening steps up to the mic and gives it a tap. The feedback is extreme and loud.

"We should probably sit back down since the speeches are starting," I tell her.

"Oh yes, of course." She kisses me on the cheek and heads back to her seat and I do the same.

If I wasn't trying my damnedest to hold it together before, I sure am now.

Thankfully, the emcee is Ryan's best man, Bishop Winslow, whom I'm sure is going to provide some much-needed comic relief. He's an interesting choice, in part because he's clearly not comfortable speaking in front of people, despite half of them being his teammates. And also because he has the bedside manner of an agitated polar bear.

"Why does he have to touch it every single time?" Stevie pushes her chair back and hikes her dress up so she doesn't trip on the hem as she rushes to the podium. Her heels are under the table, so her feet are bare.

When she reaches Bishop, she bats his hands away.

He makes a face. "Why are you slapping me, bae? What am

I doing wrong?"

She huffs, "Just let me help."

He steps away from the podium and clasps his hands behind his back, letting her adjust the mic for him while giving the crowd a shrug. Everyone chuckles, especially when he rocks back on his heels and starts whistling the *Jeopardy* theme song.

Stevie shakes her head at him and turns her attention to the waiting guests. "Sorry about that. Shippy doesn't usually do public speaking."

His mouth drops open and he holds his hands up. "Whoa, whoa. What the he—H-E-double hockey sticks?" He manages to censor his language.

She shrugs. "What? I'm not wrong. You never do."

"You called me Shippy in front of a hundred people, bae." He motions to the guests sitting at the tables. "Not cool. You're gonna pay for that later."

She rolls her eyes and spins around, but she's smiling as she walks away. "Whatever."

"You say whatever now, but later you'll be saying—"

"Don't finish that sentence unless you want me to toss your ass into the pool, Winslow!" her brother, Rook, shouts from a few seats down.

Bishop cringes. "Oh shit. I mean, shoot. Right. Sorry, grandparents and anyone with young children. I'm not the best at keeping it PG with my words, which I'm gonna have to get better at since Stevie has already told me she wants a bunch of little Bishops running around. Hopefully, they have her personality and not mine." He sends a wink Stevie's way.

"And her ability to watch her language," Ryan adds.

That gets another chuckle from the crowd.

Bishop shrugs and thumbs toward Ryan. "I told them I'm not the best at this whole speech thing. I failed it back when I was in middle school, probably because I ad-libbed with swear words. Anyway, as you all know by now, I'm the best man and Ryan's best friend. We've known each other for a lot of years. When we were teens, we played for the same team when we

21

were in the minors. Ryan is basically the reason I stayed out of trouble, not because I was particularly good at following rules, but when you're like me, and you have the personality of a rabid porcupine, not a lot of people will put up with you."

"You're more like a declawed panther, Shippy!" Stevie heckles.

He gives her a look and shakes his head. "I'm coming for you later, bae." He brings his attention back to the guests. "She's such a beautiful distraction, isn't she?" He runs his hand nervously over his tie. "Anyway, where was I?"

"You were talking about your winning personality and your bromance," Rook reminds him.

"Right. Yeah. So Ryan, being the stand-up guy he is, decided I was worth all the headaches. And an unlikely friendship began. Sort of like a bunny befriending a grizzly bear." Bishop pulls some paper out of his pocket. It's lined school paper. He unfolds it and sets it on the podium. "Anyway, I wrote a bunch of shit—I mean stuff—down, mostly jot notes and things I wanted to touch on." He clears his throat and smooths a hand over his tie, then takes a sip of his drink.

"For those of you who don't know King very well, I can tell you, he's the most responsible guy I've ever met in my life. He drives like a ninety-year-old on Sunday afternoon. Sorry if there are any ninety-year-olds out there, but man, you better not be in a rush to get anywhere if you're riding with King. Aside from his excessive caution when driving, he's a pretty great guy. And loyal. You've never let me down, buddy, except for that time you let Rook take shots at me."

The head table chuckles, and a few people look around at each other, not understanding the reference. "You see, this guy right here is the reason I'm married to Stevie. If it weren't for his advice, and his patience, I don't think I would have gotten my head out of my butt long enough to figure out how to get her to date me. Man, I'm rambling, aren't I?" He tugs at his tie again, his face starting to turn red, possibly from embarrassment.

"Back to King. He's a rule follower, through and through,

but when he met Queenie, well . . ." He waggles his brows and smirks. "Let's just say, for the first time in all the years I've known him, I watched him struggle to follow those rules he likes so much."

He takes another sip of his drink. "I wanted to talk about the way these two actually met, because everyone believes that was when Queenie started working for the team, but their first introduction came six weeks before the start of the season."

I glance down the table at Ryan, whose cheeks are on fire. Queenie's cheeks have gone pink as well, but she's hiding a grin behind her hand. She whispers something to Ryan, who arches a brow and calls out, "You might want to move this along unless you're planning to relinquish your best friend status."

That gets us another round of giggles.

Bishop smirks. "Don't worry, King, I won't give up all your best secrets. Anyway, I can tell you that Queenie must have left a lasting impression, because King is the most even-keeled guy in the universe. Not much ruffles his feathers, but Queenie lit a fire under his a—butt." He smiles, and it's no longer a smirk, but something softer. "Queenie, you came into King's life at exactly the right time. He needed someone to shake things up, and you did that in just the way he needed. You made a great guy an even better man. If there were ever two people who are meant for each other, apart from my bae and me, it's the two of you."

Queenie hugs Ryan's arm and mouths *thank you* to Bishop.

"You took my milk-drinking, khaki-wearing, straight arrow of a best friend and you pushed him outside his comfort zone. So thanks for that." Bishop lifts his drink, which is mostly empty, and toasts the couple.

More speeches follow, and when it's my turn to speak, I freeze and only manage to say how happy I am for Ryan and Queenie and how they're made for each other. It feels slightly disingenuous to talk about my relationship with Ryan as my brother, even though that's how most of our lives have been spent. Jake and my parents are the last to speak before Queenie and Ryan.

Jake takes his place at the podium and sets his glass of water to the side. He takes a deep breath and shakes his head. "I don't think I'm going to make it through this without a few voice cracks." He clears his throat. "King, you are such a lucky man to get to love my daughter."

Ryan smiles and kisses Queenie's temple.

"Queenie, what a phenomenal woman you've become. I'm always so impressed by your resilience, your compassion, your zeal for life. From the moment you were born, I knew you were destined for great things. You have this light, this way of making people fall in love with you." He pulls a tissue from his pocket and clears his throat. "There were times when I wasn't sure if I was doing this whole parenting thing right, Queenie, and I feel like we learned a lot by trial and error, especially when it came to things like hiding all the Sharpies and only leaving the Crayola markers lying around. That was a rough lesson."

"For you, not for me," Queenie quips.

Everyone laughs.

"We've been through a lot together, you and I. Lots of up and downs. Every boo-boo we put a Band-Aid on was a life lesson for me. I couldn't protect you from the world, no matter how hard I tried, so I did my best to make sure you always knew I was going to be there to help you up when you fell. You've become a strong, independent woman, and I'm so damn proud of you. And you've picked such a great partner." His gaze shifts to Ryan and he blows out a breath. "King, I know you're going to love my daughter the way she deserves to be loved, without reservations or conditions. You make her happy in a way no one else ever has. It's been a joy to watch you two grow together." He raises a glass. "To a love that knows no boundaries."

Glasses clink and then my parents get up to speak.

"Ryan, you were such an unexpected surprise, and we're so glad you came into our lives when you did. You were exactly what our family needed. Your kindness and your gentle soul enriched all of our lives so much." My mother dabs at her eyes. "Raising you was an honor and delight, and it's so humbling to see what a wonderful man you've become. You've made us so very proud. I have faith that you will be a dedicated husband, and eventually a father, exactly the way you are in every other part of your life."

It's a real battle to keep my emotions in check as my mother continues to talk about all of Ryan's accomplishments.

And I know that without their support and their guidance I would never have had the opportunities I did, and neither would Ryan. It's a bitter pill to swallow, knowing that if it had even been a few years later, I would have been able to raise him instead of handing over the reins to my parents.

Once the speeches are finished, I breathe an internal sigh of relief, thinking that we're through the hardest part. At least until the father-daughter and mother-son dance.

And that's when the reality of today truly hits me.

I will never have this moment with my son. I will never walk down the aisle beside my own child. And it stings.

I slip out of my chair, excusing myself to the bathroom as the song is coming to a close, unable to keep my emotions in check. I don't head for the pool house, which is closer. Instead, I slip around the edge of the yard and carefully make my way back to the main house. Once inside, I toe off my heels and walk down the hall, ducking into the spare bedroom. I close the door behind me with a quiet click and will the tears away.

But it's too much.

CHAPTER THREE

A Shoulder to Lean on

Jake

"WHAT'S THIS ABOUT you and King meeting before you started working as my personal assistant? And how come this is the first I'm hearing about it?" I ask Queenie as I move her around the dance floor. Mostly I'm digging for information. Queenie and I don't keep much from each other. She usually tells me what's going on in her life, and the only times she's kept things from me that I would consider important are when she's worried I'd be upset—or disappointed.

But this little piece of information and King's reaction, which was to turn the color of a beet, make me curious.

Her smile grows wry. "We met at a bar."

"King doesn't go to bars. Not unless he's with the team."

"It was the night he found out about Hanna."

"Oh." I pull back so I can see her face. "That must have been hard for him."

Queenie smiles. "It was. I didn't know he was one of your players, and he obviously didn't realize I was your daughter. He was trying to get drunk."

"King was trying to get *drunk*?" I glance across the dance floor where Ryan is expertly waltzing with his mother. Like he's taken lessons. He probably has. It seems like something he'd do.

Queenie throws her head back and laughs. "I know, right? To be fair, *trying* is the operative word. He had six drinks lined up in front of him and they were all full because he genuinely doesn't like the taste of alcohol. He said he was a fan of milk, so I ordered him a White Russian. We traded secrets and promised to keep them for each other."

"And that was it?" I arch a brow.

"The rest is history, isn't it? All you need to know is he was the gentleman he always presents himself to be, even while slightly intoxicated." She pats me on the chest. "Anyway, fate seemed to have plans for us with the way it kept throwing us into each other's paths, and now here we are, starting the rest of our lives together."

"He's a good egg."

"The best."

With each rotation on the dance floor, I catch a glimpse of Hanna sitting at the head table, a small pile of tissues sitting on top of the pale purple linen. Her gaze is fixed on the other side of the dance floor, and it looks as though she's struggling to keep it together.

I know today has been hard for her. I could see it on her face when her mother and father spoke about what a remarkable man King's become and how he came into their lives at the right time.

As the song comes to an end, we do another rotation and I notice that Hanna's chair is empty.

The deejay changes the music to something upbeat and guests flood the dance floor, allowing me to step back and survey the room. I don't spot Hanna anywhere. She may have stepped out to use the bathroom, so I grab a drink from the bar.

After a few minutes and still no sign of her, I poke my head into the pool house, but it's empty, so I make my way to the house. The bass of the music vibrates under my feet. The kitchen has already been tidied, thanks to the cleaner that Hanna hired to help manage things today. Another reason for me to thank her.

I make a stop in my bedroom and retrieve the small gift box, tucking it into my pocket. I hope if she's having a hard time tonight, this will cheer her up.

I stop at the closed door to the spare bedroom and knock three times. "Hanna?"

"I'll just be a minute. Is everything okay?" she calls.

I debate waiting in the kitchen or the living room. I decide neither is ideal. "Is it okay if I come in?"

I'm greeted with silence for a few long seconds before the door finally opens. I slip inside and close it behind me.

"Are the kids okay?" She wrings her clasped hands. Her eyes have that slightly watery quality about them. The kind I associate with tears.

"The kids are fine. They're dancing and drinking and doing what they do when they're celebrating a wedding and have no idea what the future holds for them, apart from a lot of love."

She exhales a relieved breath. "Okay. Good. That's good."

I set my drink on the dresser and take a step forward and put my hands on her shoulders. "Are *you* okay?"

"I'm fine." Her focus is on my shoes.

"Hanna." I slip my finger under her chin and tip her head up. "You don't have to put on a brave face for me." Over the past several months, our relationship has evolved in a lot of ways. We share similar histories, although the way they unfolded is very different. But we get each other in a way not many can understand. It definitely doesn't hurt that she's beautiful, and kind, and fun—both in and out of bed.

She nods once and her eyes fall closed. She breathes out slowly as her hands settle on my chest. "I know. I just need to keep it together for a few more hours."

"If you need to let it out, then let it out. I'm not afraid of tears, Hanna. I raised a teenage girl on my own. If I can handle irrational teenage girl tears, I can certainly handle reasonable, adult emotional tears. Hell, I've cried more than once today, and I don't feel like I need to have my man card revoked for that."

She chuckles and then bites her bottom lip as two tears track down her cheeks.

"Aw, babe." I sweep them away with my thumbs. "Today has

been hard, hasn't it?"

"I didn't think it would hurt this much," she whispers.

"Not being able to take the role that's yours?" I ask.

We've talked about this before—about how her relationship with Ryan has changed ever since he found out the truth about their family dynamic.

"Logically, I know it's not my place. I know that. But it just . . . I really didn't expect it to be so hard. And the mother-son dance. Without my parents' support neither of us would have had the opportunities we did. I could never have afforded the hockey teams, or the travel, or any of the stuff my parents were able to give him—" She sucks in a tremulous breath.

"But it doesn't change the fact that it hurts," I say gently.

"I thought I could handle this. I need to be able to handle this. For Ryan."

"You have been handling this, Hanna. And you can fake being okay for everyone else, but you don't have to do it for me." I pull her against me and press my lips to her temple.

She melts against me, body shaking, even though her cries are silent. "Thank you for being such a rock, Jake."

She lets me hold her for a few minutes, her breathing evening out. The emotion seems to pass as quickly as it came. She inhales deeply and dabs under her eyes with a tissue. I have no idea where it came from, but it's definitely seen a lot of tears based on how mangled it is.

She waves her hands in front of her face. "Every time I think I've got myself under control this starts up again. I thought teenage hormones were bad. They have nothing on this perimenopausal shit."

"Aren't you a little young for that?"

She arches a brow. "Now you're being obtuse."

I hold my hands up in supplication. "Seriously. I didn't think that was a thing before fifty."

"Oh. Well, that would be ideal if that were the case, but it can start way earlier than that. Just depends on how much of an asshole your body wants to be." She closes her eyes and shakes her head. "It's bad enough that I cried all over your suit. I'm not going to subject you to the horrors of perimenopause." She purses her lips. "I really need to stop talking."

"I have something for you." I figure I'll save her from having to fight her way out of a conversation that's making her uncomfortable. Sometimes I forget that Hanna is slightly older than I am.

"What?" She frowns, as if she's not quite following the new direction of our conversation.

"A gift." I pull the small, wrapped box out of my pocket. "Just a little something to say thank you. I meant to give it to you earlier, but I forgot." I pass her the box.

"You didn't need to get me a gift." She bites her lip. "I didn't get you anything."

"You don't need to get me anything. You've been so great with Queenie. With everything. I would have been totally lost without you."

"You underestimate yourself. You would have been totally fine."

"We can agree to disagree on that." And I recognize, maybe not for the first time, that through this whole thing, I've felt like I had someone I could rely on for support and who was there for my daughter unfailingly.

My mouth goes dry, and I reach for my scotch, which I set on the dresser when I first walked in. The liquid burns but makes it easier to swallow. The sudden nervousness doesn't make sense. It's just a token of my appreciation.

Hanna pulls the bow and it flutters to the floor. "Oh, wow. I don't think anyone has ever bought me something from Tiffany's."

"The last time I shopped there for Queenie's sweet sixteen."

"She's a lucky girl to have such a thoughtful dad."

"She never really had a mother figure. There were things I couldn't do for her, or be for her, and you stepped in so graciously, even when it was hard for you." I'm going to miss

Hanna's regular visits now that the wedding is over.

"I feel the same way. Lucky, I mean, to have you both in my life as well." She lifts the lid from the box and inhales sharply. The chain is thin, and a small rose gold infinity heart is suspended from a diamond encrusted bar. I didn't even ask for help picking it out. It just seemed to fit Hanna. The room in her heart for the people she cares about always seems infinite.

"Oh, Jake, this is beyond stunning." She blinks several times rapidly. "I'm totally blaming you if I start crying again." She starts to wave her hands around in the air, so I take the box from her and quickly grab a tissue from the nightstand.

"These are good tears this time, though?"

She nods. "This is so beautiful."

"Exactly like you," I tell her.

"I'm a hot mess."

"Well, you're hot, I'll give you that. And if you're a mess, you're a beautiful one." I give her a long, lingering once-over.

"Don't look at me like that right now. I'm weak, and that smirk is too tempting." She turns around. "Can you help me with the necklace, please?"

"Absolutely." I sweep her thick dark waves over her shoulder. She often wears it up in a messy bun that shows off the slope of her elegant neck. Which is exactly what I'm looking at right now. The back of her dress is cut in a V. The style of hers is different, the straps slightly thicker, the dip in the back not quite so deep. A bit more modest. But still so damn sexy.

When she's thinking, her fingers often drift along the smooth skin. And all I want to do is follow the same path, but with my lips.

I unclasp the necklace she's currently wearing and replace it with the new one. We're facing the mirror, and our gazes meet and lock there. Her bottom lip catches between her teeth as she turns her head toward my mouth and reaches up, fingers brushing the edge of my jaw.

"Should we head back?" I dip down and press my lips to her collarbone.

"Maybe not quite yet." She leans into me, her back meeting my chest.

I settle my hands on her hips. "I don't know that I should be starting something I can't finish for a few more hours."

"We could be quick. Take the edge off." She arches, her butt pressing against my erection.

"Ah, fuck, Hanna."

She spins around and grabs my tie. "I think that's a really good idea." She pulls my mouth down to hers.

Every time I kiss her it's the same. It's like the first bite of a piece of cake snuck from the pantry when no one is looking. The delicious anticipation of having something you've waited for, only to discover it's infinitely more decadent than you expected.

I wrap one arm around her waist, savoring her moan as we tip our heads and open wider for each other. Lust overwhelms, and I feel like I'm being caught up in a vortex. Even after all these months, we still consume each other with the same fierce desperation, like each time is the first and last. Because even though we know we probably shouldn't be indulging in each other like this, we can't seem to stop ourselves.

I break the kiss long enough to grind out, "I want in you."

CHAPTER FOUR

The Perfect Distraction

Hanna

IN THE BACK of my mind, I recognize that now isn't the best time for this. And that Jake and I need to have a very real discussion about what exactly we're doing and that it should also probably stop, but today has been difficult on so many levels, I can't find it in me to put the brakes on. I need this. I need him. Which is its own problem. One I'll have to tackle before I leave on Sunday night.

But for now, I give myself over to sensation, to feeling good instead of conflicted, or sad, or lost.

"We can't go back out there rumpled," I mumble into his mouth as I loosen Jake's tie.

"Good call." His hands roam my curves with familiarity.

Because we've been doing this for months now. And tonight I feel a heightened level of desperation for him, knowing we can't keep sleeping together indefinitely, that it's going to end. And I feel a lot like I'm losing something else. Something bigger than I want to admit.

I quickly and carefully unbutton his shirt, all the while we're still kissing. He tastes like scotch and faintly of cigar, probably because someone handed him one earlier and he wanted to be polite. I've never seen Jake smoke anything before.

I finally manage to get the last of his shirt buttons undone. I pull his tie over his head, messing up his hair in the process. I try to run my fingers through it to smooth it back into place, but he shakes his head.

"Don't worry about it. You know your hands are going to be in it again anyway in a minute. I'll fix it after."

I'd say something cheeky, but he's not wrong. I toss his tie on the chair and push his shirt over his shoulders and he helps by tugging it free from his arms. Just like his suit jacket, he pauses to carefully drape it over the chair in the corner of the bedroom.

For a moment, his back is turned, so I do a quick breath check, relieved that it mostly smells like the mint candies I've been eating all night to keep me from drinking too much wine and becoming even more emotional than I already am. Wine and feelings are a lethal combination for me. While I'm checking my breath, I'm also checking out Jake's back and his backside.

It doesn't matter that I've seen him naked dozens of times, I never get tired of the view. He's in incredible shape. All toned muscles and broad back. He has the body of an athlete. Which I suppose makes sense since he works out with the boys he manages on a regular basis.

He's also an avid swimmer and golfer. And every time we've gotten together for family events, summer parties, and that one weekend we all spent in Texas, he and I have ended up in bed together.

He turns back to me and I take a step forward, running my hands over his shoulders and down his chest. I lightly skip over his abs, fingers cresting the dips and planes until I reach his belt buckle.

Jake's gaze dips down to where my fingers dance along the waistband of his dress pants.

"I can't tell you how many times I've thought about this today, Hanna." His voice is low and gravelly.

"About me ogling you while I undress you?" I pull on his belt, freeing the clasp.

He chuckles and exhales a long, slow breath as I pop the

button and drag the zipper down. "About getting you out of this dress." He takes my face in his hands. "About kissing you."

He slants his mouth over mine, groaning as his tongue slips between my lips. I want to savor this experience. Drag it out and make it last. We haven't had much alone time since I've been down for the wedding, and the past twenty-four hours have been a lot of heated looks and fleeting touches. It's been building all day, like a symphony reaching its crescendo, bringing us here, to this moment.

I dip a single finger beneath the elastic of his boxer briefs and graze his erection, which kicks behind the cotton. I slide my hand inside the fabric and curl my fingers around his length. The first time we were together like this, I did a mental cheer, along with a virtual roundoff, backflip, and a booty shake, because, as I'd hoped, Jake does not disappoint.

In fact, he's firmly rooted in the boyfriend dick department— not so big that walking is a chore for the next week, but ample enough that I'll be pleasantly sore for a few days.

Jake breaks the kiss, one hand leaving my face to pull the waistband of his boxer briefs down, exposing his glorious erection, and threads his fingers between mine.

I have what he calls piano hands: long, slender fingers and narrow wrists. So his hands, which are athlete-style large, make mine look even more delicate than usual. And he really, really loves my hands on him. With his fingers between mine, he guides my strokes, moving slowly, unhurried despite what's going on beyond the door of this bedroom.

His gaze shifts from our hands to my face and back down. His forearm is taut, the veins bulging, looking like baby snakes writhing under his skin. The arm porn is out of this world, and while I can't wait to have his hands on me, watching him like this, seeing the way he reacts to my touch, is a heady, empowering feeling. One I'm going to miss.

He's still cupping my cheek with the other hand, and his fingers glide along the edge of my jaw, slipping into my hair, anchoring there. His mouth finds mine again, hungrier this time, and his slow strokes falter. He squeezes his hand around mine.

"I need you, Hanna," he groans into my mouth. "Naked."

"Same," I mutter, then smile a little. All this time spent with twenty-somethings means I've adopted some of their lazy language habits.

He untwines our fingers and goes to work on unzipping my dress. If I'd had time and a plan, I would not be wearing Spanx right now. I'd expected to have time to freshen up, maybe put on something sexy before we ended up in bed together at the end of the night. But I didn't expect him to come looking for me. And maybe I should have, because he's always in tune with how I'm feeling.

He carefully slips the straps over my shoulders, but there's double-sided tape keeping my bodysuit fixed to the dress. Nothing is worse than your bra strap peeking out. "Hold on, I'll get it."

Jake steps back, and while I peel the tape free, he loses his shoes, socks, pants, and boxers. The pants get hung over the arm of the chair and my dress goes carefully on top.

While he's distracted, I peel myself out of my bodysuit. On the upside, I wore the lacy, pale pink one, so it's not nearly as unattractive as the other, plain, skin-toned one I own.

His eyes roam over me in a hot sweep and then we're back to kissing, skin to skin, hands caressing. Hunger and desire take over, and he walks me backward to the bed, lifting me onto the edge of the mattress. He runs his hands up my thighs, and I open, allowing him to step between them. The head of his erection bumps against my stomach, close to my navel.

I drag myself backward so I'm in the center of the bed and Jake climbs up after me, settling into the cradle of my hips. The smooth, hard length rubs against my clit, and every muscle below the waist clenches deliciously. I need this, him, this connection and distraction from everything else.

Jake's mouth descends on mine again and he rocks against me, the head sliding across my sensitive skin, hot and hard and oh-so-stimulating. I roll my hips in time with him, creating decadent friction that sends little jolts of pleasure zinging through me.

He nips along the edge of my jaw and nibbles my earlobe, his voice a low growly-whisper. "I want to taste you."

I don't really process his words. Not at first. He starts kissing his way down to my breasts, his stubbled chin scraping over my nipple, sending a wave of heat flashing through me. His tongue circles the taut flesh, lips closing over it, applying suction before his teeth graze the tip. He gives my other breast the same attention before moving lower.

Which is when his words finally register.

Jake is gloriously gifted in all aspects of the bedroom, and particularly talented with his tongue. And I'm eternally grateful that I took advantage of the spa day with the girls and treated myself to the complete works in the pampering department, including a Brazilian wax. I'm smooth as smooth can be below the waist.

"Do we really have time for that?" Even as I ask, I grab a pillow and shove it under my head, carefully arranging my hair so I don't mess it up and also don't have to strain my neck as Jake kisses and nips his way past my navel.

He looks up at me, eyes dark and hooded with lust, the right side of his mouth turning up with a smirk. "There's always time for kitty snacks."

I laugh at how cheesy he is, and then groan as he turns his head and parts his lips, biting the skin on my inner thigh, and then sucking. Not hard, but with the promise of what's to come.

He doesn't go for the kill. Not right away. And as much as I just want him to *lick me*, I always appreciate the teasing. He nibbles and kisses and then finally, finally, I feel the warm wet of his tongue as it strokes up my center.

"Oh, yes, please." I turn my head and bite my knuckle to keep the moans from bubbling up, especially when he lets out a low, feral groan and latches onto my most sensitive skin, sucking fiercely.

My toes curl and my eyes roll up. I stop biting my knuckle, half-worried I'm going to break the skin. I prop myself up on my elbow, not wanting to miss out on the visual glory that is this gorgeous man with his head between my legs. This act, so intimate and vulgar at the same time, is something Jake thoroughly enjoys and is extremely skilled at. Lucky, lucky me.

I reach down and slide my fingers into his hair, gripping at the crown, rolling my hips in time with the strokes of his tongue. His gaze shifts up, those blue eyes meeting mine from under his long lashes. I drag my tongue along my bottom lip to wet it, my mouth dry from all the gasping.

"You're going to make me come if you keep it up," I rasp.

"That's the fucking point, babe." He grins, dark and primal, then resumes stroking me with his tongue, faster, harder, alternating between suction, licking and teeth until a wave of pleasure rolls through my body, stealing my breath and turning the world into a burst of stars followed by darkness.

I fall back onto the mattress, sinking into the bliss of release. When the pulsing slows, Jake moves back up my body and settles between my legs, hips pressing into mine, his thick erection sliding over my still-sensitive skin. He kisses me, and I taste myself on his lips and his tongue.

"Thank you for that."

"Your orgasms are my favorite sound." He pushes up on one arm, his face inches from mine. "I want you to ride me."

There's nothing better than being in the driver's seat when it comes to sex. "I want me to ride you, too."

He grins, then flips over on his back, pulling me on top of him. I settle over his erection and roll my hips in slow circles, teasing like he did to me.

His gaze shifts to the chair where all of our clothes are, and his eyes fall shut for a moment before they refocus on me. "Fuck. The condoms are in my bedroom."

"We can go without this time." I suppose that's the one benefit of this early menopause BS. "If you're okay with that. Or I can go down—" It won't be great for my makeup, but I'm not about to leave him like this.

"We can go without," he agrees.

He's the only person I'm sleeping with, and while it hasn't been a conversation, I don't think he's had much time for a social life outside of the wedding and me.

I nod and take his erection in my fist, giving it a couple of slow strokes before I rise up and position myself over the head. And then I sink down, slowly, taking him inside inch by inch, until my ass rests on his thighs.

His eyes flutter closed. "Oh fuck, yes." He grips my thighs, nostrils flaring, every single muscle in his body tightening. "Just stay like that. Don't move," he grinds out.

I stay put, but I squeeze from the inside.

He cracks a lid and gives me a disapproving look.

I grin. "I'm not moving."

"You're flexing."

"It's not the same as moving. You have ten seconds to get yourself under control, Jake, and then I'm going to ride you, like you asked me to."

A carnal smile turns up the corners of his mouth. "I love it when you give me attitude in bed."

"Do you now?" I plant my palms on his pecs and lean down, my hair brushing over his chest.

"You already know the answer to that." His hand smooths up my back and under my hair.

"Mm. Are you ready?"

I don't wait for his reply. Instead, I roll my hips. His jaw clenches and he tips his chin up, groaning low in his throat. And I do exactly as he asks; I ride him with slow hip rolls and long, deep strokes. I send my Pilates and yoga instructor a mental *thank you* for pushing me every single week. I need to buy her a gift when I get back to Tennessee. A present for keeping me limber and forcing me to do those freaking Kegel exercises.

Jake is no passive recipient to pleasure. He lifts and lowers me, driving his hips up to meet every single thrust. One hand leaves my waist and his thumb brushes over the base of his shaft, gathering wetness. He rubs tight circles over my clit, pressing firmly as I sink down and rock over him, the head of his erection hitting that spot inside, sending me over the edge. Again.

I'm in the middle of an orgasm, unable to control my body anymore. Jake reaches up and pulls me down, then flips me over so I'm under him. His expression is fierce, lips curling up as he pumps his hips, fast and hard. The world is hazy and soft around the edges, but I manage to keep my eyes open and fixed on his stunning face as every muscle in his body locks up and he groans through his release.

He collapses on top of me, sweaty and breathing heavily. My heart pounds in my chest and I relax into the mattress, sated.

Best distraction ever.

CHAPTER FIVE

That Was Great Until it Wasn't

Jake

EVERYTHING FEELS HEIGHTENED today. Emotions, sensations, the need to just be inside Hanna. Maybe because yesterday all we managed was a quickie in the bathroom before my house was filled with people and wedding preparations.

Whatever the reason, with all emotions come a certain level of clarity. Feelings that have been lurking at the periphery seem more real tonight.

Needless to say, my post-orgasm high is a welcome release.

Hanna, who's currently half under me because all I've managed to do is roll to the side and trap her leg under mine, glances at the clock on the nightstand. "How long have we been gone?"

Shit. My high pops like a balloon. "I don't know, but it's definitely been a while. We should probably head back before someone notices we're missing." I can't believe I've disappeared from my own daughter's wedding reception to have sex. Although, to be fair, that wasn't my plan when I followed Hanna into the house.

And yet, here I am. But I can't find it in me to regret my actions. Not even a little. We both needed this. And Hanna needed a break from the dump truck of reality she's had to contend with today.

Hanna slides out from under my leg and rolls gracefully off the bed, hopping to her feet. She nabs her lacy business from the floor and her dress from the chair and heads for the bathroom.

I tuck an arm behind my head. "You getting all shy on me now?"

She laughs. "Hardly. I need to clean up and get dressed. I'm a little messy." She winks and disappears inside the bathroom, the door closing with a quiet click.

I get up and get dressed as well. I'm in the process of putting my tie back on when Hanna comes out of the bathroom, looking exactly like she did before I got her out of the dress—apart from the flushed cheeks, anyway.

"Here. Let me help you with that." She steps in and takes over tying my tie. Not that she needs to. I've done it nearly every day for the past two decades. But it's nice to have someone want to help if for no other reason than it's an excuse for closeness. She tightens it and rests her hands on my chest. "Thank you."

"No thanks necessary. We both needed that." I adjust her necklace so it sits in the hollow of her throat.

"I should have jumped you this morning when I had the chance." She smooths the lapels on my shirt, then drops her forehead against my chest. "This was probably really stupid, wasn't it?"

I wrap my arms around her. "Why do you say that?"

"Why couldn't you be shitty in bed? Or have an abnormally small penis?"

"Why would you want me to be either of those things?" I'm trying to get a read on where this is coming from and what her mood is, so I go for light. "Also, this means you think I'm phenomenal in bed, right?"

She laughs. "I love that not being shitty is automatically equated with being awesome in your man-brain."

"You come every time." That's just me stating facts.

She gives me the same *duh* look Queenie does, usually when she's referring to something that has to do with technology I don't understand. I'm in that weird middle-ground generation who sort of gets technology, but also sort of doesn't. I have a smart TV and half the time I have to look up how to use it. Or I give up and read the paper instead.

"You're right, I do." She pats my chest reassuringly. "You're an excellent lover, Jake. It's hard not to lose my head with you."

"Well, we're two peas in a pod then, aren't we? Otherwise, we wouldn't be locked in here right now." I tip her chin up and drop a kiss on her perfectly tempting lips.

I mean for it to be chaste, but after a few seconds we tip our heads and allow it to deepen. I stop before I get too excited and leaving the bedroom will be a problem.

Hanna glances at the clock again. "We should head back to the reception before we're missed."

"Smart plan." I'm halfway out the door when I remember I don't have my suit jacket. I grab it and shrug into it.

"Oh! Your hair. Let me fix it." Hanna stops me so she can run her fingers through it, and I settle a hand on her hip.

A shadow darkens the hallway. I drop my hand from Hanna's waist and she stops fixing my hair, stepping back until she bumps against the wall.

We both glance at the suit-wearing figure taking up most of the hallway. I sigh with relief when I realize it's not King. But that relief is short-lived.

Bishop Winslow's gaze shifts between Hanna and me. His brow furrows and his lips turn down. "Well, isn't this cozy." He crosses his arms.

"It's not what you think," Hanna blurts, which only makes it worse, and makes it seem like it's exactly what he thinks.

Hanna has been very clear that she doesn't want Kingston, or anyone else, to know what's been going on between us. She hasn't wanted to add any layers to that already challenging dynamic. And she also didn't want us to distract from the wedding festivities. I understand her reasons, even if I haven't felt quite the same way.

He arches a brow, and his gaze moves from Hanna, whose

face has gone a telling shade of red, to me. "So I didn't catch the two of you leaving a bedroom, making sure you don't look at all conspicuous after you've been missing from your kids' wedding reception for the past hour?"

He holds up a hand before either of us can speak, which is probably good because Hanna seems likely to dig our hole deeper and I'm not sure how bad she is at lying. Although, she did keep the fact she's King's mother under wraps for nearly three decades. "Don't say anything else. The less I know, the better, because I sure as fuck don't want to lie to my best friend. But if you want to keep people from talking, I would *not* show up out there together." And with that, he disappears down the hall, shaking his head as he goes.

"Do you think he'll say something to Ryan?" Hanna's eyes are wide.

"No. And it's not like he actually saw anything. He's jumping to conclusions right now."

"No, he isn't."

"He doesn't know that, though. You head back out; I'll be there in a few minutes. I'll see if I can catch him and talk to him."

"Okay." She doesn't wait for me to placate her further, just turns and walks briskly down the hall.

I go the other way, hoping I can stop Bishop before he has a chance to talk to anyone else.

CHAPTER SIX

Yours Until the Weekend Is Over

Hanna

THE REST OF the night is a blur. I spend it in a state of mild anxiety and arousal. Thankfully, it seems as though no one apart from Bishop noticed our extended absence from the reception. It's nearly two in the morning before all the guests have left.

Queenie and Ryan are headed to a hotel, and they're leaving for their honeymoon in Hawaii first thing in the morning. My parents took my brother, Gerald, back to Ryan's place two hours ago. He started doing shots at ten, and by eleven he was doing the worm on the dance floor. By midnight, he was passed out on a plate of sandwiches.

The cleanup crew isn't expected until noon tomorrow, so at least we'll be able to sleep in. I've basically spent the rest of the night avoiding Jake, worried that I'll do or say something incriminating. I wait until the last guests leave before I let myself get within touching distance.

"You okay?" he asks, taking a sip from his glass. He was drinking scotch earlier but seems to have switched to water.

"I'm fine. Did you get a chance to talk to Bishop?"

"He won't say anything to Ryan. I told him nothing was going on."

"Do you think he believed you?"

Jake shrugs. "It's not like he caught us doing anything." He sets his glass onto the counter. "Besides, we're adults. We don't have to answer to Bishop, or anyone. What we do behind closed doors is no one's business but ours." He said the same thing before, when we first gave in to the chemistry we share.

And he's right. But I really don't want Ryan to find out, and this confirms what I already know—that as much fun as we're having, we're going to have to stop.

He takes a step closer. "Are you worried?"

I bite my nail, my gaze roaming over his face and down his dress shirt-covered torso. He lost his suit jacket a while ago and his tie hangs loose.

I run my hand down his tie and wrap the silky fabric around my hand. "I trust you when you say he won't tell Ryan."

"He won't. And anything he has to say would be based on conjecture, not fact." He wraps his hands around my waist and pulls me into him. I tip my head up and he tips his down, his lips brushing over mine. "I want to take you to bed again, make you forget about all your worries."

"I want that, too."

I CANNOT BELIEVE how sore I am. Everywhere. Jake and I spent the rest of the weekend having marathon sex all over his house.

Even when my ex-husband Gordon and I were happy and totally in love, I still can't remember a time where we spent an entire weekend—minus a few hours spent with my parents and my brother—having nonstop sex.

I feel like I've done six back-to-back Pilates workouts. There's a very good chance I've lost five pounds this weekend.

Jake sets a plate of bacon, eggs, and homemade hash browns onto the table and takes the seat catty-corner to me.

"How are you feeling about going home?" he asks.

"Eh, going to work on Monday morning is pretty weak in

comparison to a wedding and a weekend of hot sex."

He grins. "You are definitely fun in bed."

"So are you." His sexual appetite is voracious, his prowess unmatched. "I can't even fathom what your stamina must have been like two decades ago."

His grin drops and he leans back in his chair, crossing his arms. "What does that mean?"

I cover my mouth and laugh, then set my fork down and push my chair back. He glares at me, clearly unimpressed with my comment. I imagine being over forty and feeling like one's virility is in question could easily sour a mood.

I shimmy my way onto his lap. I'm fairly tall, and I have hips, and curves, but Jake somehow manages to make me feel petite with his broad shoulders and defined muscles. His eyes are narrowed, and his jaw is set. The only time I've seen Jake lose his cool is when his players aren't performing the way they're capable of—namely starting fights on the ice instead of staying focused on the game. It's pretty sexy. And I find irritated, unimpressed Jake is rather appealing.

"Look at how angry you are."

"I'm not angry." He stares at me through dark, hooded eyes.

"Hmm." I trace the shell of his ear. "I had to take Tylenol this morning because my entire body aches. And do you know why that is?"

He cocks a brow and his gaze heats. "Because you had me turn you into a human pretzel last night?"

"Well, yes." I can feel my cheeks heat at the memory. I don't know what got into me last night—other than I haven't been that ramped up…in…well…I guess the last time we spent a weekend together. "But also because you're an animal between the sheets. Which is a compliment, by the way. I'm not sure if I should be jealous or feel sorry for the women you dated in your twenties."

"There weren't a lot of opportunities for dating during that decade of my life."

"Mm." I run my fingers through his hair. "So making up for missed opportunities then?"

He shrugs and grins. "Or maybe you bring out my wild side." He laces our fingers together. "What do you think the chances are of you coming out this way for another visit in the next few weeks?"

This is the conversation I've been avoiding. The one I can't put off any longer. And probably the reason I was so voracious this weekend, knowing that it was going to be the last time. "I don't know if that's a good idea, Jake."

He drops his head, eyes on our twined fingers. "I think another weekend with you in my bed is a great idea."

I settle my palm against his cheek and wait until his gaze lifts to mine again. "I like you, Jake." Maybe a little too much. "And this chemistry has been so much fun to explore. But the wedding night was a close call. And I know we're adults and we can do whatever we want, but our kids are married now, and I don't think it's a good idea for us to keep doing this." My chest aches as disappointment settles behind his eyes. "Ryan and I have finally gotten to a good place again in our relationship, and I can't jeopardize that. And I can't lie to him, which is exactly what I've been doing and what I'd have to keep doing if I started flying out here to see you. I can't come to Seattle and not spend time with Ryan, and more than that, I don't want to hide things from him. He's had secrets kept from him his entire life, and I don't want to do that to him again. I can't. My life is in Tennessee, and yours is here. I think we need to stop before it gets more complicated than it already is." And based on the way my heart clenches, I know this is exactly the right thing to do. I'm getting too attached, and someone is going to get hurt if we keep going the way we are.

He gives me a small smile. "I understand. And you're right, about all of it." His fingers drift up and down my arm. "I'm just being greedy."

"If things were different—"

"—but they aren't," he finishes for me.

I shake my head.

His gaze moves past me to the clock on the stove. His palms

smooth down my back. "Can I take you to bed one last time before I drive you to the airport?"

I should say no. It would be the smart thing to do, especially after this conversation. But I don't. "Please."

"TELL ME ALL about the wedding! How was Hottie McDaddy? Did you take pictures? Did you get to at least dance with him?" Paxton, my colleague and very close friend, props her chin on her fist, eyes alight with excitement. Hottie McDaddy is the nickname she's given Jake.

We've been working at the art studio for years, teaching classes together. It's a hobby and a passion for both of us. We've been friends for decades.

Paxton was one of the first girls I met when I was finally able to return to school after Ryan was born. She was also the only friend I had who knew the truth: that Ryan wasn't my baby brother. And she kept that secret for our entire friendship, until Gordon let the cat out of the bag. She's always been someone I can confide in.

We're at her place, sitting on her back deck, eating tortilla chips and guac, sipping bubbly water. She offered me a glass of wine or a margarita, but after the wedding, I need to dry out for a week, or three. It's been two days since I arrived home. Two days to think about the way I left things with Jake. How, on the way to the airport, he commented that he knew something felt different this weekend. And when he'd kissed me goodbye, it had felt like heartbreak.

Over the past two days, I've gone over and over every single encounter. In the spare bedroom, in his bed, in the shower, in the pool, the hot tub, the kitchen counter, the living room. We had an exceptional amount of sex. I feel like I'm going through some kind of withdrawal.

And I miss him.

Which is so bad. And stupid. And exactly the reason I needed to stop things when I did. Because clearly, I'm starting to have real feelings for him, and I need to put those in a box and bury them six feet underground.

"I did something stupid." I poke at the lemon slice floating in my glass with my straw, mostly so I don't have to see her reaction when I spill the beans. Especially since I haven't exactly been forthcoming about the fact I've been sleeping with Jake for months.

"Like get drunk and make an emotional speech while sobbing kind of stupid?" she asks.

"No. That would actually be tame in comparison."

She stops trying to chase a piece of tomato around the bowl of guac. "Did you murder someone?"

I give her a look. "Of course not."

"Then it can't be that bad."

"I slept with Jake."

Confusion makes her eyebrows try to meet each other. "I'm sorry, what was that?"

I lift my hand in front of my mouth and repeat myself, "Jake. I've been sleeping with him."

Paxton frowns. "We're not talking about Hottie McDaddy, are we?"

I clasp my hands to stop from biting my nails or shoving another handful of chips into my mouth. "Yes, we are."

Paxton's chip breaks in half. "Holy shit."

"I know." I scrub my hand over my face.

"Whoa. Wait. Back this bus up. First you said you slept with Jake, and then you said you've been sleeping with Jake. Does that mean this wasn't a drunken one-off?"

I shake my head. "It wasn't a one-off."

"And you're just telling me *now*? How long has this been going on?"

I start chewing on my nail. "A while."

She narrows her eyes. "What's a while?"

"Since the engagement party." It sounds so much worse when

I say it aloud, which is probably why I haven't until now.

"Not to point out the obvious or anything, Han, but your kids are married to each other."

I raise a hand. "I know, I know. I told him this weekend we had to stop."

"Okay. Wow. How'd he take it?"

"He said he understood." And then we had more sex. The desperate tear-each-other's-clothes-off kind.

"Do you believe him?"

"I do. He understands the challenges with my relationship with Ryan."

Paxton blows out a breath. "Did you talk about how you were going to manage the next family gathering? I know with the wedding being over, you won't see each other *as much*, but there are still holidays and birthdays."

"I know!" I throw my hands in the air. "Hence the reason I can't believe I did something so stupid." For months. A lot of months. "I'm forty-six. I should not be thinking with my hormones at this age!"

"Eh, I mean, we're heading into the menopause stage of things, so really, we're all hormones."

"You're not helping!"

"I'm deflecting with humor because I honestly don't know how to help. He must be pretty damn good in bed if you've been sleeping with him all this time. I still can't believe you kept it from me. No wonder you were always so giddy about going to freaking Seattle. Is this why you started taking Pilates?"

"I started taking Pilates because it makes me feel good." And also because I needed to limber up for all the sexy times. "And yes, he's amazing in bed. He's in really good shape. Not just for a guy in his forties, but in general. He still has a six-pack. Well, it's more like a four-pack, but still. And he's definitely got it going on."

"You mean he's hung?" She props her chin on her fist again.

"Oh yes."

"Is that why you're walking all funny?" she asks.

"I'm not walking funny!" Although I was yesterday. And the day before that.

"Come on, Han, give me some details! You've been sitting on this for months! Is he so hung you were uncomfortable the next day? Or does he have the kind of penis you'd like to get more of on a regular basis. You know, boyfriend dick. If he wasn't your daughter-in-law's father and Ryan's father-in-law, that is."

"Oh, he definitely has a boyfriend dick. And he's very skilled at oral." I point under the table. "And multiple Os."

"Multiple Os?" She slaps the table. "Oh man, are you sure you want to stop riding that ride?"

"No, but I have to. I can't do that to Ryan."

She sags in her chair. "Dammit. Oral skills, multiple Os, abs, and a boyfriend dick? You found a unicorn and you have to give him up. That's just tragic."

"It is. He really is the whole package, pun completely intended." I scrub a hand over my face. "We almost got caught by Ryan's best friend *during* the freaking wedding."

Paxton's mouth drops open. "During? What'd you do, sneak off for a quickie?"

It all sounds so sordid. I explain what happened, the speeches, the mother-son dance, how Jake came to find me.

"Do you think he'll say anything to Ryan?" Paxton manages to pick most of her chip parts out of the guac.

"He didn't see anything, but it was too close for comfort, you know? Ryan and I have spent so much time trying to rebuild our relationship and trust. I don't want to put this kind of strain on it."

Paxton regards me for a moment before she asks, "Do you have feelings for Jake? Aside from wanting to jump his bones."

My throat feels tight and that ache in my chest tells me the answer to that question. "It doesn't matter. I won't compromise my relationship with Ryan." It's bad enough that it's gone on this long. It was only supposed to be that one weekend, but obviously that wasn't how it panned out.

"Ah. I see." She flips a chip between her fingers. "You don't think Ryan would understand?"

"Jake and I live on opposite ends of the country. It was never going to be anything but casual."

"Have you heard from him since you've been home?"

I nod. "He wanted me to message when I got home, so I did. And then he messaged again today to ask how I'm doing. We were friends before we started sleeping together, so I'm hoping we can go back to being friends again. I know it'll probably be weird for a while, but I'm sure everything will be fine."

It'll just take some time for us to get used to the fact we know what each other's come faces look like when we're sitting across from each other at family dinner in the future.

No biggie.

CHAPTER SEVEN

Baby, Don't Lose My Number

Hanna

OVER THE WEEKS that follow, Jake and I continue to message and talk like we used to, before we started sleeping together. It's an adjustment, especially when he's still his flirty self and I'm determined to keep us in the friend zone. It's not easy, but I remind myself that if I keep falling into bed with him every time I see him, I'm being selfish. Ryan is more important than my sex life.

But I can't pretend that I don't miss the trips out to Seattle and all the time Jake and I spent together.

A couple of months after the wedding, he calls on one of my exciting Friday nights. I'm relaxing in the tub, reading a book. I was supposed to go out for dinner with a few colleagues, but I didn't feel up to it. My lower back has been tight, probably because I skipped a couple of Pilates workouts last week. I was just too tired. I'm blaming it on long hours at work.

Jake and I haven't had a reason to speak on the phone since the wedding, and my stomach flip-flops as his name flashes across the screen. I put him on speakerphone. "Hey, how are you?"

"I'm good. Getting ready for preseason training, trying to enjoy what's left of my summer, but I'm not very good at the whole relaxing thing."

"Mmm. I'm very familiar with what relaxing looks like when it comes to you." Even though it's not meant to sound suggestive, somehow my tone makes it so.

He chuckles softly. "That you are." I hear a repetitive tap, maybe a pen on a desk. "I wanted to run something by you."

"Sure. Is everything okay?"

"Oh yeah. Everything is fine." He clears his throat. "Queenie's birthday is coming up next month."

"Ah, yes. Ryan was telling me he's planning a surprise party for her. Is there anything I can do to help?"

"I think we've got it all covered. Ryan's got a friend who owns this axe throwing bar and he's renting out the entire place."

"Oh! I remember he took her there when they started dating. That's a great location!"

"It is, and there's this cupcake place that's connected to it. So food and dessert are all taken care of. The only thing that needs to be dealt with are some minor decorations, but Stevie and Lainey are taking care of that."

"How fun. Ryan told me he's taking her on a day date, so I don't think she's expecting it to be a big thing." He's always so thoughtful when it comes to birthday celebrations. Every year he sends flowers to my work and makes a point of flying home on my birthday, or flying me out to a game.

"That's what he told me, too. Does that mean you'll be coming out to Seattle?"

"Absolutely. I wouldn't miss it." Although seeing Jake for the first time since the wedding is definitely going to be interesting, if not a little awkward, much like this conversation.

"Good, that's good. I'm glad to hear that. I'm looking forward to seeing you."

"Me, too." And I mean it. I am looking forward to seeing him, even if it's challenging. I set the phone on the tray that sits over the tub, where I keep my e-reader and my glass of wine. Although tonight I'm sipping ginger tea since my stomach has been bothering me.

"I don't know what your plans are, but you're still more than welcome to stay here if you want. With me." At my silence he rushes on. "I know we agreed that we need to stop… sleeping together, but, uh, that doesn't mean we can't still spend time together. With our clothes on." He chuckles at the end, sounding nervous.

I close my eyes and fight a sigh. I want to say yes. I want to spend the weekend at his place, hanging out in his living room, relaxing in his hot tub, drinking coffee on his back deck in the morning. "I don't really know if that's a good idea, Jake."

He's quiet for several long seconds. "What if I told you I would be on my best behavior?"

"Do you really think you can do that?" He's always been flirty with me. And even over the past couple of months he's sent the occasional picture that looks innocent enough, but they always remind me of the weekends or nights we've spent together.

"I'd like to try," he says softly.

"Jake." I wish he wasn't so persuasive.

"Hanna." His voice is gravelly and low.

"I don't know if I can trust myself to be alone with you," I tell him honestly. It's easy to convince myself that I can see him and keep him in the friend zone when there are literally thousands of miles between us, but it's not the same when we're sleeping under the same roof.

"I won't let you do anything you regret."

"You say that now, but what happens when we've both been drinking and we're stumbling through the door at two in the morning and there's no one to stop us from tearing each other's clothes off?" I sink down in the water and groan. "And now that image is going to be burned into my head for the rest of the night."

"It's definitely an image I'm a fan of," he says.

"This is exactly what I'm talking about, Jake. I think we need to learn how to be friends again, before we put ourselves in a position that's going to make us feel bad about our decisions. I want to say that I can handle staying at your place and that I won't come knocking on your door in the middle of the night, but I don't feel ready to test that hypothesis. And I don't want to put you in a position where you have to turn me down and then we'll both feel terrible, and I'll gain five pounds afterward from drowning my embarrassment in ice cream."

He's quiet for a while and then he sighs. "That's fair. And I don't think I'd be able to turn you down. But I'm still looking forward to seeing you, even if you're fully dressed the entire time."

I laugh. "Me, too." More than I should be.

THE NEXT MORNING, my phone buzzes and I grumble about people messaging too early on weekends. I blink a few times and am slightly confused when I notice I'm on the couch in my living room, rather than in my bed. I must have fallen asleep watching TV last night, which makes sense since baths always knock me out.

I leave my phone where it is and drag my groggy self to bed. The next time I open my eyes, the clock on the nightstand reads eleven o'clock. The last time I can remember sleeping in this late was when I was in my early twenties. Those were the days when I used to go out with friends and stay up until three in the morning. I'm pretty sure I passed out before ten last night.

Work has been busy, especially since I'm being considered for a promotion. I've been working for the same accounting firm for the past fifteen years, and when the chance to move into a management position became available, I decided to throw my hat into the ring. It comes with more responsibility and a significant pay increase that could accelerate my retirement plan. On top of that, I've been spending a lot of hours at the art studio, and clearly not getting enough sleep.

I'm teaching painting lessons this afternoon, and I need to be at the studio before one, so I roll out of bed, head for the bathroom, and turn on the shower. Once I'm dressed, I make a coffee, but the cream must have gone bad, because it tastes funky. I dump it out, grab a bottle of water and a banana, and leave for the studio.

Paxton is already there by the time I arrive, which isn't a surprise because it's ten to one. Usually, I'm half an hour early so I have time to help set up.

"Hey! I messaged you earlier. Everything okay?" Paxton gives me a once-over.

"Oh shoot! I'm so sorry. I haven't checked my phone at all today." I rummage around in my purse for it but come up empty-handed. "And I don't even have it with me. I'm a bit of a hot mess." I set my purse down and shrug out of my coat, hanging it on a hook so I can help Paxton finish setting up.

"Late night?"

"Really early night, actually. And I slept until eleven."

"Wow, channeling your inner teen, huh?"

"Seems that way."

Students begin to arrive—our first class is for kids—and we spend the next hour teaching eight to ten-year-olds how to work with watercolors. After that, we have a group of seniors who are loads of fun. It's been my side gig for a lot of years. It's not something I've ever considered as a full-time job because as fun as it is, I think it would put a damper on my love of painting. But the studio is my outlet, and being here, helping people create, is my happy place.

"Want to head to Charlie's for a bite to eat?" Paxton asks when we're finished cleaning up.

"Sure. That sounds great." My stomach rumbles. I haven't eaten much apart from that banana at breakfast and a bag of chips from the vending machine in the breakroom between classes.

Paxton lives close to the studio, so we take my car to Charlie's and settle into a booth in the back corner. I order a ginger ale and Paxton orders a glass of white wine.

"It's Saturday. You're not having a drink?" Paxton asks.

I shrug. "I've been tired lately. Don't want to add alcohol to the mix when I'm already a yawn factory." I cover my mouth with my hand and yawn so wide and so hard it brings tears to my eyes.

"Oooh, late night chats with Hottie McDaddy?"

"Actually." I arch a brow.

She stops browsing the menu to look at me. "Wait. I thought you said the sexy times were over."

"They are." I poke at my ice cubes with my straw.

"But?" Paxton prompts.

"Queenie's birthday is coming up, and I'm planning to fly to Seattle for the party. Jake called last night and invited me to stay at his place."

She sets her glass down and gives me her full attention. "You mean as friends? What did you say?"

"I told him I didn't think it was a good idea."

"Would it really be so bad if you had one last, last roll in the hay with him?" She wiggles her fingers and smiles like a villain.

I chuckle and then sigh. "I don't know if I could limit myself to one last roll, which is the problem. When I first met Jake, Queenie made some sort of comment about how well he and I got along, and Ryan told her that his family was already messy and not to go planting seeds. It was innocent enough, but I can't see him being okay with it."

"But you still want to sleep with Jake."

"It doesn't matter what I want. It's a colossally bad idea to continue sleeping with Ryan's father-in-law."

"When you put it that way." Paxton makes a face. "I'm sorry."

"Me, too. I really would have loved another weekend of hot sex with a guy whose number I didn't need to lose."

CHAPTER EIGHT

I Can't be Reading that Right

Hanna

WORK IS INCREDIBLY busy in the weeks leading up to Queenie's birthday party. With the promotion on the table, I'm pulling longer hours and taking on more responsibilities. I end up having to move my flight to Seattle to the morning of the party, thanks to an unexpected audit on one of my bigger clients. It means I'm up until one in the morning getting all the paperwork in order.

My alarm goes off at the crack of dawn on Saturday morning, my bag already packed for the weekend and waiting at the door. However, I hit the snooze button more than once on account of the exceptionally early hour and am forced to get dressed in a rush. Thankfully, I already programmed my coffee to brew last night, before I went to bed, so I pour a to-go cup, grab a banana, and head for my car. The drive to the airport isn't long, and I won't have to contend with rush hour traffic.

I pull onto the freeway and move into the center lane. I take a first sip of my coffee and make a face. My luck with cream has sucked lately. I make a mental note to throw it away when I get home on Sunday. I can grab a fresh cup at the airport.

Unfortunately, I got the time wrong for my flight. It doesn't leave at eight thirty-five; it leaves at eight oh-five, so I only have minutes to spare once I'm through security to get to my gate. Ryan has upgraded my ticket, but I'm aware that airplane coffee is not the best, even in first class.

I end up passing out—I blame the comfortable seats—and sleep the entire plane ride to Seattle. Thanks to the time change, I still arrive well before noon.

As soon as I step off the plane, my phone blows up with messages. I have a couple from Jake telling me to have a safe flight and to message when I've landed. It's almost disappointing when there's nothing inappropriate or suggestive in his texts. I fire one off, telling him I'm in Seattle and I can't wait to see him later.

The group chat with Lainey, Violet, and Stevie is a different story altogether. There must be more than a hundred missed messages in the chat. Ryan is taking Queenie out for the day, so we won't see her until later at the restaurant. But Ryan, being as thoughtful as he is, has scheduled an afternoon of pampering for the girls and me.

I stop at Ryan's first, even though he and Queenie have already left, so I can freshen up before the girls pick me up for our afternoon at the spa. We'll start with massages and facials, then mani-pedis. Queenie has made such wonderful friends here, and I love that they've pulled me into their group and adopted me as one of their own.

Stevie, Lainey, and Violet pick me up after I've gotten myself settled into what will eventually be a nanny suite, I'm sure. It's almost like a self-contained apartment on the main floor of the house, and usually where my parents stay when they visit.

Stevie leans over and gives me a side hug as I slide into the back seat. Her hair is a different color every time I see her, and today it's pale blue. "Yay! I'm so glad you could make it!"

Lainey smiles at me in the rearview mirror. "We were just talking about how nice it would be if you lived closer and we could all see you more often. We'd all gotten used to you being here more than once every three months."

"When the boys play Tennessee, you'll all have to come out

and visit." If my whole life wasn't in Tennessee, including my job and my art studio, I might consider moving this way. But at the same time, NHL players aren't guaranteed to stay in one place. Ryan is lucky he's been on the same team for as long as he has, and while his contract is going to keep him in Seattle for the next several years, there's no saying where he'll go after that.

"We'll have to do that before this one gets herself knocked up." Violet points at Lainey, who is busy driving with her hands at ten and two. Ryan would approve.

"You're trying to get pregnant again?" I ask. She just had her little girl Aspen not that long ago.

"Kody was a happy accident, but it took forever for me to get pregnant with Aspen." She smiles slyly and her cheeks go pink. "Not that I mind the trying part, but I don't want another big gap between Aspen and the next one. And RJ, while accommodating, has said he'd like to have spontaneous sex before the end of this decade."

"You can say goodbye to spontaneous sex until the kids move out," Violet says. "Robbie stays up later than me half the time these days, which means zero privacy unless we farm them out to the grandparents."

"You do realize these conversations are like birth control advertisements, right?" Stevie snickers and pulls up the hockey schedule for the season. "There's a game in Tennessee in November. Maybe we could come out then, if that works for you?"

"It could definitely work."

"Is it mid-week or on the weekend?" Vi asks.

"That one is on Friday," Stevie says.

"Don't you teach painting classes on the weekends? Are you missing one today?" Lainey asks.

"My friend Paxton is running it solo this weekend," I explain.

"Maybe we could sit in, so you don't have to change your schedule. It'd be so much fun to spend a weekend with you in Tennessee." Lainey smiles warmly.

"I think it's a great idea." I really love how easy they all are to be around, and how, even though I don't see them often, we have such a great time together and I always feel like part of things.

Our conversation is put on pause when we arrive at the spa and go our separate ways for our massage appointments. I almost fall asleep again during my massage, probably because it's so relaxing. It's followed by a heavenly facial. Afterwards, we meet up again for our mani-pedis.

Our manicures are first, and once our nails are set, we're given snack plates and plenty of drink options while our toes get pretty. I have a headache, so I opt for water.

After our pedicures, we're moved to the lounge, where we're supposed to wait for our toes to dry. I take the opportunity to make myself a coffee, adding a spoonful of sugar and a smidge of cream. Then I take a small sip. Just like this morning, it tastes sour. I take another sip. Nope. Still tastes wrong.

"Everything okay, Hanna?" Lainey asks.

"Twice today I've had coffee that tastes like the cream is off."

"Want me to give it a taste?"

"I don't know if that's a good idea. What if I'm coming down with something?" It's entirely possible with the way I've been burning the candle at both ends lately.

"I can do a cream sniff test?" she offers.

"Sure." I pass her the tiny pot of cream and she wafts it toward her nose.

"Smells fine to me."

"Maybe my taste buds are off."

"Every time I was preggers, three things happened," Violet says and motions to her chest. "My bras stopped fitting because my boobs turned into giant balloons and I'd punch Alex every time he tried to touch them because they were so sensitive, dairy always tasted funky, and I could sleep like a teenager."

"Oh! Yes! My boobs were so sore. I couldn't sleep on my stomach at all," Lainey says.

"Wow, way to sell me on *not* getting pregnant any time soon," Stevie deadpans. She and Bishop have been together for years, but they still haven't jumped on the baby train. Yet.

I chuckle, but it turns into something like a croak. I covertly press on my chest and cringe at how tender my breasts are. I assumed my body was being its weird self by making it seem like my period was coming. I've been having phantom PMS symptoms for the past year, and only once every three months do I actually get a "period."

I've been exhausted lately, sleeping for twelve hours and still feeling like I could sleep longer. And then there's the coffee.

"Hanna? Are you okay?" Lainey asks.

"I-I don't know." I cover my mouth with my palm. "Everything Violet said, that could be me."

Silence follows, thick and heavy.

"I'm sure it's nothing. I'm just run down," I rush on. "I've been working long hours at my accounting firm. One of my big clients had an audit, and I'm being considered for a promotion."

"That's exciting, about the promotion," Vi says. "I miss the constant work sometimes, but I like picking and choosing what jobs I want to take." She's also an accountant, but she mostly does freelance work.

"I thought it was a good move," I agree. "But it means late nights and early mornings to keep on top of things, you know?"

"That's really wonderful about the promotion." Lainey glances toward the door as she shifts in her seat, turning to face me. It's the four of us in here. "But is there a chance you could be pregnant?" Her expression is full of gentle concern. It's very much the way she is, always maternal.

"I don't know?" I swallow down my uneasiness. "I've been perimenopausal for a long while. My periods are irregular, and really short when I do have them."

Lainey's smile is soft. "Even during menopause you're still releasing eggs, and sometimes your body goes a little haywire, so they lose the steady rhythm they once had. Or your cycle can be influenced by others around you." She motions to Stevie and Violet. "I'm synced up with these ladies because we spend so much time together."

"What are the odds, though?" I wish I had a paper bag to

breathe into.

"I didn't know you had a boyfriend," Stevie says.

I'm not sure if I imagine her suspicion or if I'm being paranoid. "I don't." I give my head a shake. "I mean, it's casual. It's not a serious relationship. What am I going to do if..." I can't bring myself to finish the sentence. Then it's far too real.

"It could be that you're tired, or that your body is following a stronger cycle. Hold on." Lainey grabs her purse from the floor and roots around in it.

At first I think she's looking for her phone, as if she's going to do some research on the subject, but I'm surprised when she pulls out a pregnancy test.

"I've been buying these in bulk for years. I carry them with me everywhere." She rolls her eyes at herself and hands it to me.

"Do you think I should take this now?" I hold it like it's a dismembered limb, not a tiny device to pee on.

"They're most accurate when they're taken in the morning, but false positives aren't really possible, so if you are pregnant, you'll know right away. I can stand outside the bathroom door if you want," she offers.

"It's okay. I'll be back in a couple of minutes." I push up out of the chair on unsteady legs.

Violet jumps up and takes my arm. She's a head shorter than me, and a tiny thing, apart from her chest. "We're all here for you, Hanna," she says, her voice softening. "Whatever happens, we've got your back."

I appreciate that I have a girl gang to rely on right now. I wish Pax was here. She's been my go-to forever.

I slip inside the bathroom and lock the door. It's a nice bathroom, much nicer than the one I was in thirty years ago where I found out for the first time that my entire life was about to change.

I take a deep breath, reminding myself that I'm not a teenage girl. And that I haven't had a regular period in two years.

There's no way I can be pregnant.

In less than five minutes I'll be laughing about my paranoia.

And chugging a glass of champagne. Or a bottle.

I unwrap the test and read the instructions. One blue line means not pregnant, two blue lines that cross mean I am pregnant.

Got it.

I take a deep breath and try to force the pee out. Of course, now I'm having pee stage fright. I turn on the tap, hoping it's going to help me out. It does the trick.

I manage to get my hand as well as the stick, which is gross, but not unexpected considering the day I'm having.

I grab a handful of toilet paper and set the test on the vanity. Then wipe myself and wash my hands, humming "Happy Birthday" twice, all the way through.

I take a deep breath, not wanting to look at the test until the two minutes is up.

I take a quick peek.

Then another one.

Looks like that mimosa is off the table.

CHAPTER NINE

Complicated, Times Two

Jake

I'M STANDING BY the bar, away from the axe throwing enclosures, where all the young kids are. And by young kids, I mean King and Queenie's friends who have come to celebrate her birthday. For a guy who drives a Volvo and is usually fiscally responsible, he sure does like to go all out for my daughter. I was relieved to find out they don't allow alcohol in the axe throwing enclosures and they close that part of the restaurant off after ten. The lighting is low and there's a cozy, homey feel. I can see why King chose this place. The name is even cool—The Knight Cap.

I don't know what's going on, but pinning Hanna down is harder than trying to catch a fly with a pair of tweezers tonight. Lainey and Violet are practically glued to her, like they're her personal bodyguards. I knew things were going to be a little awkward between us, but it feels a lot like she's purposely avoiding me. Which isn't what I want. Not when our kids are married and we've got a lot of years of shared family functions in our future.

I resorted to texting her about half an hour ago, but I don't know if she's carrying her phone at all since all I've seen in her hands is a glass of what could be water, or gin and tonic since she's a fan of those.

"You all right? You've been checking your phone all night." Alex Waters, my head coach and one of my good friends, leans against the bar, sipping a glass of scotch.

"I'm fine, just, uh . . . waiting on a message."

"Work-related or personal?"

"Personal. If it was work related, you'd already know about it."

He gives me a casual shrug. "You never know. Could be one of those NDA type deals you can't tell me anything about."

"I'd still tell you if something was up. Especially this close to training camp."

"Okay." He sips his scotch again. "This personal thing, is it something you need to talk about?"

I give him a look. "What are you now, a therapist in training?"

"Might as well be, with these kids and all their hormones and not knowing their ass from their armpit." He motions to the group of players milling around the bar.

"They look so damn young, don't they?" Some of the rookie players still have remnants of teen acne.

"That's because they are."

"Not for long, though." I rub my chin. "It feels like yesterday when I was dealing with midnight feedings and changing diapers, and now Queenie's in her mid-twenties. I can't imagine it's going to be long before she and King start a family either."

"King definitely gives off a strong family man vibe," Alex agrees.

"He'll make a good dad. Shit. I can't believe this is the kind of conversation I'm having at my daughter's birthday party." I run a hand through my hair.

Alex claps me on the shoulder. "As long as you don't start talking about erectile dysfunction at poker night, I think you're fine."

"Screw you." I shrug off his hand. "I'm in my forties, not cashing my pension checks."

Alex chuckles. "I'm kidding. And forty is creeping up on me like a bad wedgie."

"At least you'll be forty and married. Dating at my age in the twenty-first century is not my favorite."

"I can't even imagine trying to meet women now. I'm pretty sure Violet would have taken a restraining order out on my ass if I was trying to get her to fall in love with me now." He gives me a sympathetic half-smile. "Which begs the question, this personal message you're waiting for, would it happen to be from a woman? And if so, when the hell did you start dating her and why haven't you said anything until now?"

Alex is one of the very few people who knows about my dating life. I keep it pretty low profile, mostly because of Queenie. It's not that I don't think she can handle me dating someone. In fact, it's the opposite. My worry is more that she'll get attached to whomever I'm seeing, and then if it ends, there will be double the disappointment to contend with.

I don't want to bring women into Queenie's life who aren't sticking around, since her mother has been a perpetual abandoner at the worst of times and a shit disturber at the best.

"I've hardly had time for dating."

"Queenie's wedding was three months ago. That's a lot of weeks to get back out there. And it's the off-season."

"I'm busy with the upcoming season."

He coughs the word "bullshit" into his fist.

"Why are you on me about this?" In the months since Hanna put an end to what was going on between us, I haven't so much as tried to go on a date. I realized, after the fact, that it had started to feel like an actual relationship. Which I guess made sense, since we were spending a lot of time together, and not just between the sheets. I miss having someone constant in my life, and for a while Hanna was that.

"'Cause you've been distracted all night. If you're not dating someone, does that mean you're setting up a booty call during your daughter's birthday party?" Alex raises a brow.

I shoot him a glare. "Seriously?"

"Why are you being so secretive? Are you hooking up with someone the same age as Queenie or something?"

I nearly choke on my drink. "I'd have to be a special kind of stupid to date someone my daughter's age. Like I need that level of drama in my life. And I'm not hooking up with anyone. Not anymore, anyway." I glance around the room, searching for Hanna. Not that sleeping with her had any less potential for drama. But we're mature adults. We knew what the limitations were. Although I'm having trouble coming to terms with those, apparently, based on the way I'm incessantly checking my phone.

He perks up. "Not anymore? So you *were* seeing someone?"

"It was casual."

"How come this is the first I'm hearing of it?"

"Because we didn't want it to be a thing."

"Is she here tonight?"

"Why does it matter?" I need him to drop it.

"Because that would narrow it down by a lot." He scans the room. "Wait a second, have you got a thing for Ryan's Momster?"

This time I don't manage to stop the scotch from entering my windpipe. I start coughing and tears spring to my eyes. "What the hell, Alex?"

He slaps me on the back a few times. "Shit. Sorry. It was a joke."

I put my hands on my knees and try to clear my throat, which burns. Inhaling scotch is not advised. "Not funny, man. Not funny."

I roll my shoulders back and pull on my tie. It feels really tight right now. Tight and uncomfortable. And my palms start to sweat.

"Jake, man."

I give him the side-eye. "Whatever you're thinking, don't."

He pokes at his bottom lip with his tongue. He does it when we play poker and gives away his shitty hands every single time.

"She's a good-looking woman."

"Stop."

"I'm just saying I can see the allure."

"There's no allure." There's plenty of allure, which is exactly the problem.

"Right. Okay. Well, in that case, maybe the next time we're in Tennessee, Ryan should invite her to a game and I can introduce her to Karl Halpern, the owner of their team. He got divorced a few years back. You remember that, right? She left him for some guy she met in Paris." He shakes his head. "He's a good guy. It's probably time he gets back in the game."

"I don't think he's her type."

"Really? Why not, Jake?"

"Drop it, Alex."

"That's what I thought." He grins and takes another sip of his scotch. "Your secret's safe with me."

"It doesn't matter because it's over anyway. Our kids are married to each other. It's too complicated." It's what I keep telling myself, anyway. "Don't tell Violet."

He scoffs. "I know better than to say anything to my wife. I love her, but she's about as good at keeping secrets as a sieve is holding water."

Five minutes later, I spot Hanna on her own, heading toward the bathrooms. I excuse myself and follow her, not needing to explain myself to Alex.

I manage to catch her on her way back out.

"Oh! Jake!" She nearly crashes into me. But to be fair, I was lurking in the shadows, which there are a lot of since the restaurant has low lighting.

"Hey. I've hardly had a chance to say hello tonight." I steady her by putting a hand on her hip, but her eyes dart to the hallway and she steps back, severing the connection.

"I know." She gives me a small smile and bites her bottom lip. Her eyes move over my face, but dart away before she can meet my gaze. "The girls have been keeping me busy."

"Is everything okay?" It's too dark in the hallway for me to see her face clearly, but based on her body language, things are definitely off.

She looks exhausted and nervous as hell. And her teeth keep finding her bottom lip, which is something she does when she's worried. She did it a lot when we were discussing the guest list for the wedding—every time Queenie's mom was brought up. And her own mother.

"Yes. No. Can we talk later? Maybe after the party?" She fiddles with her necklace, which happens to be the one I gave her at King and Queenie's wedding.

I'm very accustomed to tackling issues head-on, rather than letting things fester. It doesn't help either of us if I'm concocting scenarios in my head that may or may not have a legitimate basis. "Can we find a place to talk now? Even if it's for a minute? I feel like you've been dodging me all night and I know things are different." I motion between us. "But I think we need to figure out how to make this work. I still really value your friendship, Hanna. I don't want to lose that."

"In there?" She inclines her head toward the small room to the right, likely where intimate private dinners are held—when this place isn't being rented out.

I follow her into the room and she tucks herself into the corner, out of sight from anyone passing by. I take a seat beside her.

She runs her hands down her thighs and exhales a long breath. And another one.

"Are you okay?"

She closes her eyes and shakes her head. "I'm so sorry."

"For what?" I don't understand what's making her so emotional.

She reaches into her clutch, pulling free a tissue. She dabs at the corner of her eyes, stopping the tears before they can fall. She pinches the bridge of her nose, like she's trying to use it as a stop button. "All the freaking hormones are making me ridiculously emotional."

Aside from the wedding, I've never seen Hanna cry. But this seems different. She's practically vibrating with anxiety. "It's okay. You know I'm not afraid of tears." I go for light, because I honestly don't know what else to do.

"I know." She tips her chin up and dabs at her eyes again.

"Thank you. I'm sorry."

"What are you so sorry about?" This is the second time she's apologized in the past two minutes.

She takes another deep breath, and when her gaze meets mine it's so…forlorn? Torn? Sad? Worried? So many emotions pass over her face, and I don't know what to do with any of them because I have no idea what's going on.

She clasps her hands in her lap. "There's no easy way to tell you this, so I'm just going to come out with it."

"Okay." I have to wonder if maybe she's reconciling with her ex or something. Although I can't see her doing that after the shit he pulled. Unless she's sick? Or maybe she regrets putting an end to things? But I don't know why that would make her this emotional.

She meets my questioning gaze. "Jake, I'm pregnant."

I don't say anything at first. I don't know what to say. For a few very long seconds, the only sound in the room is Hanna's unsteady breathing. And the laughter and chatter of the party happening down the hall.

The first question I ask is a stupid one. "How did this happen?"

She blinks a few times, fingers twisting in her lap. "I honestly didn't think I could get pregnant. I haven't had a regular period in two years. I'm so sorry, Jake. I didn't mean for this to happen. I thought we were safe. I can't believe I was so stupid." Her bottom lip trembles and she raises her hand to cover her mouth and turns her head, fighting to keep her composure.

The last time I got news like this, I was in college. I was on track to get my degree and being signed to a team. I had my entire life ahead of me. I was going to live the dream. NHL career, making millions a year, traveling all over the country. Kimmie and I were going to wait until we were finished with college, get married, and move to whatever city I was playing for. We had it all planned out. And then I went from carefree college kid to soon-to-be father.

"Are you sure? I thought you said you were menopausal?" I don't know what to do with this information. It all seems impossible, and I'm still in a state of shock.

"Perimenopausal. And I am." She keeps twisting the tissue in her hands, shredding it.

Panic starts to set in, exactly like it did more than two and a half decades ago, when Queenie's mother announced, tearfully, that she was pregnant. She'd been afraid and wanted to terminate. I'd told her we would make it work. That I would take care of both of them. She'd agreed, although she'd had reservations. Ones that didn't wane.

And my entire life changed.

And now it's going to change again.

"I don't get how this could happen. And you're positive it's mine?"

Hanna flinches. "You're the only person I've slept with, so yes, it's yours."

I run a hand through my hair. "I just…how is this even possible? You said we were fine to go without the condoms." I wince at my accusatory tone and try to dial it back. "Are you sure you're pregnant and it isn't just some hormone glitch?" I don't know why I keep asking idiotic questions, apart from the fact I can't believe this is happening. Again. Maybe she'll give me a different answer if I keep asking the same questions. Like miraculously she'll say she's kidding. "Please tell me this is your idea of a bad joke."

"Do you really think I would be sitting here, telling you I'm pregnant for shits and giggles?" she snaps.

I'm aware that Hanna does not, in fact, have a morbid sense of humor. But this is taking me right back to when I was nineteen and Kimmie had forgotten to take her birth control for the better part of a week. I would have worn a condom if I'd known, but I hadn't.

And once again, I'd thought we were safe, only to find out we clearly weren't.

"I was done doing the raising a kid thing. Freedom was knocking at my door." I drag a hand over my face, remembering the conversation we had all those months ago when this thing between us started. "Queenie just got married. She should be the one getting pregnant, not us. And we're not even an *us*." I keep pointing out the obvious, and Hanna seems to shrink into herself and get her back up at the same time.

Her expression is flat. "Trust me, I'm as shocked as you are."

I glance at her stomach. There aren't any outward signs to give away the fact there's a baby in there. "How far along are you?"

She rubs her temple. "If I had to guess, I'd say I'm about twelve weeks, but I won't know for sure until I see my doctor."

"So you got pregnant the weekend of Queenie and King's wedding?" I run my palms down my thighs, which are now sweaty, along with the rest of me.

"It seems that way, yes."

"We only went without a condom that one time," I mutter. Hanna and I were always careful. In fact, it's the only time I've gone without a condom since Queenie's conception.

Before I can admit that it's an idiotic thing to say, Hanna scoffs and says, "Well, Jake, we both know that's all it really takes, don't we?"

I don't bother answering that, since it's clearly full of sarcasm. And horrifyingly accurate. "When did you find out about this?"

"The cream in my coffee tasted off this morning, and then the same thing happened when I was with the girls at our spa day. I figured I was run down, or maybe coming down with something, but Violet made a comment about knowing she was pregnant when dairy tasted funky. I didn't think anything of it at first, but I've been sleeping so much lately. And my stomach has been off. I thought I was nervous about seeing you, which I was, but then I realized that there might be more to it."

"Wait, you found this out *today*?"

"This afternoon. I took a test."

"Well, that's a whole lot of irony that you find this out on my daughter's damn birthday." I shake my head in disbelief. "Wait. Weren't you with the girls all afternoon? When would you have time to take a test?"

"Lainey's been trying to get pregnant, and she's been carrying around tests with her. She gave me one, and I went to the bathroom...and it came back positive," Hanna explains.

"Lainey and Violet know you're pregnant?" That's not ideal. Especially considering the conversation Alex and I had about his wife's inability to keep secrets.

"And Stevie." She holds up her hand to keep me from interrupting. "But they don't know it's yours. I told them I was casually involved with someone, and they assumed whomever it was is from Tennessee. I made them promise not to say anything because I wasn't sure what to do."

I remember what it was like when Queenie's mom walked out on us when Queenie was only three months old and all of a sudden I was on my own, raising a kid. All the sleepless nights at twenty were hard enough. The idea of having to do that now is mind-boggling. "Do you know what you want to do?"

Her brow furrows. "Do as in...?"

"How you'd like to move forward? What your plan is? We're in our forties." And I'm back to stating the obvious. "Are you going to keep it?"

She recoils, as if I've slapped her, which tells me everything about my tone. "I don't expect anything from you, Jake. I'm not asking you to take this on with me. I'm telling you because you need to know."

"I didn't mean it the way it came out. And if it's my kid, I'm obviously going to take a role in his or her life." And how am I going to manage that? Hanna lives a five-hour plane ride away.

"*If* it's your kid? I haven't been with anyone except you," she practically spits at me.

I'm about to respond when Hanna raises a hand to stop me from saying something stupid. Again. "I need to see my doctor before we start talking about how this child is going to be raised. Even if I'm through the first trimester, which I think I am, I'm high risk and there's a chance I could still lose this baby."

"But your plan *is* to keep it?" Do I want her to keep it? Why am I asking her these questions when I don't even know the answers myself?

"Barring any complications, yes." She reaches for her necklace and fingers the rose gold heart. "I know this is very unexpected, but this is the last chance I'm going to have. I didn't even think I still had a chance. I know there are a lot of potential complications, but I'm going to go through with the pregnancy, high risk or not."

I don't even know what the risks are. Does this pregnancy put Hanna in danger? And if something happens to her, then what? I could be looking at the same scenario as last time. Except potentially worse if something bad happens to Hanna in the process. "Do you want me to get you in to see a doctor here? I could arrange something for tomorrow? I could call the team doctor."

She shakes her head. "I'd rather see my own doctor. She knows my history."

"Right. Okay. Should I fly back with you? Do you want me there?" Judging by the look on her face, the answer to that question is no.

The sound of voices coming down the hall alerts us that this conversation isn't as private as we'd like it to be.

"Should we find a more private place to talk this through?" I ask. My head is a swirling mess of memories and worries. The last time this happened I ended up losing my girlfriend, my career, and becoming a single dad. It's a giant mindfuck I don't know how to handle.

"I'm staying at Ryan and Queenie's. Do you want to come back there?" She exhales a tremulous breath and checks her phone. "It's after eleven. It wouldn't be a stretch for me to say I'm tired in say, half an hour?"

"And I'll leave with you." I need some kind of plan and a minute to get my head around this whole thing.

"Okay." She pushes to her feet, running her hands down her thighs and then motions to her face. "Do I need to manage this? Does it look like I've been crying?"

"No. You look beautiful as ever." It's probably the first thing

I've said to her that hasn't made her cringe.

She gives me a small smile. "Now you're just trying to make me feel better."

"Untrue. You're always stunning, Hanna." Out of habit, I place my fingertips at the small of her back as we step back out into the hall.

At the same time, the door to the men's bathroom swings open and out steps Bishop.

He raises an eyebrow. "Seriously? Why is it every time there's an event the two of you disappear together? You know you're making it impossible for me to ignore this."

"We were talking, just like last time," Hanna says.

He rolls his eyes. "Uh-huh. You know, if you two are hooking up, can you please keep it on the downlow and keep me out of it? Like King's family isn't messed up enough as it is without you two making him and Queenie stepbrother and sister."

And with that he turns around and stalks off.

Hanna's eyes go wide with horror. "Oh my God, Jake. What the hell are we going to tell the kids?"

CHAPTER TEN

What's the Plan?

Hanna

THE NEXT HALF hour is the longest of my life. To say Jake's reaction is not what I anticipated would be an understatement. I didn't think he'd jump for joy, but I also didn't expect . . . that. Or maybe I'm hypersensitive. I don't know. But it makes the time between telling him and leaving the bar tense.

"You okay?" Ryan slings his arm over my shoulders and pulls me into his side. In his other hand is a White Russian.

The thought of dairy makes my stomach turn, which is sad because I usually love all things dairy. Especially ice cream. "Yeah, just tired. You know how I am about flying. Nothing a good night's sleep won't cure." I hate that I'm lying to him. Still. *Again.* But I can't stand the idea of ruining Queenie's birthday with this kind of news. Not that it's bad news, exactly. It's just a shocker is all.

"You don't have to drag yourself through to the end of the night. We'll see you in the morning anyway. And you're not flying out until later, right?"

"Late afternoon." And I won't get home until after midnight, but Monday is a work from home day and I've made sure all my phone meetings are scheduled in the afternoon, so I can sleep off the jet lag.

"We can get in some quality time over brunch. And I'll drive you to the airport." Ryan smiles down at me. He's definitely tipsy. He doesn't drink very often, and when he does, it's usually dairy-based drinks that taste more like a milkshake than an alcoholic beverage.

"Okay. That sounds great." I give him a kiss on the cheek and say my goodnight to the girls, quietly thanking Lainey, Stevie, and Violet for their help today and wishing Queenie a happy birthday. Jake uses my leaving as an excuse to take off as well, and we head out to the parking lot together, Jake calling us an Uber.

As soon as I'm in the car, I wilt. I'm beyond exhausted. My brain is a foggy mess, and I have no idea what kind of conversation to expect tonight. I dropped one hell of a bomb on Jake, not to mention myself. Everything was different when we were just sleeping together, having a bit of fun. Now our lives are irrevocably intertwined in a new way. No matter what happens, whether this baby happens, our relationship will never be the same as it was.

"How are you?" Jake asks. The ride has been pretty quiet so far, mostly because this isn't a conversation either of us would like to have in the presence of Jett, the Uber driver with the bad haircut and terrible taste in music.

I shrug. "I've been better and I've been worse." Reality is setting in and it scares the hell out of me. I don't know whether I should feel any excitement at this point. There's a part of me that's really overjoyed, but that's being stepped on by all my worry now.

He leans in, his lips at my ear, dropping his voice to a whisper, "Should we stop at a CVS on the way home? Should you take another test to make sure?"

I shake my head, then turn and tip my chin up as he bends so his ear is at my mouth. My nose brushes his cheek and I breathe in his cologne. Even as stressed as I am, my body warms to his proximity. "There's no point in me taking another test. It's rare to get a false positive when it comes to pregnancy tests. Either the hormone is there or it isn't."

"Oh." He backs up, looking…stunned maybe. "I didn't know that."

I remind myself that it's been a lot of years since either of us has done this. And he wasn't the one taking the test.

I'm grateful the ride to Ryan's isn't long. As soon as we're out of the car and inside the house, I turn to him. "Like I said before, I don't expect anything from you."

He tucks his hand into his pocket and his lips mash into a line. "I raised a daughter on my own, I'm not about to shirk my responsibilities this time around. I'm just trying to get my head around it, that's all, Hanna." He blows out a breath. "I'm not trying to be a dick. But we're both in our forties. Last time I was thirty with a teenager, this time I'm going to be sixty. It's a bit of a mindfuck."

I haven't thought much past the shock of this to consider what it will be like to care for a baby at my age, let alone a teenager when I should be considering retirement. My head is spinning. "That's if this pregnancy goes to term. The chances of a miscarriage are a lot higher." I need to keep myself grounded and keep my expectations low.

I tap my lips with my fingers, trying to get a handle on my emotions and my anxiety level. I head for the kitchen. I need . . . something in my hands so I don't chew my nails down to stubs. "And I've miscarried before, so that increases my odds of having it happen again." It was such an emotional blow. One I struggled to recover from for months.

Jake follows me, eyes wide. "You miscarried before? When did that happen?"

"When I was forty-one."

"I'm so sorry. I had no idea."

"It's really not something I talk about." Especially not with the guy I've been having a clandestine relationship of sorts with.

He rounds the island and comes to stand beside me. "We probably should. Even though I'm sure it's difficult."

I nod and look out the window, into the backyard where string

81

lights hang over the outdoor dining area. "I'd basically given up on the idea of having my own baby at that point. Gordon and I had been trying for so long, with no success. I said I was done with the fertility treatments and the doctor appointments. I couldn't handle any more disappointment. I stopped keeping track of periods because they'd started to get all wonky anyway. One day I went to the grocery store and I had these awful cramps. The kind that took me to my knees. I was nine weeks." I blow out a breath. "I was devastated. I'd been pregnant and I hadn't even known. Again. It was too much emotionally to handle something like that again."

Jake rubs his bottom lip, and his eyes are sad. "I'm so sorry, Hanna. I can't even imagine how hard it was for you."

I give him a small smile. It's always strange, the feeling like I need to console the other person or protect them from my pain. "Me, too." It was the beginning of the end for Gordon and me. He couldn't understand my grief. He'd suggested adoption, and I hadn't been opposed, but we'd had friends who had gone down that path and faced horrible disappointment when the mother decided at the last minute to keep the baby. Their hearts had been so broken, and I couldn't fathom any more loss.

It had been a dark time in my life. My mom had been there to support me, and so had Paxton. And, of course, Ryan. But I'd taken it much harder than I expected. I shut down for a while and decided I couldn't go through it again. Except now I am. "So, when I tell you that I don't expect anything from you, Jake, I mean it. Neither of us meant for this to happen, but this is my very last chance to have a baby of my own. I'm very aware that it's risky for the baby and me, but I didn't think I'd get another shot at being a mom, and now I'm being given one."

He leans against the counter, his expression pained, but it's hard to get a read on him. "I see why you want to go through with this."

I feel like I'm about to start crying again, which isn't going to be helpful to this conversation. So, I shift gears. "Can I get you something to drink?"

"Why don't you have a seat, and I can get you something instead?"

"I'm pregnant, not an invalid, Jake."

"I know. I'm just trying to be helpful." He moves to the cupboards and pulls out two glasses. Of course, he knows where everything is here. He has dinner with Ryan and Queenie once a week. Queenie is incredibly close to her dad, and Jake and Ryan get along really well. I hope this doesn't change that. At least not in the long term.

Jake opens the fridge. There are three gallons of milk—not a surprise—and pressed organic orange juice, as well as sparkling water. "I'm guessing you're going to pass on the milk." At least one of us still has their sense of humor intact.

I smile. "Water is fine."

"Are you hungry? You didn't eat much at dinner," Jake asks as he passes me the glass of water.

"Thank you." I take a sip. "How do you know I didn't eat much at dinner?"

He shrugs, his expression sheepish. "I might have been watching you."

I duck my head. I wish things weren't so complicated. Ironic that I can long for the days when the hardest thing to contend with was not giving in and sleeping with Jake again. "I'm sorry that it seemed like I was dodging you. I would have called you this afternoon, but I honestly didn't want to ruin your day."

"You didn't ruin my day, Hanna." His voice is flat, though, and it sounds more like lip service than anything.

I give him a disbelieving look. "I don't think either of us started today and ever once thought 'Hey, wouldn't it be awesome if I found out I was going to have a child again.'"

He sighs. "It's definitely a surprise."

I don't know what I expect from him, but this apathy isn't it. I guess it's better than how things went when I was a teen and my ex-boyfriend was insistent I get rid of the baby, and then he accused me of trying to tie him down. "I'm going to change into something more comfortable. Then we can talk this out."

I leave Jake in the living room while I change into a pair of leggings and an oversized shirt. I'm about done with jeans and anything that isn't comfortable and non-restrictive. At least now I know why my pants have been fitting snugger these days. Jake is sitting on the couch when I return. He's still wearing dress pants, a button-down, and a tie, but it hangs loose around his neck and the top two buttons are undone.

"Tell me what you're thinking," I ask.

"That this morning I was looking forward to celebrating my daughter's birthday and hoping things weren't going to be too strained between us." He picks a pen up off the coffee table and flips it between his fingers.

"I wasn't sure how easy it would be to be around you and not end up in bed with you."

"I guess we know where our lack of restraint gets us." Jake motions to my stomach. "At least this time the condoms really wouldn't be necessary."

I cringe and he sighs and shakes his head. "That came out wrong. I'm not trying to be a jerk with all the asshole comments and the shitty jokes, Hanna. I'm just…struggling here. Earlier I was talking to Alex about how soon Queenie and King will be starting a family and here you are, telling me that I'm back at square one. It's going to take me more than an hour to get a handle on this."

"I really don't have expectations from you, Jake. But it wasn't like not telling you was actually going to be an option. In a couple of months, it's going to be pretty obvious what's going on." I rub my belly, trying to find a way to soothe myself. "You know, I looked it up and there's literally a five percent chance that I can get pregnant at my age. Five percent. The odds were so slim."

"Are you sure you don't want to see a doctor tomorrow? Bill is our team physician, and while he doesn't specialize in prenatal care, we could have another test. To be absolutely sure."

I raise a hand to stop him. "I'm already sure. And I'd really rather see my doctor. I'm sure she'll get me in right away, all things considered. She'll want to do blood work and schedule an ultrasound to make sure everything is okay so far."

"It's a lot to think about, isn't it?" Jake runs his hand through his hair.

"It is," I agree.

"If you're already at the twelve-week mark, the ultrasound should be soon, right?"

"I would assume she'll want me to have one right away. And we'll have to test for chromosomal abnormalities."

He rubs the space between his eyes. "And if there are issues?"

"It really depends on what they find, if anything, to be honest. Finding out something is wrong with the baby isn't necessarily the thing that scares me the most. It's thinking everything is okay, and then suddenly they're not. I'm even higher risk than I was last time, but I'm already past the twelve-week mark, so I'm willing to take the chance and hope things are going to be okay."

He taps the edge of the couch. "How risky is this for you? Physically and emotionally, Hanna, how hard is this going to be on you if it doesn't work out?"

I settle my palm over my stomach, not wanting to think about how painful it will be if this doesn't go the way I want it to. "It's happening, whether we like it or not. And I'm not terminating, not unless there's no other option to protect the baby's quality of life."

"What about *your* quality of life?" he asks, voice cracking at the end.

"I'll deal with whatever is thrown at me."

"What are the medical risks in your forties? And even if everything goes smoothly, you're talking about midnight feedings and dealing with a toddler. That's a lot of energy with a partner, let alone trying to do it on your own, which, you've implied more than once is something you're prepared to do." His tone shifts again, and I can't quite read it.

Is he angry about that, scared, frustrated? I don't know enough about how things went with Queenie's mother to understand how he's feeling. All I know is that she left them when Queenie was an infant and Jake raised her on his own.

"Because I don't want you to feel beholden to the baby or me."

"How will I *not* feel that way at every damn family gathering we're at together?" He runs both hands down his face. "I should have stopped and got a damn condom."

I laugh in disbelief. "You know what? I don't think this is a particularly productive conversation right now. I think we're both tired and emotional, and I'm very close to saying things I'm probably going to regret in the morning. You should go home."

"We need to figure out what we're going to tell the kids."

"Come back in the morning. We can talk then, but I'm done with this conversation and you tonight." I push up off the couch.

"Hanna." Jake grabs for my wrist. "I didn't mean—"

"Don't." I hold up a finger. "I get that you are in shock. And I understand that you feel blindsided because I felt the same way earlier today. But you are being thoughtless and entirely self-absorbed. Sleep on it. Get some perspective. We'll talk tomorrow." With that, I storm down the hall, slamming the bedroom door behind me and flipping the lock.

I'm shaking and angry. I take several deep breaths, trying to calm down.

A few seconds later, there's a quiet knock on the door. "Hanna?"

"I'm done tonight," I call out.

"For what it's worth, I'm sorry."

Sorry isn't going to fix this problem.

CHAPTER ELEVEN

Let's Try that Again

Jake

I ORDER AN Uber and go home. I feel like shit, but I also don't seem to be able to say anything to Hanna without sticking my foot in my mouth and coming off like a jerk.

Sleep is evasive. I maybe manage an hour or two of restless dozing, but my mind is spinning on an endless loop of what-ifs and why nows. I finally give up at four and make myself a coffee.

I watch it drip into the cup and consider Hanna's past experiences—Ryan being raised by her parents, getting pregnant only to wind up losing the baby before she could celebrate it, her marriage ending, and now this.

I don't know what it's like to be in her shoes.

But I do know what it's like to think I was doing all the right things with Kimmie where her pregnancy was concerned, only to have her tell me I shouldn't have pushed her to keep the baby and walk away from both of us, leaving me to raise Queenie on my own. I don't necessarily think that's something Hanna is likely to do, but I can't help that's where my mind goes.

My parents were awesome, and supportive, but while other twenty-year-olds were going to bars, getting drunk, and having girlfriends, pulling all-nighters studying for exams, or hanging out with friends, I was juggling my degree, hockey, and dealing with sleepless nights thanks to midnight feedings and learning how to manage being a single parent.

While my teammates were sleeping off hangovers, I was meeting with my lawyer and filing for full custody of my daughter. I wouldn't leave Queenie without two parents.

Instead of starting my career on the ice, I took a lower-level position in administration and dealt with the terrible twos and things like potty training and trying to get her to sleep through the night.

Over the past few months, I've finally had a taste of freedom, of feeling secure in the knowledge that my daughter has found a great partner to navigate life with. I'd just gotten used to quiet mornings and living alone. I'd been looking forward to getting back on the dating scene. Eventually. After I'd given myself some time to get over the whole Hanna thing ending, which, to be honest, was taking a lot longer than I thought it would. Maybe because we weren't just casual lovers, we were friends, too.

But now the Hanna thing is even more complicated. And I didn't think that was possible.

All it took was one impulsive moment. And now I'm facing at least another eighteen plus years of raising a child with someone who lives halfway across the country. I don't even know what that's going to look like.

"What the fuck am I going to do?" I scrub a hand over my face and take my coffee with me into the living room, pausing at the wall of photos that Queenie thinks is a ridiculous homage to bad fashion over the past two and a half decades.

It chronicles my daughter's life, from newborn to college graduate to the wedding photo I hung last week. I shifted all of the photos around to make that one the focus. My baby girl all grown up and starting her life with her partner.

I don't even have one picture of Queenie with her mother. Not because I didn't take any. I did. But Kimmie never smiled when she held our baby girl. She would give me a look and tell me to put the camera away and do something useful.

Even after Kimmie left, I still tried to keep her in our lives, for Queenie's sake. I would take Queenie to see her mother and tried my best to be civil and cordial, but it was never about time with her daughter. It was always about us. How I failed our relationship because I put Queenie ahead of everything—my career, relationships, friendships, a social life.

I don't know the first thing about having a partner. I have no idea what it's like to raise a child with someone else who is as equally invested, maybe even more so based on our conversation last night. And it scares the hell out of me.

There's so much to think about. To worry about. I'll be seventy when this kid is the same age as Queenie. She'll be more parent appropriate than I will be by then. When I drop the kid off at school, people will think I'm their grandfather.

But as I stand here, bleary-eyed and uncertain, I realize one very important thing. I may have been ready to move on with my life, but I made a choice, exactly like I did back when I was nineteen. And choices have consequences. Just because I'm having a hard time wrapping my head around this, doesn't mean I should be a selfish asshole about it.

Which is exactly how I acted last night with Hanna.

I can't imagine how she must feel right now. How nervous she must be. How alone she must feel. I don't want this to be an echo of her teens, when she found out she was pregnant the first time. Or an echo of mine, where I pushed my own agenda and forgot to take into account that it's more than just being a good dad, it's about being a reliable partner, however that looks. I don't want to have the same regrets with Hanna as I did with Kimmie.

"Ah, shit." I press the heel of my hand to my eye and rub. "Way to be an asshat." I think I handled this news better the first time around.

I head down the hall to the bathroom. I need a shower to clear my head. And then I need to talk to Hanna, and hopefully be less of an idiot than I was last night.

I ARRIVE AT Queenie and Kingston's house at six-thirty. Based on Ryan's social media, they closed down the bar at two in the morning. I doubt they'll be up anytime soon.

I let myself in with the entry code—dad privileges—and reset the alarm. I make my way to the bedroom Hanna is staying in, grateful it's on the main floor and King and Queenie are upstairs, so my being here won't wake them.

I knock on her door and am unsurprised when I don't get a response right away. Before I think about what I'm doing, I send her a text and hear the phone's muffled chime from inside the room. There's a song attached to my messages.

I'm about to leave my post and make myself comfortable in the living room, and maybe grab a nap, but the sound of feet padding across the floor makes me pause.

The door opens and Hanna blinks at me blearily. "Do you know what time it is?"

"I'm sorry."

"It's not even seven." She scrubs her face with her hand and smacks her lips.

"I know. I couldn't sleep. I shouldn't have woken you. I wanted to apologize for the way I acted last night. I was an asshole."

Her eyes fall closed and she nods, whether in agreement or acknowledgement, I'm unsure. She's wearing an oversized night shirt that reads *I like sleep more than people*. Her long hair is pulled up into a ponytail that's half falling out of the tie.

"I'll be in the living room when you're awake enough to talk." I take a step down the hall, but Hanna grabs my wrist.

"Come in. Give me a few minutes." She drops my wrist and leaves me standing in the middle of the bedroom as she disappears into the bathroom.

There's a small sitting area to the right, so I take a seat and survey the space. Her clothes from last night lie in a heap on the floor. The sheets are rumpled and twisted, and there's a pile of tissues littering the pale blue comforter, as well as a few on the floor.

Which means there were tears.

Caused by me.

A few minutes later, she reappears, her hair smoothed out, and she's wearing a long shirt and leggings.

"Are you okay?" I ask.

She shrugs and pads across the room, dropping into the chair across from me. "I've been better, and I've been worse."

"I'm sorry about the way I handled things last night. Or didn't handle things. I know it's not an excuse, but I'd just started getting used to having an empty house, and Queenie having her own person to rely on. And it took me back to when she was a baby and I was doing it all on my own and how hard it was then. I wasn't thinking about how you felt or how hard this must all be for you."

Hanna is silent for a few seconds. "It's a lot to process, and I don't expect you to feel good about it, or particularly enthused, but you needed to know. Do I wish the timing was different? That I was five years younger? That our relationship wasn't already complicated enough without this? Absolutely. But like it or not, Jake, I'm having this baby."

I wish I'd reacted to the news differently so she isn't on the defensive. "And I'm going to be here to support you through it. I know there's still a lot to figure out, but maybe once you've seen your doctor we can start making a plan? I'd like to be able to come to the important doctor's appointments. I don't want you to have to do this alone."

She rubs her eyes and exhales a slow breath. "I don't expect you to fly to Tennessee every time I have an appointment."

"I know you don't. I *want* to be there, Hanna. As much as my schedule will allow. We can use that shared calendar we set up for all the events leading up to the kids' wedding, so I can keep track of all the important stuff with you." With Kimmie, I was the one who had to make all the appointments and make sure she went to them. I'd assumed, naively, that once Queenie was born, she'd fall in love with her the way I already had. I don't get the feeling it's going to be the same with Hanna. In fact, if I had to guess, I'm going to be the one who has to work to earn her trust back after last night and my jerk behavior.

"Oh. Yeah. Okay. We can definitely do that." She rubs her temple, her posture relaxing a little.

I knead the back of my neck. "Speaking of the kids, when do you think we should tell them what's going on?"

She fingers the heart around her neck. "I'd really rather not keep more secrets from Ryan, so the sooner the better, I guess?"

"This morning then?" I suggest.

"That would be best, I think," she agrees.

I wish she was here longer, so we had more time to get comfortable with this new version of us. Whatever that's going to look like. I have so many questions, none of which I feel I can ask yet. "Do you want to tell them together or separately?"

Hanna taps her lips. "I think it would be best if we presented a united front, unless you feel differently?"

"United is good." I move my chair closer and rest my arm on the small table, palm facing up, fingers stretched toward her. "What are you most worried about right now?"

"Everything?" She tips her chin up, eyes on the ceiling as if she's fighting back tears. "I'm worried for the health of this baby. I'm worried about how Ryan is going to take this and what it's going to do to our relationship. I'm afraid to get excited or hopeful because I know how quickly things can change. The last time I was pregnant was the beginning of the end of my marriage."

"Is that why you ended up divorcing?" This isn't something Hanna and I have ever talked about. I know about her divorce, but I don't know what happened to end her marriage in the first place. And in some ways our experiences seem to echo each other. We both lost the person who was supposed to be our partner, but I still had Queenie, and Hanna ended up alone.

She slips her fingers into my palm and I curl them around hers and squeeze.

"I don't talk about this much because it makes me emotional." She takes a deep breath before she continues, "When I miscarried, I had to divulge that I'd had a baby before. I hadn't told Gordon that I was Ryan's biological mother."

"Why not? You didn't think he would understand?"

"So many reasons, but I think most of it stems from guilt. The not being able to raise Ryan the way I wanted to. And I guess that secrecy tells me more about that relationship than I'd ever been willing to admit. At least while I was still in it." She's quiet for a moment. "Gordon felt . . . betrayed. Which made sense. We'd been married for fifteen years, and it was a big secret to keep from the person you share your life with. When he found out that Ryan was actually my son, he didn't handle it well. And I was grieving the loss of our baby. He sat on that information for a couple of years, but when I told him I wasn't happy in our marriage and thought we should separate, he told Ryan the truth, and well, there was no way for our marriage to recover after that."

After everything Hanna has been through and the ways she's been let down and betrayed, I'm surprised she's even willing to talk to me this morning. "That must have been hard for you."

"Harder for Ryan. I always knew I was his mother, and he always believed I was his sister. It threw his world into upheaval."

"Why didn't you ever tell Ryan before that?" That's one thing I've always wondered but never felt I had the right to ask.

"When I was young, I thought it made sense for my parents to take on that role. I didn't want to give him up for adoption, but raising a child when I was fifteen was so daunting. So when my parents said they would adopt him, I thought it would be best for Ryan. For all of us. He'd still be in my life. But as he got older, things changed. I never moved away for college. I was there for every milestone. And when he made it to the NHL, well, I was so proud." She smiles, like she's caught up in the memory.

"By the time I was in my thirties, I started to look at things differently. And I talked to my parents about maybe telling him the truth. But he'd just started his career, and they were worried it would do too much damage. They'd made sure he would have everything he needed to be successful in life, and I didn't want to be selfish. So I didn't tell him."

"That selflessness came at a pretty steep price for you." She must have felt handcuffed by that choice. Stuck between two roles.

"And I would pay it a thousand times over knowing that Ryan is where he is because he was loved and cared for. He's a great man, and he has a great partner. I have so much hope for Ryan and Queenie."

"So do I." And I mean it. He's the balance Queenie needs. He's her anchor, and she's his buoy.

"I really don't want this to strain their relationship." Hanna motions between us.

"Are you worried it will?" King always seems to be able to roll with things.

"Our lives are completely intertwined now, on so many different levels. We're their parents, and now we have this unexpected baby on the way. It's a complex and delicate situation. What exactly are we going to tell them?"

I brush a few stray hairs away from her face, and I am relieved when she leans into the touch instead of shying away. "We tell them the truth. That we share an attraction. That we acted on it and you're pregnant."

"You make it sound so simple."

I wish that it were. "With a situation like this, I think simple is best. We tell them that you're planning to see a doctor when you get back to Tennessee and that we're going to go from there. I know we can't predict the future, Hanna, but we'll find a way to make it work." I take her other hand in mine. "Now I have an important question for you."

"Okay." She's still guarded and uncertain.

"Can I give you a hug?"

She covers her mouth with her hand and nods.

This is what I should have done yesterday. I stand and pull her up with me so I can wrap my arms around her. "We'll figure it out, Hanna."

"Thank you," she murmurs into my chest.

"For what?"

"Being you."

CHAPTER TWELVE

I Didn't See That Coming

Jake

IT'S ONLY SEVEN-thirty in the morning, and considering the late hour the kids came in, I don't expect they'll be up anytime soon. Since both Hanna and I are woefully underslept, she suggests a pre-conversation nap. I assume I'll be taking mine on the living room couch, or in one of the spare rooms upstairs, but she pats the space beside her and we both pass out.

I wake up several hours later.

Hanna is propped up on the pillows beside me, her phone in her hand.

"Time's it?" I mumble.

She chuckles. "It's after eleven. We should probably get up and face the music, huh?"

The haze of sleep is quick to lift. "It feels a lot like we're the kids again and we're about to get grounded for bad behavior."

Hanna grins. "Seems rather fitting. And Ryan has this disapproving dad look that makes you feel like a scolded child when you do something he doesn't like."

I think about that for a second. "Shit, you're right. He really does. He's totally going to be the bad cop in that relationship when they have kids."

"He won't even have to be the bad cop. He'll give them

the look, and they'll feel like garbage for whatever it was they *thought* about doing wrong but didn't."

She rolls out of bed and makes a face as she stands there.

I sit up in a rush. "You okay?"

She holds up a finger and her whole body curves in for a second. It reminds me of a cat horking up a hairball. "Hanna?"

She shakes her head. "I forgot about the joys of morning sickness. I'll be back." She rushes to the bathroom and closes the door. The water comes on a second later, but it doesn't quite cover the sound of her retching.

I knock softly and ask if I can do anything for her, like hold her hair, but she tells me she's okay and it should pass fairly quickly.

I cautiously step into the hall, wanting to give her some privacy. Queenie could always sleep until noon on weekends, but King is regimented. I tiptoe down the hall and am relieved to find the kitchen empty when I get there.

I pour Hanna a fresh glass of water and search the cupboards for dry, salty carbohydrates. I remember Kimmie having terrible morning sickness with Queenie. The kind that lasted all day, which makes the term *morning sickness* sound pretty damn misleading. She walked around with a box of crackers until that passed.

I find saltines and plain chips. As I'm heading back down the hall to the bedroom with snacks and water for Hanna, I hear the sound of footfalls on the second floor.

The shower is running when I get back to the bedroom. A few minutes later, the bathroom door opens, and Hanna appears, hair wrapped in a towel, body wrapped in a robe.

"I brought you crackers and water." I hold them up for her to see.

"You are a saint."

"Hardly, considering the things I've done to you while you're naked." I internally cringe at the bad joke, but she chuckles.

"In bed you're the Oracle of Orgasms. Right now, you're the Saint of Saltines." She takes the package from me and kisses me on the cheek before she pops a cracker into her mouth. Her eyes fall closed for a moment as she chews.

When they pop back open, I pass her the water and she takes a sip, then another and another.

"Are the kids up yet?" she asks.

"I heard them moving around upstairs when I was in the kitchen."

"Okay. I'll get dressed and we can do this." She blows out a breath. "I don't know if the nausea is actually morning sickness or nerves at this point. Or both."

She eats another cracker before she disappears back into the bathroom to change. She's been naked in front of me plenty of times, but there's a shift in our relationship now. One I'm going to have to learn to navigate.

Her hair is brushed and she's back in the clothes she was wearing earlier. She comes to stand in front of me. My shirt is wrinkly from our nap, and I don't look nearly as put together as she does. She smooths her hands over my chest. "Ready?"

"Ready." Or as ready as I'll ever be to tell my adult daughter and my son-in-law that I'm about to be a parent for the second time.

My palms start to sweat as we head for the kitchen. I can hear the low sounds of laughter and the clinking of dishes.

"Morning," Hanna says as we step across the threshold.

"Morning, Momster, you have a good sleep?" King's back is to us as he pulls a pint glass from the cupboard and sets it beside the gallon of milk on the counter.

But Queenie is facing us, chopping fresh pineapple for a fruit platter. Her smile turns inquisitive as her gaze shifts from Hanna to me. "Hey, Dad, when did you get here?" Her eyes move over my outfit.

King spins around, brow furrowed as he takes us both in. Like Queenie, his gaze moves over my rumpled shirt. He's wearing jeans and a t-shirt, and Queenie is dressed in a long, flowy shirt and leggings, the same as Hanna.

"I came over early, but I didn't want to disturb you, so I let myself in."

"Oh." The furrow in King's brow deepens, eyes flitting between Hanna and me.

"Come have a seat, I'll pour you a coffee." Queenie motions to the stools at the island. "We were going to make bacon and eggs for breakfast."

Ryan's suspicion is clear in the way he keeps glancing at us as he sets two mugs onto the counter. It reminds me a lot of the time I found him sneaking out of Queenie's room when they first started seeing each other. He'd been painfully honest about the allergic reaction he had to a milkshake that my daughter had been drinking. His face was a swollen mess. Or at least I'd thought he'd been honest. I got a lot more information the next day on the ice when I saw exactly where that rash led. That's filed under things I never wanted to know about my daughter and my goalie.

And right now, with the way King is looking at us, I can relate in a way I never have before to exactly how shitty it must have been for King and Queenie when they'd been trying to toe a line and fight their attraction for each other.

King spoons sugar and adds a dash of cream to the cup on the right that reads *#1 Momster*, and is clearly meant for Hanna. He fills it with coffee and passes it to her.

"Thank you." Her smile is strained as she takes the coffee from him and brings it to her lips. She takes a tentative sip and grimaces. "Oh, that's . . . oh no." She sets the cup onto the counter and pushes her stool back, rushing to the bathroom off the kitchen. A moment later, a door slams shut.

"Is Hanna okay? What the heck is going on?" King asks.

"She's not feeling great this morning," I say.

"Momster?" he calls out. "Are you okay?" His narrowed eyes shift my way.

"I'll just be a second." Her voice is muffled. The toilet flushes, and a minute later she comes out of the bathroom, wiping her hands on her thighs. She's pulled her hair back into a messy ponytail.

"Geez, Han, what's going on? Do you have food poisoning or something? Do we need to take you to urgent care?" Ryan rushes over and takes her arm, guiding her to the couch.

"I don't have food poisoning."

"Are you coming down with something? Is this the flu? You can't fly like this. We need to reschedule your flight. You can stay here until you're feeling well enough. And we can call the team doctor, right, Jake?"

"We need to talk to you." Hanna avoids answering any of the questions and directs a small smile at Queenie. "Both of you."

Ryan drops onto the couch beside Hanna, which is where I'd like to be. "What's going on? You've been off all weekend. Please tell me it's something I can fix. Whatever kind of medical attention you need, Han, I'll take care of it."

He's such a good kid. Always putting his family ahead of everyone else, himself included.

I take the chair opposite Hanna, and she gives me a nervous smile before her attention shifts back to King. "I'm not sick, Ry."

"Then what's going on?"

The pause before Hanna speaks feels like it lasts an eternity, and the two little words she utters might as well be a sonic boom with the effect they have on King.

"I'm pregnant," Hanna says softly.

Ryan sits there, like a deer in headlights, blinking, saying nothing at all.

At the same time, Queenie's mouth drops open and a range of emotions passes across her lovely, expressive face. Her mouth forms an "oh" as she puts things together. Her hands come up as if she's getting ready to clap, and then she covers her mouth as her gaze shifts from Hanna, to me, and back to Hanna.

"Pregnant?" Ryan finally echoes. It's almost croak-like. Similar to a parrot.

Hanna nods and licks her lips.

"But how?" Ryan, who is usually composed and eloquent, seems to have been reduced to phrases and questions consisting of one or two words. "Who?"

"I'm the father," I say, desperate to fill the silence. And then equally desperate to shove those words back from where they came.

Queenie squeals with something like delighted excitement.

Ryan's lip curls in an angry sneer and he pushes to his feet. I've never been intimidated by his size before now, but he's more than a decade my junior and he's got a few inches on me, not to mention a good thirty pounds of bulk. He's an all-star goalie for a reason.

"You got Momster *pregnant?*"

I might as well be holding a red cape as he charges me.

CHAPTER THIRTEEN

Not the Reaction I Was Hoping For

Hanna

I DON'T HAVE a chance to react before Ryan rushes Jake.

Queenie hops off the couch and gets between them before Ryan has a chance to throw a punch, thankfully. "King! Settle the F down!"

Ryan's eyes are wide and wild. He's livid and practically snarling at Jake.

I rush around to his other side, ready to grab his arm, although I've never actually seen Ryan punch anyone or anything.

"What the hell is going on? Are you two a thing?" His gaze turns to me, and under that anger is hurt. "How long have you been hiding this from me?"

"We weren't trying to hide anything from you," Jake says quietly. Calmly.

"Bullshit!" Ryan runs his hands through his hair. "That is fucking bull! How could you two do this? And behind our backs?" He spins back to Jake. "I trusted you to have Hanna's best interests in mind and you get her *pregnant*! Does this mean you're together now?"

Queenie's expression is torn. She glances among the three of us and steps in front of Ryan again, settling her palms on his chest. Her voice is gentle but firm. "My King, I need you to take a breath. I know you're hurt right now, and blindsided, but if we can't listen to what they have to say, then we can't understand. And this reaction isn't going to help any of us, and all it's going to do is make you feel bad later. Let's take a breath and a moment, and *listen*."

Ryan drags both of his hands down his face and blinks a bunch of times. He looks restless in his own skin.

He doesn't take a seat on the couch again. This time he crosses over to the chair and drops down into it, pulling Queenie onto his lap like she's some kind of human shield or his personal support human. Which I suppose she is.

I'm so glad he has her by his side to navigate life with. He deserves to be loved the way she loves him.

Jake takes a seat beside me. He puts his hand on his knee and glances at mine, which is in my lap.

I move it to the cushion beside me and he covers my hand with his, squeezing. I can hear Ryan's teeth grinding together from where he's sitting. I try to put myself in his shoes. He's spent so much of his life in the dark, and we've had to rebuild our relationship since he found out he's my son and not my brother. I know it's been hard on him, and this must feel very much like a betrayal.

He's unfailingly loyal. It's one of the things I love most about him. It's also challenging because Ryan often sees things only in black and white. There's no room for grey when it comes to trust and honesty with him.

"Ryan, I understand that you're shocked, and to be honest, so are we."

"How long has this been going on?" His voice is quiet and raw, the hurt clear on his face.

"It was only supposed to be casual." Jake rushes to my defense, then adds, "We'd been spending a lot of time together, as friends."

"Planning for our wedding," Queenie says softly.

"Obviously that changed," Ryan says with a bite.

"It wasn't intentional," I tell them. "We didn't mean for any of

this to happen. We didn't want to make things . . . complicated."
It's not untrue. We truly had tried our best to stay on the right
side of the friendship line. But staying at his house, spending
time with him, late nights talking—eventually a late-night hot
tub hang out turned into a late-night romp. And those romps kept
happening until the wedding.

"Hanna and I have a lot in common, and we understand each
other in ways not many people can," Jake explains. "I can't
pretend I know how this feels for you, Ryan, but we did try to
keep things platonic."

"So you accidentally slept with my . . . Hanna?" Ryan blows
out a breath. "You know what, you don't need to answer that.
How long have you known about the baby?" He looks between
us.

"I found out yesterday afternoon, and I told Jake last night,"
I say.

"Oh." He rubs the space between his eyes, clearly struggling
to digest all of this. "What the heck happened to using condoms?"

"We didn't think it was something we needed to worry about,
seeing as I've been menopausal for two years." It's not entirely
true, but explaining what actually happened isn't something I
feel the need to do. That this is even a conversation I have to
have, with Ryan of all people, is mind-boggling.

"There's definitely some irony in that," Queenie says with a
chuckle. She moves to the chair next to Ryan, probably because
his knee is bouncing with his anxiety.

He gives her a dark look. "This isn't a joke, Queenie."

"I know, but it's not like it can be undone. And it clearly
wasn't intentional." Queenie puts her hand over his and gives it
a squeeze, likely to remind him that she's on his side. "Does this
mean that you'll be moving to Seattle?"

The question is directed at me, and she looks both hopeful
and expectant.

Jake and I glance at each other.

He starts with, "I think eventually that will make the most
sense—"

"My life is in Tennessee." Jake stiffens and moves his hand back to his lap. Ryan rubs his jaw and glares daggers at Jake, and I swallow down the desire to backtrack. By their expressions, I know it's the wrong thing to say, but I'm already facing so much change, and Jake and I had never planned for this to be anything more than some fun between the sheets.

"Not all of it," Queenie says flatly.

"There are a lot of potential complications with this pregnancy. It's reasonable to hold off on a move until we've seen the doctor and had all the necessary tests," Jake explains.

"I've lived in Tennessee for thirty years. I have a job, and a house, and half of my family lives there," I tell Jake. And the last time I was pregnant I was hidden away at my aunt's, and then moved from Ohio to Tennessee. "And let's all be realistic about this. I'm very high risk because of my age and I've already miscarried once. I'm not uprooting my entire life and moving across the country when there are still so many unknowns."

"I don't think we need to make that decision right now." Jake's expression reflects his disquiet.

"Does this mean you're not planning to raise the baby together?" Queenie bites her lip, her gaze flitting between us.

Ryan huffs an annoyed breath. "Why the hell should Hanna have to give up her entire life for you? Maybe you should consider moving to Tennessee instead of the other way around."

"And maybe you need to back off and let Hanna and me decide what we're going to do, since it isn't up to you," Jake snaps.

"Don't you dare talk to my son like that," I fire back.

"It's not up to him to make decisions for you," Jake retorts.

I roll my shoulders back. "It's not up to you either."

"I have a right to be part of this." Jake points to himself. "I've raised one daughter on my own. I'm not going to back off and passively wait for someone else to decide what my role gets to be in this kid's life."

"If you want to be part of those decisions, I suggest you change your tone. I would never speak to Queenie the way you're speaking to Ryan or me. You might not like the questions he's asking, or agree with what he has to say, but you don't get to talk down to him."

"You know, maybe it would be a good idea for my dad and me to go grab a coffee and have a chat," Queenie says, before turning her attention to me. "And then you and Ryan can have a chance to talk, too."

"That's probably a good idea," Jake says. His knee is bouncing restlessly and he looks a little green.

Queenie turns to Ryan and whispers quietly. He nods but doesn't say anything.

Queenie and Jake gather their things, leaving me alone with Ryan. I don't love the way that went down, but I understand this is emotional for all of us.

"Why didn't you tell me you had feelings for Jake?" He doesn't sound angry anymore, more hurt and disappointed than anything else, which is infinitely worse.

I realize this is less about the actual news and more about feeling like he's been lied to. Ryan is very good at making it seem like he's handling things well, but sometimes the truth is very different than how he presents. I slide down the couch so I'm closer to him. "We never intended to act on them."

"What changed?" He spins his wedding band on his finger.

"I don't know that there was any one thing." It doesn't make sense to be anything but honest with him. "We were talking more often when the wedding plans started, and he was there for me when I needed a sounding board."

Ryan rests his elbows on his knees. "A sounding board for what? Why couldn't you come to me?"

I give him a small smile. "Because it was your wedding, and I wasn't going to put my insecurities and worries on you. I knew it was hard enough on you trying to juggle Mom and me and making sure we both felt included. And I appreciate the lengths you went to in order to make sure I felt like I was part of the day . . . but I'm not going to lie to you and tell you it was easy to stand on the sidelines. And not because of anything anyone did or didn't do. I didn't expect it to be as hard as it was, and Jake was there for me." Being with him helped distract me from the stress of it all. And we connected in ways that no one else could really understand. And now we're linked in ways that neither of us intended.

"I would have been there for you," he says.

He seems stuck on this point, and I get it, because I have always been open and honest with Ryan, just like he's been open and honest with me. About most things. Apart from how he and Queenie actually met—which I learned from Queenie and the girls on one of our many pre-wedding activity dates. "You had more than enough on your plate, Ryan. Your focus needed to be on the wedding, and putting you in the middle of everything more than you already were wouldn't have been fair."

"I would have found a way to make it easier if I'd known, though," he argues.

"I know, and I love you for it, but that is exactly why I didn't come to you about it." I hate that I've made him question my loyalty to him, and all I can do is hope that our relationship can heal from this new blow.

I cover his hand with mine. His is more than twice the size. My heart hurts that I'm so torn. I'm scared, elated, and worried, not just about the baby, but about Ryan, too. "I made choices when I was young that had consequences, and one of them was realized when you got married and I couldn't be the mother of the groom. I didn't get a mother-son dance. Mom is still a mom to both of us, and we couldn't undo thirty years just because you knew the truth. Or take that away from her. And that was tough for me, but I didn't want to make it hard for you, too. So, while I understand that you want me to be able to talk to you like your peer, the difference is that I've *always* been aware that I'm *not*, even though you weren't."

He rubs his temple. "This is kind of a mind fudge." That he's back to censoring his language is a good sign.

"It absolutely is. And I don't expect you to be okay with it today, or tomorrow, or even next week. I understand that it's going to take time to process this and that you might be angry, or hurt, or both. But please know that Jake and I never meant for this to happen, none of it. I didn't want to put stress on your relationship with Queenie or my relationship with you." Realistically, I'm aware that no matter what happens, whether I'm able to carry this baby full term or not, this will irrevocably shift things. I can only hope that Ryan and I can find our way through this and come out the other side stronger. Again.

"Are you and Jake going to be together?" I can't read him right now to know whether or not that's something he's going to be okay with. And regardless, it's a decision Jake and I will have to make, in time.

"I can't answer that yet. We understand the layers and complexity of our very interconnected families aren't simple to navigate." What Jake and I were to each other before this has changed. We're not just two adults enjoying each other's company. Now we're facing months of uncertainty and an even more complicated relationship. There are so many things to figure out, and all of it seems overwhelming. "What I can tell you is that if there are no complications, Jake and I will work together to make sure this child knows he or she is loved by both parents."

He flips his hand and closes his fingers around mine, so my hand basically disappears inside his mitt. "Not gonna lie, this is going to make our already weird family that much weirder."

"I know. I'm sorry about that." And I am, more than he'll ever know. "Aside from the whole over forty and pregnant thing, that's definitely one of the first things I thought about when I found out."

Ryan's frown turns into a grimace. "I'm so sorry, Han. I'm being a selfish brat and thinking only about myself. This has to be scary for you. Do you need me to come back to Tennessee with you? What can I do to help?"

I squeeze his hand, aware that Ryan can sometimes course correct and go overboard by doting. "You've never been a selfish brat a day in your life. Your reaction is completely understandable, so please, Ryan, don't beat yourself up for having feelings about this that aren't easy to deal with. I'm going to see my doctor as soon as I get home. I'll have to have some tests to make sure the baby and I are healthy, and then we'll make a plan from there."

"Is Jake coming back with you then?"

"Once I have an ultrasound scheduled, he'll come out." Jake and I clearly have a lot to talk about. We need a clear picture of where we are with this pregnancy before we can have the more difficult discussions.

"Right. Okay. Do you really think you'll stay in Tennessee, though?"

"Honestly, I don't know, Ryan. My life is there, and with my history, I can't start planning a move. It's too early to know." There's security and stability in Tennessee, and the thought of giving that up with so many unknowns is unnerving. And with this pregnancy I want to be a little selfish.

I can see the worry in his eyes. "I know this is something you always wanted, to have another baby. I really hope this time you get to do that."

"Me, too." I want to believe he's okay with this, but it feels like I've opened Pandora's box, and we've just scratched the surface of what's inside.

CHAPTER FOURTEEN

More Questions Than Answers

Jake

QUEENIE STARES AT the closed door for a few seconds before she slips her arm through mine and guides me to her car. I glance back at the house more than once. I'm not sure what I expect. King to come bursting out of the door like the Hulk?

"They'll be fine," she tells me as she unlocks the door and gets into the car.

"Yeah." I just don't want any big decisions being made without me. "I don't think I've ever heard King swear before."

"Oh, he swears. Not often, but he does." Queenie smirks for a second before she schools her expression. "They need time to talk. Their relationship is more complicated than most, and King can't handle being lied to. So even though that wasn't what you were doing intentionally, he perceives it differently and is more sensitive to it than would be reasonable for anyone else."

I know this about King, and until today I thought I understood it and him. "I get that he's not happy about the situation, but I hope he's a lot more subdued with Hanna than he was with me."

"Don't worry. He'll calm down. He needs to talk to Hanna without an audience." She gives my arm a squeeze, and a wide grin spreads across her face as she turns the engine over and shifts the car into gear. "How are you feeling about all of this?

Are you excited?"

I run a hand through my hair. "I don't know. There's a lot that we need to figure out. And she hasn't even seen the doctor yet. A lot could happen in the next few months."

"Are you two going to be a couple now?" She's practically vibrating with excitement, which I wish I could share more of. "I mean, eventually Hanna will move out here, right?"

"I don't know about that."

Queenie's face falls, like it did back at the house. "But how will you raise the baby together if one of you doesn't move?"

"Neither of us expected this to happen, so it's one step at a time. The risks are a lot higher at her age." Even if everything goes smoothly, there's the whole figuring out a co-parenting plan.

The possibility that Hanna will want to stay in Tennessee and do it all on her own doesn't sit well with me. Not because I don't think she's capable, but I've been there before. Even with help, it's not easy. I don't want to force her into moving, but in an ideal world, she'd relocate here and we'd be able to raise this kid together.

And maybe it won't have to be a co-parenting only scenario if that happens. Having an actual partner, someone to lean on, to trade off with in the middle of the night, being a family in the true sense is something I wanted for Queenie but could never give her. If I can do better this time, that would be great.

Queenie makes a right, and I have to assume we're heading to the local diner for a greasy brunch. "Well, I think the two of you would make a great couple."

"You do?"

"Seriously?" She gives me a look that matches the word. "I called it from the first time you met."

"You did?" I feel a tad clueless at the moment. It's almost like Queenie could see this coming. Although maybe not the baby part of the equation.

"Well, yeah. You two were smitten from the start."

"I wouldn't say I was smitten." I remember very vividly the

111

first time I met Hanna. King's entire family had come down to see him play, and they had brought along his ex-girlfriend as a surprise. I'd been sure I'd have to trade King at the end of the season. But that only lasted a couple of hours. Until he showed up at the house, looking for Queenie.

The next morning, I found his phone sitting on the front seat of his car—the window was rolled down—and I'd decided to bring it to the main house rather than knock on the door to the pool house, where Queenie was living. I wanted to respect her privacy and not see things I couldn't unsee. Like the strawberry milkshake rash.

On my way inside, Hanna had called. I already knew about their unique family situation.

What I hadn't known was how beautiful Hanna was. Or nice. And fun. And sexy.

"You were totally smitten. The two of you stared at each other like you'd just found the secret to all of life's mysteries when you introduced yourselves. It would have been awkward if it wasn't so damn cute."

"Okay, I draw the line at being called cute."

"The way you were with each other was cute."

She parks in the diner lot and we tuck ourselves into the corner booth. Queenie orders a milkshake and bacon and eggs, which seems like an odd combination, but it's what she always gets.

"You're really okay with this, aren't you?" Queenie's reaction is such a stark contrast to King's explosive anger. Neither reaction was expected. I assumed Queenie would have a lot of questions, but I didn't anticipate her excitement.

"Of course I am. Aren't you?" Her brows pull together in a slight furrow.

"It would have been better if it were planned, and not a surprise. And I would have preferred if Hanna and I were in a different place in our relationship. And I was a few years younger."

The server delivers her milkshake and my coffee. Queenie

waits until we're alone again before she responds. "You said yourself that you've spent a lot of time with her leading up to the wedding. You were friends to start with, and it evolved into more, right? Or at least that's how it seems to me."

I add cream and sugar to my coffee. "You're not wrong. It did evolve from friendship to…more. But we both knew it couldn't continue indefinitely. Besides, being friends and *friendly* with each other is a lot different than raising a baby together."

Queenie laughs. "Oh my God, you are such an old man. You were hooking up. Just call it what it is."

"Hooking up makes it sound like we met on one of those dating apps." Which I've used a few times in the past. But with Hanna it wasn't about scratching an itch. We connected.

"That's what happened, though. You two figured out you had chemistry and acted on it. When did it change?"

"Do we really need to talk about this?" I don't think this could get any more awkward than my daughter getting excited about me accidentally knocking up her momster-in-law.

"You're having a baby together. Not talking about it isn't really an option."

I decide if there's one person I can be completely honest with, and should be, it's my daughter. "Your engagement party."

"Oh my God! When Hanna stayed in the pool house instead of at our place?"

"That would be the time, yes."

Queenie slaps my arm. "I knew she wasn't sleeping in the pool house." She props her chin on her clasped hands, elbows resting on the table. "Why didn't you tell me?"

"Because Hanna didn't want what was going on between her and me to affect your wedding, or King. And telling you would have put you in an impossible position." But I wonder now, how different things would have been if we'd been honest from the start instead of trying to hide what was happening.

"That's a tough place for you to be in," Queenie observes.

I nod my agreement. "I care about Hanna. I don't want to make the same mistakes I did before."

"How do you mean?"

I sip my coffee, thinking about Hanna's reaction to her potentially moving here. "Pushing my own agenda, like I did with your mother."

"How did you push your own agenda?" She shifts in her seat, shoulders tightening as they always do at the mention of Kimmie. She's always been sensitive when it comes to her mom, which is understandable, all things considered.

"With Kimmie, I'd been determined to make things work. But we were so young. I thought I'd be able to have my career and take care of you and your mom financially. It was naïve."

"You couldn't have known she was going to take off on us." Queenie pokes at her shake.

"No, but I could have listened to her concerns instead of telling her everything was going to be fine." Because at that age, I thought it would be. I was going to be making millions a year. But I didn't take into consideration what it would look like for Kimmie. Basically, raising a kid alone while I traveled all over the world. Queenie had taken over my whole world as soon as she came into it, and it hadn't left a lot of room for Kimmie.

"But this time you know what you're up against, and you and Hanna like each other. And you'll have King and me to help out," Queenie points out.

"I know. And that's good, but there are other things I need to take into account. Hanna and I both have careers and lives that are very separate from each other. My instinct is to do what I do at the negotiating table, but I'm not making a trade, and there are a lot of people I care about involved here." I flip my spoon between my fingers, recognizing the truth and weight in that statement. "I might want Hanna to move here, but there's selfishness in that, because she'll have to give up her entire life and basically start over again. And considering her history and how things played out with King . . . I want to be careful. I want to do the right thing. I want to support Hanna and the decisions she makes; I want a role in my child's life, and I want you and King to know that we never intended to go behind your back on any of this."

"We know that. Or at least I know that. I could kind of see the direction things were going with you and Hanna, and I think King did, too, even if he doesn't want to admit it. Don't worry, Dad, it's all going to work out. I can feel it." She pats my hand and smiles. "Now let's look at baby names!"

I hope she's right. But I can't get the look on King's face out of my head, or how adamant Hanna was that her life is in Tennessee.

If that doesn't change, then how exactly was all of this going to work without someone getting hurt?

QUEENIE AND I spend two hours at the diner. She likes Rex and Jax and Hudson for boys' names, and Belle, Cinder, and Ella for girls. I go along with her because it's easier that way. And she's excited, which alleviates some of my anxiety, but creates other worries, like how preemptive is this, and what happens if Hanna loses this baby? And what happens if she has it?

I need to work on getting over the challenges of potentially being a brand-new dad again at my age. I have a routine that's been the same for a long time, and this is going to change that drastically. I'll have to travel less, and I might have to adjust my responsibilities for the team. My job has been my life for a lot of years, and babies take time and energy away from that.

I need Queenie's positivity right now. And I'm optimistic it will rub off on King.

Queenie and I head back to her house. I'm hopeful that I'll still be able to drive Hanna to the airport. We could use the time to talk. And for me to get a better sense of where King is emotionally.

He seems to be much calmer when we return.

"I'm sorry about how I reacted earlier. I don't have the right to speak to you that way, and I wouldn't accept it if someone

115

spoke to Queenie that way either," I tell King while Hanna packs up her things.

He grabs the edge of the counter, his jaw working. "Hanna's been through a lot, not just with me, but the last time this happened…it was hard on her. And asking her to upend her life when you don't even know what this is going to look like, or what you are to each other, isn't fair."

"I understand." Or at least I'm beginning to. "I don't want to push Hanna to make any decisions, not right away. We still have a lot to talk about and figure out." I take a deep breath. "And just so you understand where I'm coming from, Queenie's mom tried to fight for partial custody for the wrong reasons. I know that's not the case here, but it's hard not to revert back to that way of thinking, which I recognize isn't fair to Hanna." I'll never forget the hurt and heartbreak I felt at the thought that my daughter might be taken away from me.

"I'm always going to want what's best for her," King says.

"I wouldn't expect anything less."

Hanna appears at the edge of the kitchen, her suitcase rolling behind her. "We should probably head to the airport."

"Do you want me to drive you?" King asks.

"I think it would probably be a good idea for Jake to take me this time," Hanna says softly.

"Right. Yeah. Of course." King doesn't seem all that excited about that, but he doesn't put up a fight either. Things are definitely tense as I load Hanna's suitcase into my car while they say their goodbyes.

Queenie whispers that she'll call me later.

Even with traffic, King's house is only about half an hour from the airport, so on a Sunday afternoon it takes considerably less time.

I turn the radio down so it's barely a hum in the background. "How are you?"

"It's been one heck of a weekend." Hanna's hands are clasped in her lap and she looks tired.

It's not really an answer. "King seemed better. I'm sorry

about how I reacted, it was out of line."

"We're all a little emotional and reactive. I'm sensitive to Ryan's feelings and how he perceives all of this. Particularly the fact we kept what was going on between us from him."

"I get that, and my concern is making sure this isn't causing you unnecessary stress, especially with everything you've told me this weekend." This is going to be a difficult new line to walk with Kingston as one of my players, my son-in-law, and now this added layer. I'm definitely going to need to talk to Alex about how I should approach this moving forward, and what I can reasonably get involved with where King is concerned.

"Ryan doesn't like conflict, so he's pretty direct about things, but I also know that he's worried about me, because of everything I've already been through. I can't be sure that he won't mask his feelings to protect me."

"What about you? Are you masking your feelings to protect him?"

"Maybe. It's hard to know how I should feel. I'm scared because my age makes this risky, and the fact this wasn't planned or expected, but I'd given up on the possibility I could have this. I want to be excited, but so much could go wrong, and has in the past." She taps her lips. "I know this probably isn't something you thought you'd be contending with at this point in your life."

"My head's still spinning, but I get that you want this, Hanna, and I support that. As long as this baby isn't putting your health at risk." I pull into short-term parking and find a spot, shifting the car into park so I can give her my attention. "I'm going to be honest, I think we'll need to figure out what co-parenting is going to look like. I get that maybe now it's a little early to make decisions, but one of us is going to have to move eventually."

"I can't make any kind of plan until after I've seen my doctor and I have a better idea of what's happening." She places a hand over her still-flat belly. "Aside from Ryan, my primary support system is in Tennessee, and so are my job and my life."

"But it's my baby, too, which sort of changes the order of importance, don't you think?" I don't know how to tread this line with her, I realize.

Hanna rubs the space between her eyes. "I don't want to leave on an argument, Jake. When I was a teenager, I lost all my friends and my entire life when I had Ryan. I've spent three decades forming relationships and friendships in Tennessee. You can't ask me to give all of that up. Not right now and maybe not ever."

I need to dial it down a bit. This isn't just about what I want, or what I think is best. We're going to have to make decisions together, and steam rolling Hanna into them isn't going to work, even if I want it to. "I know you've made sacrifices, big ones. But I have, too. I gave up my career for my daughter, and while I wouldn't change how I dealt with raising Queenie, it would be hard to do it again." I implore her to understand. "All I want is to be an active part of this child's life. I don't want to be relegated to half the holidays and a weekend every month."

"I'm sorry, Jake. I don't think I truly understood what that looked like for you. And I appreciate you wanting to figure things out, but this is all so new. I think we both need some time to process."

I reach across the center console and put my hand over hers, wanting to smooth things over for her sake as much as mine. We're both bringing baggage to the table. The kind we're going to need to unpack. And it's not going to happen today. "I realize we still have a lot to talk about, but I want you to know that I'm with you on this. We're in this together."

"I don't know how to do this with a partner," she admits, her eyes soft and worried. "The last time I went through this, it ended badly and so did my relationship."

"We have that in common, the last part anyway." Although we have similar experiences, there are just as many differences. I want to protect Hanna from more loss, but set boundaries for myself, too. We both gave up a lot last time around, so I'm hoping this time we can find a better balance with each other. "We'll get through this."

Her phone pings, signaling it's time for her to check in for her flight.

I get out of the car and get her bag and I walk her as far as security.

I open my arms, a silent request for a hug. She grins and steps into me. "I'm sorry I'm so stubborn in my old age," I murmur.

"I think we both are. It makes for fun times in the bedroom, but challenges outside of it since neither of us wants to give an inch."

We both chuckle. There's so much truth to that.

When we part, she leans in and kisses me on the cheek, her lips close to the corner of my mouth. "I'll send you a message when I land."

"Have a safe flight."

She grabs her bag and walks through the security gate, looking over her shoulder once and waving before she disappears around the corner.

This distance is going to be hard.

But I'm going to have to learn how to live with it if I want this to work.

And I realize I do. More than I thought possible.

CHAPTER FIFTEEN

Permission to be Excited Granted

Hanna

THE FLIGHT HOME is much different from the flight to Seattle. My nerves over seeing Jake have been replaced with a million new fears that compound each other.

It's far too late to call Paxton when I land, and, of course, I've been vague in my texts about how the weekend went. We need a face-to-face for this conversation. I need my best friend and her perspective.

I take my phone off airplane mode as we head toward the gate to deplane. I have several messages from Jake. It's hard to keep a clear head with him, and up until now the most difficult conversations we've had revolved around wedding planning. This is life-altering, and while I appreciate that he wants to be involved, I cannot and will not let him, or anyone else, tell me what I have to do and when. Talking about moving right now is pointless. I need to see my doctor before I can make decisions about anything. I'm also acutely aware of how uncertain the next several weeks are going to be.

I pull up the messages, nervous all over again.

JAKE: I know you're still in the air, but I want you to know that whatever you need I'm going to be here for you.

JAKE: You don't have to worry about not getting the support you deserve. Emotional, or otherwise. I know you're a strong, independent (sexy) woman and you're more than capable of doing this on your own, but I will stand by your side every step of the way.

JAKE: I've set up a pregnancy calendar so we can track appointments and milestones in the coming weeks.

JAKE: Flight tracker says you just landed. Checking in to make sure you arrived in Tennessee.

JAKE: I probably look like a desperate stalker at this point with the number of messages I've sent. Five hours is a lot of time to think.

I nearly burst into tears, my relief overwhelming. I didn't know how much I needed these messages until I read them. I manage to keep my emotions under control as I message to let him know I've landed and I'm about to get my car and drive home, but that I'll text again as soon as I walk in the door.

It takes twenty minutes to get through the airport, and then I have to find my car, which proves to be more difficult than I expect because I usually take a picture of where it's parked so I don't forget. Unfortunately, I was in a rush on my way out of town, so there's a bit of guesswork involved.

An hour after I land, I walk through the door to my townhouse and drop my bag onto the floor. I fire off a message to Ryan to let him know I'm home and then do the same with Jake.

My phone rings two seconds later.

"Hey."

"Hey. I'm glad you're home safe. Was the flight okay?" Jake's voice is low and soft.

"It was good."

"Good. That's good."

I don't know how to do this with him now. Everything that was fun and light and easy suddenly isn't.

"Hanna, I need to tell you something."

"Okay." My stomach does a flip-flop at his serious tone.

"I know that we've both been through this before, and that it's a lot different this time. I don't know how this all feels for you, but if I'm overbearing or overstepping, I want you to tell me, okay? I want us to try to be as open and honest about where we're at as we can." Jake's tone is earnest.

"I'll try my best to do that." I'm already more optimistic than I was when I left Seattle.

"Good. Me, too. You must be exhausted, so I'm going to let you go, but if you need anything, I'm a phone call away."

I WAKE UP the next morning feeling like a bag of garbage. I'm very glad I don't have any meetings scheduled first thing, because I'm not actually capable of functioning.

I don't remember the nausea being this bad, although combined with jet lag and stress, it seems to be a pretty horrible trifecta. I find a sleeve of saltines and park myself on the couch, munching my way through half of them while I wait for the queasy feeling to subside.

Seattle is only two hours behind, but Jake messaged this morning to see how I slept. And to check if I got the link to the shared calendar and if I've gotten ahold of my doctor.

My head is throbbing, likely from the lack of caffeine, but I'm not sure I can handle the smell of coffee yet. I hope this phase doesn't last long. Cutting caffeine cold turkey will not be pleasant.

I decide my best plan is to call my doctor again before I do anything else. However, it turns out I've slept through a call from them already. And that I happen to have an appointment in less than an hour. It means I only have enough time to throw on some clothes and pull my hair into a ponytail before I'm out the door.

But I've left my purse on the kitchen table, along with my

keys, so I have to go back and get those. Then I'm on my way.

By the time I get to the doctor's office, my head feels like it's going to explode. Unfortunately, I don't have time to stop and grab a coffee, so I'll have to deal with what feels like a miniature Thor slamming his hammer into my temples until my appointment is over.

My doctor is a lovely woman named Roxanne Tumbler. She's in her mid-to-late fifties, and she has three children, two in college and one close to finishing high school. She was over forty when she had her third, so I know I'm in good hands.

I'm called in right away and take another pregnancy test to confirm what I already know: that there's a bun in the oven. Once that's taken care of, the nurse busies herself with weighing me and taking my blood pressure. She frowns when she sees that it's one-thirty-two over eighty-seven and takes it again. This time it's one-thirty-five over eighty-nine.

"Should I be worried about that?" I ask and try not to fidget.

"It's on the higher side, and you're usually right around normal, but we'll wait to see what Doctor Tumbler says." She gives me a reassuring smile and leaves me on my own.

I figure it's best to wait until after the appointment to message Jake, otherwise I'm bound to create more worry and anxiety where there doesn't need to be any. Yet.

But while I wait for the doctor, I send Paxton a message.

Are you free tonight?

It takes her less than thirty seconds to get back to me.

Wine and cheese at your place? I want to hear all about the weekend. Don't think I didn't notice the vague texts.

I don't say anything about the wine, or my intentional vagueness.

I'm working from home today, so come over whenever.

She replies with:

I'll head straight there after work.

I respond with a thumbs-up and tuck my phone back into my purse as Doctor Tumbler slips into the room and closes the door, my file in her hands. Her smile is questioning. "I didn't realize you were trying to get pregnant."

"It wasn't planned." Roxanne has been my doctor for a long time. She was there for all the failed pregnancy attempts with Gordon and the miscarriage.

I can both feel and see her concern as she takes the seat in front of the computer monitor. "Is this a welcome surprise?"

"I think so. Unexpected, but as long as the baby is healthy, then I would like to proceed." My biggest fear right now is that she'll tell me it's not safe for me to continue with this pregnancy.

She crosses her legs and faces me. "I know you're already aware of the risks, but I'm going to be very upfront with you, Hanna. The potential for complications is a lot higher than they were last time. And there's a significantly higher chance that you could miscarry again."

"I know. I'm willing to take that risk."

"I figured you would be." Her smile is soft and knowing. "Do you have a sense of how far along you are?"

"I think about twelve weeks, or so? If I had to guess, I'd say I got pregnant in early June."

Roxanne's eyebrow lifts. "Twelve weeks? That's positive. We'll need to get started on blood work right away. Would you like to test for chromosomal abnormalities liked we intended when you were trying last time?"

"Yes, absolutely. Barring any extreme complications, I'm planning to keep the baby, no matter what." I cover my belly with my hand.

She folds her hands in her lap. "I think you should also keep in mind quality of life. If the child has exceptional needs that could place a high demand on your energy and your resources.

You will need to take those things into consideration as well. But one thing at a time. I'll send you to the lab for blood tests immediately, and we'll set up an ultrasound as soon as possible. That way we know where we're at and what we can expect in the coming months."

"Okay. That's good. I'd like to be as informed as possible moving forward." I'm nervous about the tests, even more so now. "I just want to know if the baby is healthy."

"Any cramping or spotting? We're going to want to monitor you closely, especially over the next several weeks. The lower your stress levels, the better. Are you doing this on your own, or is the father involved?"

"He's not local, but he'll be involved."

"And he's supportive?"

"He is." The messages since I've left Seattle have been exactly what I needed but am scared to want. Having Jake's support is a double-edged sword. It means I'm not alone, but it also means I need to give him a say in what happens. Like one of us eventually having to move if we're going to co-parent effectively. I recognize there's a strong connection between losing the last baby and the end of my relationship with Gordon. I'm afraid to count on Jake too much, to get comfortable with the idea of having this baby and then have it all taken away.

"That's good. Does he understand the risks involved?"

"He does. We talked about my pregnancy history."

"Okay." She smiles softly. "This is something you've wanted for a long time, so I'm glad you have a supportive partner."

"I'm aware this pregnancy will be my last," I say.

"You are in great shape physically, Hanna, which is positive, so let's make sure everything else looks good and we can start planning from there. I'm keeping an eye on your blood pressure, though, since it's higher than I'd like."

We spend the next half hour reviewing all the risk factors, setting up my ultrasound for the following week, and then I stop at the lab to have my blood work done.

I leave the office feeling slightly more hopeful, but I'm highly aware that the next several weeks are critical.

Reducing work stress might prove to be a challenge. Especially with my promotion on the table. Although this baby could impact that. It's not easy to give a promotion to someone when they're about to take a maternity leave. And I already know that my company only gives new mothers twelve weeks.

That seems woefully inadequate.

One thing at a time, though.

Schedule appointments. Record them in my shared calendar with Jake. Blood work. Talk to Jake. Then meetings. Then Paxton.

CHAPTER SIXTEEN

So This Thing Happened

Hanna

ON THE WAY home, I call Jake and put him on speakerphone so I can fill him in on what the doctor said and reassure him that apart from slightly raised blood pressure I'm doing well so far.

"What's slightly raised?" he asks.

"The low one-thirties over the high eighties."

"What are the implications of that?"

"As of now? None. But I had a bunch of blood tests to make sure everything is normal. And I have an ultrasound scheduled for next Monday—"

"I saw that on the calendar. I've already scheduled a flight for Sunday night so I can be there. I'm going to book a hotel close to the ultrasound clinic."

"Wow. Okay. That's good." I shouldn't be the least bit surprised. Jake wants to be involved, and I appreciate that, as nervous as it makes me. "But you don't have to stay at a hotel."

"I didn't want to make assumptions or make you uncomfortable."

We had that nap on Sunday morning, and when I woke up, Jake was wrapped around me like he often was when we were sleeping together for all those months. I had to slide out from under him, not wanting to disturb him when it became apparent my bladder wasn't going to wait for him to wake up. I've missed that, and I'm not sure how I'll feel if he stays at my house in the spare bedroom. But having him in a hotel would feel worse, so I offer, but give him an out. "You staying with me wouldn't make me uncomfortable, Jake. But if you think it's better . . ." I trail off, letting the sentence hang.

"I want to do whatever is easiest for you," he replies.

We'll have more time to talk things through, and it would be nice to have the support, even if I struggle with wanting it. "Why don't you stay here then? With me."

"You're sure?" I can hear the relief in his tone.

"I'm sure."

We chat for a few more minutes and end the call with the promise to talk soon.

I spend my afternoon on calls with clients, my nerves building as I wait for Paxton to show up.

She arrives at five-fifteen with takeout from Franco's, my favorite Italian restaurant. I'm grateful for the pasta Bolognese, because there is no way I can handle eating anything with cream sauce right now. "Sorry, they were out of the deluxe mac and cheese, which sounds unbelievable, but apparently an entire hockey team came through an hour before I ordered takeout and cleaned them right out."

"I can see how that might happen."

"I also brought a bottle of red to go with the pasta because I figured you'd only have white."

"Also a safe call." I take the bottle of wine from her and she follows me to the kitchen.

We plate our dinners, and she unscrews the cap on the bottle and grabs two wine glasses. I don't stop her, mostly because I want her to be sitting down when I deliver the news. I even let her get as far as pouring me a glass. That I won't be able to drink for a lot of months.

Paxton props her feet onto the coffee table and flips her long black hair over her shoulder, dark eyes alight with excitement. "How was the weekend? How were things with Hottie

McDaddy?"

That nickname has new meaning now. I set my plate onto the coffee table. The good thing about Franco's is that it's even better the next day, so if I can't eat it now, I can definitely enjoy it later. "I have to tell you something."

"Oh man, does this mean you slept with him again? And if you did, it's totally okay, because from the pictures alone he looks like he's hard to resist." She takes a sip of her wine, and I wait until she sets her wine glass back onto the table before I answer. My couch is grey and wine stains suck.

"I'm pregnant."

Paxton's expression remains blank for a few seconds before she throws her head back and laughs. "Oh my God, you had me there for a second." She slaps her thigh and her fork flips off her plate and lands on the area rug. Thankfully, it's dark blue.

When I don't start laughing, too, she sobers quickly. Her plate joins mine on the coffee table. "Wait, are you serious? How? I mean, I thought you were menopausal?"

"I am. I was. Apparently, you can still get pregnant, even when you're perimenopausal."

"Holy . . . wow." Her hand comes up to cover her mouth. "When did you find out? How did you find out?"

I explain what happened, and how exactly I came to realize and confirm that I am indeed pregnant.

Her brow furrows. "Didn't you use condoms?"

I give her a look.

"So one of them broke?"

I scrub my hands down my face. "We went without once."

"Once? Holy hell, Hanna. What are the chances?"

"Five percent, apparently," I mutter.

"Wait." She shifts so she's facing me, eyes wide. "Does Jake know? I have so many questions. I want to be excited, but I know how hard this has been for you in the past."

I crack a smile. "It's been an intense forty-eight hours. And yes, he knows. But it's so complicated." I need this time with Paxton so I can talk this out. Especially since she's been through this with me before.

I tell Paxton all about the weekend, from finding out, to telling Jake, and then telling Ryan and his reaction.

"Ryan will adjust. He needs time." She sounds so certain, and I want to believe that she's right.

"I hope so. I get why it's hard for him. Everyone he loves and trusted lied to him for a lot of years. He doesn't like feeling betrayed, and this thing with Jake and me feels like a betrayal." And he doesn't truly know how long it was going on for, although I'm sure he and Queenie can surmise if they want.

"I can see that." Paxton taps on the armrest. "Does this mean you're going to move to Seattle?"

"That's not part of my plan. Not right now. It's too early to make that kind of decision when anything can still happen."

"But is it going to be part of the plan eventually? Or will he move here?" She fidgets with the sleeve of her shirt.

"I really don't know. My whole world is here." I don't want to think about the things and people I'd leave behind.

"So he didn't mention it at all?" she presses.

"He did, but I'm not ready to deal with what that looks like yet."

"Okay. We can come back to that later." Paxton reaches out and squeezes my hand in silent understanding. "Next hard question. Have you told your parents yet?"

"No. Not yet." My stomach does a flip-flop. My mom was such a huge source of support when I miscarried last time. She was there to pick up the pieces, and she was there when my relationship with Gordon crashed and burned. But this is very different. I can only hope after the initial shock, I'll have the same level of support again.

Paxton makes a face. "When are you going to tell them?"

I'd like to say never, but that's not possible. "Maybe I should move to Seattle."

She tips her head, pensive for a moment. "You don't think they'd be supportive?"

"I want to hope they will be. But it's the *who* I'm having

a baby with that I think is going to be the cause of the most conflict. It could literally be anyone other than Jake and I think it would be a lot easier to tell them."

"Are you stuck on the fact he's King's father-in-law?"

"It's a pretty reasonable thing to be stuck on." I reach for my necklace. "And honestly, as weird as the family dynamic is, I think what I'm least excited to talk about is the fact Jake and I were having this secret relationship and I have no idea what we're going to be to each other now. And considering what happened with my last pregnancy, I don't know that putting any kind of label on it makes sense."

Paxton sighs, her smile sad. "But he's a great guy, with a great job, and you already know he's a good parent. He passed up a career in the NHL so he could raise his daughter on his own. Won't they see that side as well? And you're an adult. You can have a relationship with whomever you want."

"I know. You're right. But beyond the confusing family circumstances, I'm scared that I'm going to tell my mom, and then she'll finally come around, but it will be just like last time." Only I already know what I stand to lose. The tightness in my throat eases with that admission.

"Oh, Han. I wish this were easier for you." She nabs a tissue from the side table and passes it to me.

I dab my eyes, not realizing they'd started leaking. "I wish I were a decade younger."

"I know there are a lot of things you're worried about, Hanna, and that focusing on all the other stuff is probably a distraction you need, but at some point, you're going to have to stop being so concerned about how everyone else is going to handle things and bring the focus back where it needs to be, on you." She squeezes my shoulder. "I can't pretend to know what this must feel like for you, but you deserve to be happy. And you deserve to have this baby. Give yourself permission to do both of those things, however unconventional that family is going to look."

"Thank you for always being here for me."

"That's what best friends are for. I'm always beside you, no matter what happens."

CHAPTER SEVENTEEN

How It All Fits Together

Hanna

THE WEEK THAT follows finding out I have a bun in the oven passes in a blur of saltines, plain chips, work, accidental naps, and a lot of phone calls. Between conversations with Jake making sure I'm okay, Ryan checking up on me—he's still off, but swears everything is fine and that he's just worried—the group chat with all the girls, and Paxton showing up almost every night of the week with dinner, I'm feeling both overly pampered and exhausted.

I've also made Ryan promise not to say anything to Mom until after I've gone for the first ultrasound and I've heard the heartbeat. There's no real logic to my *not* telling our parents, other than being nervous.

By Sunday, I'm a ball of anxious energy. I do an hour of yoga, followed by two hours of cleaning, even though my cleaner was here in the middle of the week. By the time I'm done, I'm sweaty and exhausted all over again.

Which means I fall asleep the second I sit on the couch.

And that's the position I find myself in when Jake shows up on my doorstep.

I have a slew of missed messages and six missed calls—not all of them are from Jake. It looks like my Seattle Girls, as I've named the group, were chatty this morning. I have no idea how long he's been ringing the doorbell, but considering that five of the last six calls came in the last eight minutes, I can guess.

I don't have time to do anything but stumble to the door and throw it open.

His expression shifts from frantic, to relieved, to concerned in the span of three blinks. One of his hands settles on my waist and the other lifts, sweeping wayward strands of hair off my cheek. "Hanna? Are you okay?"

I can feel my face warming with embarrassment. "I'm fine. I fell asleep on the couch."

"Oh. Okay." His shoulders come down from his ears and his smile turns wry. "You must have been out cold. I've been ringing the doorbell for ten minutes."

"It would definitely explain the dream about an alarm going off that I couldn't find." I take a step back, noticing that my neighbor to the right, who's always in everyone's business, is pretending to trim her hedge. "You should come in. I'm sorry I'm such a hot mess."

"You're hot, but you're not a mess." He picks up his suitcase and a second bag—it seems like a lot for an overnight visit—and steps over the threshold.

"And you're a liar, but I still like you anyway." I give my neighbor a wave, so she knows I'm on to her, and close the door before she gets the idea to come over and ask a million questions.

Jake stands in the middle of my foyer, looking ridiculously delicious for someone who spent five hours on a plane. I glance beyond him, to the mirrored front hall closet door. My hair is pulled into a messy ponytail. I'm wearing a baggy shirt and a pair of sweats that are better suited for a twenty-five-year-old, not someone in their mid-forties. But Queenie gave them to me for Christmas and they're comfortable, so I can't resist wearing them.

"Oh wow, I need five minutes to freshen up." I cringe at my reflection. "It's a wonder you didn't turn around and head right back to the airport. I look like yesterday's garbage that's been baking in the sun all day."

One of Jake's eyebrows pops.

I spin around and take a step toward the hall leading to my bedroom, where there's a shower, a brush, and clothes that are presentable.

"Whoa, whoa. Hold on a second. Where are you going?" His fingers close around my wrist.

"To change."

"You don't need to change. Come here." He takes a step closer and tugs me toward him at the same time. His arms come around me, strong and solid. He smells faintly like plane, but also like laundry detergent, cologne, and cinnamon, or mints, or possibly both.

"I probably smell horrible," I mumble into his chest, but I melt into the embrace, needing it more than I want to admit.

"You smell a lot prettier than any of the hockey players I work with." He drops his head, and I can feel his warm breath in my hair.

"King smells like the inside of an old shoe after he's played a game or worked out, so there's a lot of room left for various levels of disgusting in there." I absorb the comfort of his presence like a salve to my worries.

He chuckles. "Those boys actually smell like used jock straps."

I make a gagging sound and Jake releases me and takes a quick step back, eyes wide. "I'm sorry. That was too far, wasn't it?"

I laugh, in part because his expression is priceless, and he's jumped back about four feet. "I guess I can't really make that sound right now, can I?"

"You can, but I might take cover. Not very chivalrous of me, but there you go."

"That seems fair. And I think I was better off not connecting that smell to that particular part of their uniform."

"To be fair, the odor is a combination of a lot of things." Jake purses his lips and closes his eyes. "And we're going to stop talking about it, because it's not an appealing topic." His eyes pop open and he smiles almost shyly. "I couldn't stop thinking about you this week."

"Seems reasonable since I'm carrying your baby and all." We have yet to address what exactly we're doing here, apart from having a baby together, and I know we're going to need to talk that through, too. I've thought about it a lot this week, and while trying to be a couple could be good, it also has the potential to go very, very wrong. And I have no idea where Jake stands on any of that. Despite all the potential hurdles, I think I at least want to try to see where it goes. "And I've been thinking about you all week, too," I confess.

"Because you're carrying my baby?" His gaze moves over me in a slow sweep that I feel like a caress.

There's some relief in knowing the attraction we share hasn't disappeared in the wake of this new, unforeseen development. "That is definitely at the top of the list."

"What's at the bottom?" he teases.

Whether or not I should invite you to share my bed tonight or offer you the spare room.

When Jake and I first started talking more frequently, it revolved around King and Queenie's engagement party. I kept sending him shared task lists so we could keep track of what needed to be done. For a while, every time he went to start a task, he'd find it had already been ticked off. He couldn't understand how I managed to get to everything before he did, especially since I was doing it all remotely. After a while, he started at the bottom of the list and we'd meet in the middle.

"I should probably keep what's at the bottom to myself," I mumble.

"What was that?"

"Nothing. Do you want a tour?"

"Nice deflection." He smirks. "I think the bottom of both of our lists is probably the same based on how pink your cheeks are right now."

I give him the side-eye and continue deflecting. "You don't

135

make lists."

He sets his keys and sunglasses onto the side table and points to the bucket and the mop leaned up against it. "Were you cleaning before I got here?"

"I might have forgotten to put that away the other day." It's a small fib.

His left brow arches. "You don't forget to put things away."

He's not wrong. Whenever I stayed at his place, I'd basically follow him around the kitchen, or whatever room we were in, and put things away. Even after sex sometimes I'd try to get out of bed and pick our clothes up off the floor. Often that would result in full body hugs from Jake to keep me from leaving the bed. Which isn't something I should be thinking about, but the memories are already surfacing.

I clear my throat. "I'm pregnant, Jake. I forget my own name these days."

He pokes at his lip with his tongue and stares at me until I have to look away. It's a thing he does when he thinks he's being bullshitted. Usually that look isn't directed at me, and I find myself struggling not to fidget under his scrutiny. He reaches out and skims my cheek with his knuckle. "Based on your blush, I'm calling BS. Why are you mopping your floors? Shouldn't you be taking it easy?"

"I'm pregnant, not made of glass. And mopping isn't particularly taxing."

"Still, you're already working full-time, and you have your art studio. You have enough on your plate without all the extra stuff that comes with maintaining a house, don't you think?" His question is soft, not demanding, and he's taken on a tone I recognize. It was the same one he used every time I would try to take on another wedding project for Ryan and Queenie.

Could I delegate some of it? Would one of the other girls be able to help with that? I didn't need to take on everything myself.

He would always put a hand on my shoulder and step into my personal space, just like he's doing now. It was as disarming as it was welcome.

I tip my head up so I can meet his concerned gaze. "I have a cleaner, and she was here on Wednesday, but I was restless this morning, and when I'm restless I tidy. It's what I do. Which you already know. And then I wore myself out and fell asleep. Hence this exceptionally sexy look I'm sporting." I motion to my less than appealing outfit. "I'd planned to be wearing something that doesn't scream *too lazy for real clothes*, but I didn't have time to change on account of my spontaneous napping."

"I happen to like this outfit." He tugs at the sleeve of my shirt. It's loose and hangs off one shoulder, exposing my black bra strap.

"You can thank Queenie, then, since she's the one who picked it out for me."

"Speaking of my daughter, it looks like she's messaging you." He nods at my phone, which buzzes on the side table, right next to the mop and his keys.

I've missed a lot more than calls from Jake during my nap. "She's probably checking to see if you made it here okay."

"She knows I did. She's already messaged me sixty times since the plane landed. She wants me to share her list of baby names with you," he says wryly.

I smile. Her excitement has helped balance out my fears. "She did that earlier this week."

"She has a new one on the go, and recently she's been retracting her choices and telling me she'd like to reserve the names for her own baby, which is fine by me, because I don't really think I want to call our kid Jax or Ambrosia. I know I was a little out there with the whole Queenie thing, but it suits her, you know?"

I laugh. "It does. And I'm very glad to hear that both Jax and Ambrosia are off the table."

He swipes a hand across his forehead. "Phew. That's a relief. I was hoping for something more traditional, like Jacob Junior."

"I wouldn't have a problem with that, unless we're having a girl. Then it would require an annoying amount of explanation." I settle my hand low on my belly. There isn't movement yet, but soon, if all goes well, I'll get to feel him or her doing acrobatics in there.

"Hmm." Jake taps his lips. "You make a good point. What if we add an A to the end if it's a girl?"

"Uh, I'm vetoing Jacoba right now."

"Maybe it'll grow on you."

"Like fungus?"

He laughs and I grin, glad that despite everything, we still seem to have fun together.

"If you need me to tell her to dial it down, I can," he offers. "I know she's excited, and I think it's good that she is, but I don't want it to overwhelm you either."

"It's okay. It's actually been really nice. And I'm comfortable enough with Queenie to be honest with her about things like that."

"Okay. That's good. I figured, but I wanted to put it out there." He rocks back on his heels. "She, uh . . . sent some stuff for you. I can get settled, and then you can check out the gifts from Queenie?"

"That would be great. Maybe we can talk about how we're feeling now that we've had time to digest things? Go over what to expect tomorrow?"

"That sounds perfect." His smile is gentle and warm.

I lead him down the hall and push open the first door on the right. "This is the spare room." I put fresh sheets on the bed this morning. The frame is simple, whitewashed wood. The comforter is a very pale yellow, and the pillows are different shades of yellow and orange. The walls are white and so is the dresser set. "It's a bit bright. And feminine." Not that he needed me to tell him that since he's standing in the middle of the room.

"Seems appropriate since you happen to fit into the bright and feminine categories as well."

I poke him in the side. "My ex only liked grey and blue when it came to color themes, so I made some serious adjustments when I bought this place."

"I like the yellow."

"You don't necessarily have to sleep in here." I rub my bottom lip and look at him out of the corner of my eye. Way to make things awkward. "Unless you'd prefer to."

Jake's gaze moves slowly from the bed to me. There's heat in it, but softness, too. "Do you have a preference?"

"My hormones have a preference." I rub the bridge of my nose.

"I see how it is. You just want to ride this ride." He motions to himself, grinning.

I bite my lips together. He's not wrong, but he's not right either. "I've missed you," I admit.

"I've missed you, too." He takes a few steps toward me, close enough that I can smell his cologne. He dips his head, wearing a smirk. "And I think this probably warrants a discussion, which we should probably have before we make a final decision on where I should be sleeping tonight."

"Okay." I exhale an unsteady breath. In the past, whenever we saw each other, the first thing we'd do was get naked. It was always a flurry of clothing removal, roaming hands, and battling tongues. Half the time we didn't make it to the bedroom. Sometimes we didn't even make it past his front entryway. And then I put an end to it. Except now I'm trying to un-end it. And I'm pregnant. It's a lot. And he's right. We definitely need to have a conversation. I wish I had an inkling as to how he feels, so I don't go embarrassing myself.

I motion to the door beyond the bed. "There's an attached bath through there. I'll let you get settled and I'll meet you in the living room in a few?"

"Sounds good."

I leave him in the spare room and rush down the hall to my own. My plan is to have a quick shower, but once I get started, I end up washing my hair.

And then I make the stupid decision to check my phone. The messages from the Seattle Girls are blowing up. There are two group chats: one with all the girls, including Queenie, and one without—we set up that one when we were working on a surprise group gift and her wedding shower. The most recent messages are in the group that doesn't contain Queenie.

Violet: Girl, you have some explaining to do. I just finished extorting information out of my husband (you don't want to know how) and I have it on good authority that JAKE IS IN TENNESSEE RIGHT NOW.

Lainey: *wide eyes* OMGee. You and Jake?

Stevie: Bishop said he caught you two making out.

Stevie: Wait. He said he caught you fixing Jake's hair. Not the same.

Violet: IS THE BABY JAKE'S????

There are surprise emojis and a range of mind-blown gifs, along with a picture of Bishop frowning and holding a sign that reads I KNEW IT.

I send one message in response:

The baby is Jake's. He's here with me now. Queenie and Ryan know, but can we keep this on the DL, please? I promise we will have a video chat in a couple of days.

I leave my phone in my room and find Jake in the living room. He, too, looks freshly showered based on his damp hair and change of clothes.

I offer him something to drink, and even though I picked up the scotch he likes, he declines and opts for ginger ale, which happens to be what I'm drinking.

There are several boxes sitting on the coffee table.

"As you can see, Queenie got click-happy." One corner of his mouth quirks up and his cheeks flush. "She tried to send me with more, but I told her she should hold on to them for a bit." He hands me the first box.

By the time I'm done unwrapping, I have several new cute

shirts with sayings like *Momster in the making* and *Mama to be* and *carrying precious cargo*. I pull my current shirt over my head—I'm wearing a tank underneath—and replace it with one of the new shirts that reads *ICE ICE* with an arrow pointing down. It's a couple of sizes too big at the moment, but in a few months, it'll fit perfectly.

"This was really sweet of her."

"Do you mind if I take a picture and send it to her?"

"Not at all." I hop to my feet and pose for a picture, which he sends to Queenie before I take my seat on the couch again.

Thirty seconds later, he gets several messages from Queenie in return, full of heart-eye gifs.

"It's sweet that she's excited."

"She tends to look at the positive side of things." He taps the armrest and gives me a chagrinned smile. "She's been very clear that she's Team Jake and Hanna. And I apologize if that's been . . . awkward at all for you."

"I feel like that's the word of the year for us." I prop my cheek on my fist. "And it's not awkward. I mean, I think we can agree that this whole thing is pretty weird as a whole. But it's also very different from my other experiences."

"Can you tell me more about that? I don't really know much about how things went for you with Ryan." Jake stretches his arm along the back of the couch, his attention on me. "I know the basics, that you got pregnant as a teen and your parents adopted him and raised him as theirs, but that's a very tidy version of a complex situation."

Jake and I talked about Ryan finding out, but not about how I ended up in the situation in the first place. And maybe telling him will give us both some perspective, because for as long as I can remember, this has been a closed subject. One to be put in a box and tucked away. It came with shame and fear, both of which I don't know I've ever truly come to terms with. "I didn't realize I was pregnant until I was over four months along."

Jake's eyes flare with surprise. "You were almost halfway through the pregnancy."

"I was." Memories surface, taking a trip backward through time, to the day I finally figured out what was going on with my body. And how my entire life basically felt as though it had fallen apart. "I didn't start getting a period until I was fourteen, and my cycle was never very regular, at least not for that first year, so what should have been a red flag wasn't all that uncommon. Plus, I was involved in all kinds of sports, which can affect regularity. I didn't have any of the usual symptoms, or at least not the kind I expected." I blow out a breath, aware now of things I hadn't been back then.

"You were only fifteen, though, right?"

"Just barely. Way too young to be having sex," I mutter. "At the time, my parents had their hands full with Gerald. He was younger but such a troublemaker."

"King mentioned that he used to get up to a lot of no good."

"He tried to take our dad's truck on a joyride. He couldn't reach the pedals or see over the steering wheel at the same time so all he managed to do was ruin my mom's rose bushes. I wasn't an angel, but I didn't give my parents the same kind of hard time he did."

"So they didn't pay much attention to what you were doing and who you were doing it with?" Jake asks.

"Exactly. In my freshman year I started dating a senior."

Jake's brow furrows. "That would make him almost four years older than you."

"Yup. And when you're in your twenties and thirties, or even your forties, those four years don't mean a lot. But when you're fourteen and he's eighteen . . ." I trail off.

"I would have lost my mind if Queenie brought home a senior when she was fourteen years old." Jake clenches and releases his fists. "What the heck were your parents thinking, letting you date that guy?"

I shrug. "It was different times, I guess? We lived in a small town, Kurt was captain of the football team, and I was a cheerleader. Before he went off to college, I was invited to go with his family on a mission trip. I'd just turned fifteen. Gerald had just been caught shoplifting, so my parents were dealing with that. Kurt's dad was a pastor, so of course, my parents thought it was safe to send me with them. But we were camping in a trailer and his parents spent the entire trip at church events."

"You were left to your own devices," Jake says knowingly.

"We were teenagers with nothing to do for hours every day and a lot of hormones. And sex education back then wasn't what it is now."

"Which is how you ended up pregnant."

"Yup. And by the time I was sure, Kurt had already moved out of state for college and his family had followed. We'd broken up a few weeks after we got back from the trip. I honestly thought the nausea and being tired and emotional was heartbreak."

"I can see how you could make that mistake." Jake slides his fingers under my hair, his thumb smoothing up and down the back of my neck. "How did you figure it out?"

"My cheer coach pulled me aside and asked if I'd had my period."

"Holy shit."

"Yeah. It was . . . not the best. I guess she noticed the weight gain and sort of put two and two together. She gave me a pregnancy test and I took it into the girls' bathroom."

"What the hell was your cheer coach doing with pregnancy tests?"

"Would you be surprised to hear that I was not the first girl in cheer to end up pregnant?" I lean my cheek against his forearm. "Anyway, the test was positive. I had no idea what to do. The coach called my parents, and the next thing I knew, my dad transferred offices from Ohio to Tennessee."

"What about Kurt? Did you tell him?"

"Oh yeah. I called him before we moved and begged him to let me move in with him. In my head we were going to get back together and raise the baby. But he wanted me to terminate the pregnancy. He didn't want a baby ruining his chances at a pro football career. Plus, his dad would have killed him if he found out."

Jake's lip curls up in a silent snarl. "He's an asshole."

"He wasn't my smartest boyfriend choice. And I suppose karma intervened in her own way since he never made it to the pros."

"Have you seen him since you were teenagers?"

"Only once, and that was when he signed over his parental rights so my parents could formally adopt Ryan. I had to be there to sign the papers, too, otherwise it wouldn't have been legal."

"That must have been awful for you." His expression is full of sadness and empathy.

I'd agreed to the adoption before Ryan was born. It seemed like the best way to keep him in my life and give him a stable, normal childhood.

"It was hard, but I didn't know any different at the time. I had to leave all my friends behind, and I couldn't tell anyone what was going on. There was a lot of ruling by fear in my family, at least with Gerald and me. It was different with Ryan. But I spent the last half of my pregnancy pretty much in isolation." I had a midwife, and never even went to the hospital. The doctor came to the house for all my checkups. I was friendless and alone.

"What do you mean, isolation?"

"When my parents moved to Tennessee, I went and stayed with my aunt on their farm in Kentucky. I took most of my courses through distance education that year. It wasn't until Ryan was born that I was allowed to come back home. I had a week with him before that happened. And the moment I walked through the door to my parents' house—the baby that had grown inside of me, that I had given birth to and fell in love with—stopped being my son to the rest of the world."

But my heart knew he was mine, even if no one else was supposed to.

And that was the hardest part. Grieving a loss that no one could ever know about.

CHAPTER EIGHTEEN

Innie or Outie

Jake

I TRY NOT to let my horror show on my face, but it isn't easy. I'm very right about the neat and tidy version of that story being a hell of a lot different than Hanna's reality. I can't fathom going through that as an adult, let alone at the age of fifteen. I clear my throat. "That sounds like it was pretty hard on you."

I'm glad I didn't know any of this about her parents until now. Although, moving forward, I'm not sure how I'm going to deal with them the next time we're at a family function. I'm also aware I'm seeing this through my own lens, and my perception of her experience and how she feels about it are two very different things.

As if she can read my mind, or possibly my facial expression speaks volumes without me uttering a word, she runs her hand over my forearm, as if I'm the one in need of reassurance.

"My parents aren't bad people, Jake. I believe they had my best interests at heart, even if the way they managed it wasn't necessarily great for me emotionally. They didn't want me to have the stigma of being a teen mom hanging over my head. They saw what it looked like in the small town I grew up in and they didn't want that to be my life. And frankly, neither did I." She drags her finger back up my arm, following a vein, her voice soft. "They also worried I'd end up on the same path as Gerald, who I love dearly, but he had a criminal record by the time he was eleven and he still can't hold down a job for longer than six months."

She's not wrong about that. He acts more like an unruly nineteen-year-old than an adult who has it together. "But you're not Gerald."

"I know, and so did they, but kids don't come with an instruction manual. Gerald was particularly difficult, and I think they overcorrected with me out of concern. And then Ryan was a dream child, so doing it right with him was easy. He was loved and had the chance to achieve his full potential, and that's what matters the most." The way she says it makes me wonder who she's trying to convince, herself or me.

"Thank you for sharing all of this with me, Hanna. I feel like I know you a little better." And I can see why this baby means as much as it does to her. "You're a pretty incredible woman."

"I made a mess of my teen years."

"You had some help making that mess," I remind her. "I feel like knowing this is going to help frame my actions moving forward. I couldn't understand at first why you were so opposed to moving to Seattle, but it makes more sense now."

"I don't want to commit to uprooting my life and everything I've worked so hard for when things are still uncertain," she replies, her bottom lip slipping through her teeth.

I can see how much stress this conversation puts on her, and I want to reassure her, at least for now, that we don't need to make those decisions. Eventually, yes, but not yet. For as strong as Hanna is, there's a fragileness about her, and it's tied to these pieces of her history. "I understand. Especially knowing how your first pregnancy went, and then miscarrying. Both of those experiences were traumatic. You're going in with eyes wide open and protecting your heart from more potential damage."

Her smile is soft and sad. "You know, I don't think I truly connected all the pieces until right now, but you're absolutely right. That's what I'm trying to do, not just with the baby, but with you, too."

"Can you explain that?" I need to know where we stand.

She nods and looks away, absently fingering the pendant at her throat. The one I gave her. She closes her eyes and blows out a breath. "This is hard."

"I'm a big boy, Hanna. I can handle whatever it is you need to tell me."

"I knew we couldn't keep sleeping together because it had stopped being just about the sex. Which, I have to be honest, is out of this world. You're so fun." She glances at me from the side and her tongue peeks out to wet her bottom lip. "And I was worried about seeing you again on Queenie's birthday because I knew it would be hard not to…relapse, for lack of a better term." She smiles cheekily for a second before her expression sobers. "I didn't know how to go back to being friends like we were in the beginning. It was too complicated, and I didn't want to do that to Ryan."

"And then you found out you were pregnant," I supply.

"It changes everything, but it's no less complicated." Her eyes lift to the ceiling and she blinks a bunch of times. "I had feelings for you, Jake. I still do, but I'm terrified of what might happen with this baby, and my last experience saw my marriage implode, so my head's a bit messy over you. And my heart, well, it feels a lot like it's made of glass right now."

I stroke her cheek and she leans into the affection. "For the sake of transparency, I have feelings for you and have for a while. A long while, actually. And I gotta be honest, I was pretty disappointed when you ended things, but I wanted to respect your relationship with King. Finding out you were pregnant took me back to what happened with Kimmie. I did a lot wrong with that relationship and made mistakes I don't want to repeat with you. I put so much focus on Queenie because Kimmie was so reluctant that I think I had a hand in dooming us. Although, I don't think that relationship would have lasted regardless, but I made Queenie my entire world. It didn't leave a lot of room for anyone or anything else."

"As someone who had to step back from the role of mom, I can tell you that it was the hardest thing I've ever done. And while I knew it was right, I don't think there's ever been a time that I haven't wished it had been different," Hanna says softly.

"The thing I'm most afraid of is the potential for loss. I got over losing my career, and after a while I got over losing Kimmie, but I really don't want either of those things to happen again." I drag my fingertips along her collarbone. "I'm aware that the road ahead of us isn't going to be an easy one, and that we are part of each other's lives in an inextricable way. But I think we could be good together."

"I'm scared, Jake," she whispers.

"Of what?"

"Of falling for you, of what could happen with this baby, of the possibility of getting my heart broken again." Her throat bobs with a thick swallow before she continues, "But I still want to try to be an us."

"That's good. Me, too. On all fronts, but I want this with you."

"So do I."

I take her hand in mine and bring it to my lips, kissing her knuckles. "Does this mean we're dating? Officially?"

"I think it does." Hanna exhales what sounds a lot like a relieved sigh.

It echoes the weight that's lifted from my shoulders. "Do I get to call you my girlfriend then?"

She ducks her head and smiles. "That seems reasonable."

"I think so, too. Does this mean I don't have to sleep in the spare bedroom anymore?"

"You didn't have to sleep in the spare bedroom in the first place," she reminds me.

"Yeah, but that was before, when I was just the ride you were riding, not the boyfriend."

She tips her head back and laughs, but when her gaze meets mine, her expression is suddenly serious. "You were never just the ride, Jake. You should know that by now."

"And you were never just a secret I was keeping." I slip my

hand into her hair. "Now that we're dating, can we make out?"

"Absolutely." Her fingers curl around the back of my neck and our lips meet.

It feels like a promise sealed. A kiss for a kiss.

IN THE MORNING we head to the doctor's office for the ultrasound. The majority of the people sitting in the waiting room are in their mid-to-late twenties. There's one couple where the husband looks to be close to my age, but the wife doesn't look to be more than thirty-five.

When Hanna's name is called, the attendant asks me to remain in the waiting room, and I'm told they'll call me in during the last few minutes of the appointment. I'm not the only one waiting to be called in. There are two other guys, the one who also looks to be closer to my age and another guy who's maybe twenty-five at best. The younger one has earbuds in and is playing some kind of game on his phone. The guy closer to my age is clicking away on a mini tablet, probably answering emails.

Neither of them seems particularly worried or excited. Or anything really.

I'm an anxious wreck by the time an attendant calls me in. And that ratchets up another several notches when I step into the room and the first thing I see is Hanna dabbing at her eyes with a tissue.

"Is something wrong?" I feel like my heart is suddenly in my throat and the room seems to shift under my feet.

"Everything's okay, Jake." She holds out her hand and I step forward to take it, gripping it tightly. "These are relief tears. Come here and have a look at Jake Junior."

I bend and kiss her forehead, then the tip of her nose and her lips. "Thank God. I'm going to need to learn how to differentiate between sad and happy tears over the next few months, aren't I?" I cup her face in my hands and am about to kiss her again when someone clears their throat.

I glance to the right, where the technician is standing with the ultrasound wand in her hand.

"Oh, hey. Sorry. I was a little nervous waiting out there." I thumb over my shoulder to the door.

She gives me an understanding smile. "Jitters are normal."

I blow out a breath and Hanna's words when I first walked in finally register. "Wait a second. Did you say *Jake Junior*? Are we having a boy?"

Hanna's grin lights up her face. "It looks that way, and so far he's meeting all the important milestones. We very well may have another little hockey player on our hands with how active he is." She tips her head. "Come around the other side so you can see."

I move around the table, taking in the mostly flat expanse of her belly and a small, faint scar, maybe from an appendectomy.

I crouch down beside her and kiss her temple again. I know I need to cut it with the PDA and being overly touchy, but for a very brief second, I thought something bad had happened. That's all it takes for me to realize the ambivalence I first had about this has shifted. I want this baby, not just because Hanna does, but because I've become invested.

The technician moves the ultrasound transducer over Hanna's stomach, stopping when she gets to a small baby-shaped shadow on the screen. And then the sound of our son's heartbeat fills the room.

I'd like to say that I keep it together. That I don't get emotional. But that would be a lie. "You're sure it's a boy? I didn't think we'd be able to tell yet."

"I would say we're more than ninety-five percent certain it's a boy," the technician says while wearing a smile.

Hanna smirks and I have to wonder what the conversation was like before I entered the room.

"Like father, like son then?" I murmur in her ear.

She barks out a laugh, and our son bumps around in her stomach before he settles again. Hanna grips my hand tightly.

"Don't make me laugh like that. I'm holding a liter of water, and I'm about ready to pee my pants."

"Sorry." I kiss her cheek again. "We're having a boy." I understand better now how she must feel. Excitement and worry take up equal space in my head. Knowing the gender makes it more real.

"We really are."

"How far along are we?" I try to remember the markers with Kimmie, but it's been so long. "We must be out of the first trimester, right?"

"That's right," the technician says. "You're just over fourteen weeks, and the due date should be around March second."

"Okay." I filter through the game schedule in my head. "I can make sure Alex is set up so I don't have to travel with the team when we get close to your due date."

"I don't expect you to do that. I know how important your job is."

"You and our baby are my top priority, and there's no way I'm going to risk missing him coming into the world. But we can talk more about that later." I'm jumping ahead, but I'd been at a game when Kimmie went into labor and I only managed to get to the hospital as Queenie was being born. I don't want that to happen again.

The technician leaves, and Hanna takes a trip to the bathroom while we wait for her doctor.

The excitement over finding out that we're having a boy is replaced by anxiety all over again when her doctor arrives to discuss the results of her blood tests.

I take Hanna's hand in mine as her doctor takes the seat across from us. I feel like I'm holding my breath. I've done plenty of reading over the past week, and I'm very aware of the potential genetic complications we might be facing.

As soon as the introductions are done, Dr. Tumbler says, "I have some good news."

Hanna's grip on my hand loosens enough that my fingers start to tingle with the renewed blood flow. "What kind of good news?"

"The blood tests have all come back negative for abnormalities."

Hanna's hand comes up to cover her mouth, and she turns her head, her cheek pressing against my arm. "Oh, that's a relief."

I wrap my arm around her shoulder as she makes a squeaky sound and takes a deep breath.

Dr. Tumbler holds out a box of tissues, and I pluck one from it and pass it to Hanna, who dabs at her eyes.

"I know we're not out of the woods yet, but this feels like a good step forward," Hanna says.

Dr. Tumbler nods. "I do think it's advisable to do further testing in the coming weeks. We can schedule the second part of your integrated screening in a few weeks, but I'm also going to suggest additional blood tests, an amniocentesis, and tests for neural tube defects."

"Yes. Of course. I want to be as prepared as possible."

"I'd like to keep a very close eye on your blood pressure, and your sugar levels are higher than normal. Nothing concerning at this point, but something to monitor."

I ask the doctor as many questions as I can, wishing I could record her answers, because I'm not sure I'm taking it all in the way I'd like to. Once we've exhausted all the questions, we head back to reception to make follow-up appointments and set up new ones for blood tests and the next ultrasound. All of which we add to our shared calendar.

We're also given an envelope with pictures from the ultrasound, as well as a video, complete with heartbeat. We didn't have these options with Queenie, and I plan to take advantage of every one of them in this technologically advanced age.

"Are you hungry? Do you want to grab something to eat? We could get takeout and bring it back to your place if the smells in a restaurant are going to be too much." I ask once I've helped her into her car and I'm behind the wheel.

"You are honestly the most considerate, conscientious man I have ever met. Do you even have time for that? I don't think I asked when your flight out is."

"Not until tomorrow morning."

"Oh. Well, that's good. I didn't realize I was going to get another night with you." Her cheeks color with embarrassment. "I'm really sorry I passed out so early last night."

"That's okay." I give her hand a squeeze. "I'm happy to be your personal body pillow any night of the week, Hanna."

She laughs, the tint in her cheeks deepening. "How did that even happen?"

"You pulled me into bed with you and wrapped yourself around me and wouldn't let go." I could have easily slipped out from under her, but I wasn't particularly motivated to leave the bed. Not after the emotional conversation we had and our newly established relationship status.

"I can't believe I did that." She holds up a finger. "Well, I can, because you're a hard man to resist. But I will say, I didn't peg you for a cuddler."

"Oh? And why is that?" In all honesty, I don't think I've ever been much for spooning or letting someone use me as their body pillow. But in the past, I've always kept some walls up between the women I chose to date and me. It helped me manage my own expectations and theirs. With Hanna it's different. I want the closeness with her.

"Maybe I should have suspected you'd be a closet cuddler. I just figured you didn't get where you are by being a softie, and I've seen how you are with the boys when they're not pulling their weight on the ice. It's a lot different from how you are outside of your job. And definitely different than how you are with me." She runs her thumb over my knuckles.

"My job is to keep my team in line and make sure they're working together and unified. I can't afford to be soft with them or they'll walk all over me. Not because they're a bunch of assholes, but because the only way you can be a successful elite athlete is by having guidance, structure, and rules." It's something I've had to learn how to balance carefully, and not let that hardass attitude seep into my personal and family life.

"Oh, I get it. Leading a team is a big deal. And watching you and Alex together . . ." She shakes her head and rolls her eyes to the ceiling. "Let's just say my friend Paxton and the ladies in my painting class are big fans."

"What do you mean they're big fans? Of hockey? Do you want me to get you extra tickets for a few Tennessee games?"

"I'm pretty sure those women would love that." Her smile widens. "Some of those ladies ship you and Alex."

I'm sure I must look confused. "Doesn't that mean they want us to be a couple? Or does *ship* mean something else? I'm too old for today's slang. Why can't things be rad and awesome and cool?" I can also feel my face warming.

Hanna props her chin on her fist and her eyes glint with humor. "Sort of, they dig on your bromance."

"We don't have a bromance."

"You're two very attractive men who manage and coach a hockey team. When you're on the road, you're always together. And Alex has four kids and a wife, and you have a daughter in her twenties who is always at the games, and it's very clear that you're close. Women of all ages find that incredibly sexy."

"Wait, you think Alex is attractive?" I don't know why I bother asking. Queenie always talks about his hot dad status.

Hanna arches a brow. "That's your takeaway?"

"But not more attractive than me, right?"

"No, Jake. I don't find him more attractive than you. Besides, I've heard more than enough about Alex's man business to know that I would not want to be in Violet's shoes." She motions in the general vicinity of her crotch.

I don't need to ask what she's talking about. Alex had several endorsements when he was a top player, including one for prophylactics, all before he started coaching. Once, when he hosted a poker night, his wife thought it would be funny to put the life-size cutout at the door to the garage, sort of as a welcome. I can't unsee him holding up a box of extra-large condoms wearing only a pair of tighty-whities. I've heard enough semi-drunk discussions between the wives about his grower versus show-er status to believe there was no photoshopping in that ad.

"Right. Yeah. I vote we stop talking about Alex and his junk."

"Are you jealous?"

"No." Maybe a little. "Queenie does this whole swoon thing whenever he brings the kids around and talks about ovaries exploding." Which is an off-putting thing to think about.

Hanna barks out a laugh. "You should see my group chat with the girls. It was full of ovaries exploding gifs during every event where the kids were present." She puts her hand on my arm. "Don't worry. It'll be the same when it's you holding little JJ."

"Little JJ?"

"Jake Junior. That's what I'm calling him until we settle on a name."

"I thought that was going to be his name." I'm kidding, but apparently she doesn't take it that way.

"I can get on board with JJ. I'll put it at the top of my list."

We make a stop at one of Hanna's favorite cafes and pick up lunch.

By the time we get back to her place, my phone has half a dozen new messages from Queenie asking how the ultrasound went and if we have any news. It's followed by a range of gifs from nail biting, to the one with the elderly lady that reads *it's been eighty-four years*.

Hanna checks her own phone. She has a single message from King, asking how she's doing.

We spread our lunch out over the dining room table.

"Should we see if they're both home and we can share the news?" I ask.

"Sure, that would be good." Hanna tucks her hair behind her ears and then starts folding the napkins into triangles.

"Are you okay?"

She smiles. "A little nervous, that's all."

"About King?"

She nods and her bottom lip slides between her teeth.

"Is there anything in particular that you're worried about?"

"I don't know exactly." She smooths the napkin out again. "I

155

think I'm just worried about Ryan's reaction to finding out that we're having a boy."

"Why do you think the gender would matter to him?" I want to understand her thought process here.

"I don't think it would be conscious on his part. But having another boy...the parallels might be difficult. I know that as excited as I am for this, I also feel...some guilt, I guess? Because I can take care of this child in a way I couldn't with Ryan. And if I'm feeling that way, then how is he feeling? And will he even recognize those feelings, and if he does, will he be able to share them with me?"

I lean over and press a kiss to her temple. It's becoming my default move and a way to show her affection. "Would it be better if we called them separately, so you two can talk privately?"

She taps her lip, contemplating for a few seconds. "I don't think so?" It's more question than statement. "I'd rather tell them together if that's okay with you. That way he has Queenie as a buffer, and hopefully her excitement will help him process. Then he and I can have a conversation later, after he's had time to digest it."

"Okay, whatever you think is going to be best." This is a hard line to toe; wanting to protect her and understanding there are more variables than just us and how we're going to deal with the way this unfolds.

I message Queenie and ask if they're both home and if they have time for a quick call.

Queenie FaceTimes me right away and I move my chair so both Hanna and I fit in the small screen. Hanna has this little stand she puts the phone on and adjusts it so they're not looking into our nostrils.

"I want to know everything! How did it go?" Queenie's sitting in the middle of the couch, legs crossed. Her hair is pulled up into a loose ponytail and she's wearing a shirt dotted with paint splatters. Her fingernails hold traces of pink and blue paint.

"Good. It went well. Where's Ryan?" Hanna asks.

Queenie cups her hands around her mouth and shouts, "King,

get your ass in the living room. Hanna and Dad are on the phone!" She turns her attention back to us and rolls her eyes. "Sorry. He literally walked in the door thirty seconds ago. You know how he is post workout. Needs to carb load like he hasn't eaten in a month."

"Just give me a sec," he calls out.

"Did you get to hear the heartbeat? Is everything okay with the baby?"

Hanna's hand slips below the table and comes to rest on my leg. I turn to make sure she's okay and Queenie sighs.

"You two are so freaking cute I can't even stand it."

King's legs appear and the sound of a plate and cutlery hitting the table close by filters through the device. A second later, his mammoth frame fills the other half of the screen. He stretches his arm across the back of the couch. His gaze shifts between the two of us and he smiles, but it looks strained. "Everything go okay this morning?" His fingers wrap around Queenie's shoulder and he pulls her into his side.

"Everything went well. I'm just over fourteen weeks and due at the beginning of March," Hanna says.

"Oooh! A water sign baby!" Queenie claps. "This is so exciting!"

"And the baby is healthy?" King asks.

"Yup. The initial blood tests came back negative for abnormalities, which is a relief. There will be more tests in a few weeks, but so far so good."

"That's good. And you're healthy?" King's thumb rubs back and forth over Queenie's shoulder. He has yet to make eye contact with me.

"The doctor is going to watch Hanna's blood pressure because it's high, but otherwise she's doing great," I say.

His gaze flicks to me and then back to Hanna. "High blood pressure? Is that dangerous? Has that ever been a problem for you before?"

Hanna shakes her head. "It's usually right around normal. Sometimes it happens in pregnancies over forty, but I have appointments scheduled every two weeks with my doctor to keep a close eye on things."

"Okay. That's good then." His tongue slides over the chip in his front tooth. "Have you told Mom and Dad yet?"

Hanna's fingers flex on my thigh and she shakes her head. She smiles, but it wavers a little. "Not yet. I wanted to wait until after the ultrasound."

"Did you get ultrasound pictures? What about a video? Did you find out the sex? Are King and I going to have a little sister or a brother?" Queenie jokes about having a mutual half-sibling. I think it might be her way of trying to normalize this very strange situation we've all found ourselves in.

King rubs at his bottom lip, possibly to hide his grimace, as he grumbles, "Queenie."

She pats his leg. "It's the truth, might as well get comfortable with it."

King seems to pull himself together and his gaze bounces between the two of us. "Did you find out the gender?"

"We did," I say and stretch my arm across the back of Hanna's chair.

She leans into me and tips her chin up, eyes on me instead of the screen. "Do you want to tell them?"

I can't tell how she's feeling. I want to take the pressure off of her and give her and me permission to be excited to share this news. "Why don't we tell them together?"

"On the count of three?" Her smile is full of silent gratitude.

She counts down from three to one while I do the drumroll on the table. "We're having a baby—"

Hanna and I look at the screen as she says, "Boy!"

Queenie screams her delight and King, to his credit, plasters a smile on his face and tries his best not to get elbowed in the junk by my daughter, who's flailing around like Kermit the Frog hopped up on methamphetamines.

"We're going to have a baby brother, King! I'm so excited! Don't you think Jax is a great name for a boy? But if you don't use it, maybe we should use it when we have our first boy."

"First boy?" King arches a brow.

Queenie rolls her eyes his way. "You've been talking about how we're probably going to need a bigger house, and this place has five bedrooms. For sure, we're going to have more than one boy." She turns her attention back to the screen. "Are we the first to know? Are you telling anyone else?"

"Not yet. I think we want to wait a few more weeks before we do that."

"Okay. Your secret's safe with us, right, King?"

"Yup." He makes a zipped lip gesture.

We talk for a few more minutes, until King reminds Queenie that she has another art therapy session soon.

It doesn't escape my notice that when King says goodbye he doesn't address me, and he refers to Hanna by her first name instead of "Momster."

I get this is hard for him, but my biggest worry is that he's going to inadvertently cause Hanna more stress and steal her joy. I don't want to overstep, but I think he and I need to talk this out so I know where he's coming from and we can work on figuring out our ever-changing relationship.

CHAPTER NINETEEN

Stand by Me

Hanna

JAKE AND I spend the rest of the day organizing our schedules for the next few months. The plan is for him to fly here for ultrasounds and important doctor appointments, and for me to go to Seattle once a month, provided it remains safe for me to fly.

He mentions the possibility of one of us moving again and makes a case for me coming to Seattle. With Ryan there for the foreseeable future and his job being there, it would make sense to consider it. But I'm not ready yet to have this serious discussion. I'm still worried about the health of the baby, and I need to ensure his safety before I think about making major life changes.

I spend the week following Jake's return to Seattle fretting over the upcoming family dinner on Sunday, which is when I plan to tell my parents that I'm pregnant. I skipped it last weekend and lied about why I couldn't go since telling them I had company for the weekend would have resulted in questions I didn't want to answer. I know my mom will support me, like she has the past two times, but she's going to be worried about all the risks. And then there's telling her who the father is. As if our family isn't wonky enough.

On Sunday afternoon, I drive over to my parents' place. We're having steak and baked potatoes on the barbecue. So far most of my cravings have been for fruit and chocolate. But I've always had a weak spot for chocolate, so I'm not sure if it's a pregnancy craving so much as it's my comfort food and my go-to when I'm stressed. Needless to say, I've eaten a lot of chocolate today.

Gerald is sitting in one of the Adirondack chairs, nursing a beer and tossing a Frisbee to Burton, my parents' ancient golden retriever. "Hey, sis! How's it going? Did you bring a pie? Is it cherry pie? I love cherry pie."

I hold up the pie plate. "Sorry, Ger, it's apple, do you think you'll survive?"

"I have a feeling I'll live through the disappointment since apple is my second favorite." He grabs the Frisbee from Burton and tosses it again.

I take the plate straight into the house so neither Burton nor my brother gets any ideas. It's happened before, with both of them.

My phone buzzes in my purse. I have messages from Jake wishing me luck. He actually offered to fly back down this weekend for moral support, but I told him it would probably be best for me to share the news on my own first. Explaining the complexities of my relationship with Jake to my parents, while he's here, is a level of awkward no one needs.

I also have messages from my Seattle Girls—they've been incredibly supportive—even when they found out that Jake is my baby daddy. It's a lot easier now that most of the people I would consider close to Jake and me know what's going on. And in some ways, I question how different things would have been if I'd allowed us to be something more months ago. But I'd wanted to protect Ryan, which I'm beginning to realize is a bad habit that only seems to cause more conflict instead of less.

I have a message from Paxton sending me good vibes.

Even Ryan has messaged to wish me luck with a series of crossed finger emojis.

He knows what our mother is like. We love her, but she has a very strong opinion on everything.

"Hanna Banana! How's my favorite daughter!" My dad pulls me in for a hug.

I'm his only daughter, hence he can call me his favorite. "I'm good, Dad. How are you? How's your forever Saturday treating you?" My dad retired last year, and I think he's busier now than when he was working full-time.

"Good. Good. Did I tell you I'm taking up stained glass? Your mother used to do it when you were young, so we have all the stuff lying around in the basement. I was cleaning it out and figured I'd give it a shot. See if I'm any good at it."

"That sounds fun." For a while, we all got stained glass lamps and night-light covers for our birthdays.

"It probably would be a lot more fun if your mother didn't take over every single project I start, but I'm getting the hang of it." He gives me a conspiratorial wink.

I laugh, but I know exactly what he's talking about. My mother is an expert on basically everything and loves to be "helpful." Usually, it means she elbows you out of the way and finishes what you started.

"Hanna! Oh good. You're finally here. Can I get your help in the kitchen with the biscuits? I need you to cut in the butter for me," Mom calls from the kitchen window.

"Sure, Mom. I'd be happy to."

I leave my dad and my brother sitting in the backyard and set the pie onto the kitchen counter, far from the edge so Burton can't knock it off, which has happened before. My mom comes behind me and wraps an apron around my waist. She makes a noise as she ties it into a bow.

"Thanks." I don't bother telling her I'm more than capable of tying my own apron. Part of my mother's shtick is that she will forever be a mother. Being a mom was always what she wanted to do. And she was fully committed to that role when we were growing up.

"Have you been eating too many sweets lately, honey?" she

asks in that tone that makes Gerald and me roll our eyes.

"Probably." I just smile and start cutting the butter into the flour mixture.

"Did I tell you that Delores lost almost fifty pounds on some new diet where you only eat certain foods at certain times of the day? She looks amazing! And she started dating again. Did you know that the Walravens' son divorced a couple of years ago? They're having a birthday party next month. You should come and I can introduce you to him."

"Aren't the Walravens over eighty? Isn't their son retirement age?"

"I think he'll be in his mid-fifties this year. He's got a great job. I believe he's the VP of his company, which means he makes excellent money. If you two ended up together, you could consider early retirement." She scoops the filling out of the potatoes and into a large glass bowl. She's always been very traditional, and there's nothing wrong with that, but we have different wants out of life.

"I like my job, Mom." And I don't think dating someone while I'm pregnant with another man's baby will go over very well, with anyone, especially Jake.

"I know you do, honey. I just mean that it would be nice if you didn't have to run a household all on your own. I'm glad you have your career. It was good for you to have the distraction after what happened with Gordon. You needed somewhere else to put your focus after all that heartbreak." She pats my shoulder as she leans over it. "Make sure the dough is in pea-size bits before you start rolling it out. And only half an inch thick or they'll be too doughy." She tosses in a handful of cheese and chives. "I'm sure Ryan and Queenie will be announcing a baby soon, don't you think?"

"They've been married for three and a half months, Mom."

"Ryan's already thirty, though. And Queenie doesn't have to work, so it's not as though they need to worry about financial stability, which is usually one of the reasons so many people put it off. That's what happened with you and Gordon. You were both so absorbed in your careers you waited too long. I don't want the same thing to happen with Ryan. He'll make such a wonderful father." She sighs and starts slicing a cucumber for the salad. "I can't wait to be a grandmother. It'll be nice to have little babies around again. And you'll be such a wonderful auntie."

I bite back the nasty retort sitting on my tongue like a bitter pill. These pregnancy hormones are making me edgy and prone to snippiness. And stupid tears. It's like being a teenager all over again, minus the perky boobs.

I can't imagine a better segue than this. Ideally, I'd like to tell my parents at the same time, but my dad's reaction to everything is pretty much the same: either *that's nice* or *that's too bad*. I love him, but he's the most passive man on the face of the earth.

Well, here goes nothing.

I set the pastry blender down and wipe my hands on my apron. "Actually, you're going to be a grandmother by early next year."

She stops what she's doing. "Is Queenie pregnant already? Why didn't Ryan tell me?" She reaches for her phone, which is sitting on the window ledge.

I put my hand out to stop her. "Queenie's not pregnant, Mom."

"Oh my heavens." She makes the sign of the cross. "Please tell me Gerald hasn't gotten someone pregnant."

"Probably pretty unlikely since the only women who can tolerate him for more than half an hour are related to him," I mumble and instantly regret it.

"That's not nice, Hanna. You know it's not your brother's fault he is the way he is."

"I know, Mom. I'm sorry." I need to get a handle on the mean vibe I'm throwing out there. Gerald is just Gerald. And we love him no matter what.

"So what is this you're talking about? Are you thinking of adopting? Or maybe fostering? Do they allow single women to do that?" This is what my mother does: ask seven million questions and never let you answer one before the next one pops out of her mouth.

"*I'm* pregnant," I blurt, needing to get it out already.

For once in her life, she doesn't have a cheeky response. At least not right away. It takes about three seconds before her lips pull together as though she's sucked on a lemon. "That's not something you should joke about, Hanna."

"It's not a joke. I'm fifteen weeks." I fight to keep my cool.

"How in the world is that even possible at your age?" She blinks several times in a row.

"Lots of women have babies well into their forties these days, Mom." Although forty-six is definitely on the late side. I try my best to be calm and patient, but I'm starting to feel like it would have been a lot better to have someone on my side here with me. Even Paxton would have been a good buffer. Anyone outside of family members to force my mother to think before she speaks.

"Just because other women do doesn't mean you should! Is it even safe with your history? You know what happened with little Tammy Van Wallen's baby and she was only thirty-six, a full decade younger than you!"

"There was a history of chromosomal abnormalities in her family." I could really use a glass of water and maybe a chair.

"Why would you put yourself at risk like this, Hanna? Have you forgotten what happened the last time? I can't see you go through that again. It was devastating for all of us! Whose baby is it even? Are you and Gordon getting back together? After everything that happened? Why would you do that without even telling me about it?" Her hand goes to her chest, as if the idea that I would make this kind of decision without her is mortally wounding.

I cross over to the kitchen table and take a seat. My legs feel unsteady, and my throat grows tight. "I'm aware of the risks. And yes, I've seen my doctor. I've had all the tests, and so far the blood work and the ultrasound show that the baby is healthy. And no, it wasn't Gordon."

"How long have you known, and why didn't you tell me until now? And who in the world is the father? I didn't even realize you were dating anyone!" She crosses her arms, her hurt clear on her face.

This isn't how I expected her to react. I assumed, maybe naively, that I would have her full support. So this aggressive inquisition is both frustrating and unnerving. This isn't about her, and yet, somehow she manages to make it that way. "I've only known for a little while, and I thought it would be best to tell you in person rather than over the phone."

She breathes heavily through her nose. "I would have gone with you to the doctor. You still haven't told me who the father is."

"Jake is the father." I feel like I'm holding my breath, waiting for the axe to fall.

"Jake?" She makes the lemon-suck face again. "Is he someone you met at work?"

"No, Mom." I could not be any less excited to explain this. "Jake, Queenie's dad."

Her eyes go wide and she blinks. And blinks again. "You're pregnant with Ryan's father-in-law's child?"

"It was an accident." I don't know why I say this. It doesn't matter that it was unintentional. It's happening. I'm having a baby with Jake. End of story.

"An accident? I can't believe you would do something so thoughtless! Poor Ryan. How is he going to handle this?" She presses her hand to her heart again and gives me the disappointed look I got three decades ago when I had to tell her I was pregnant the first time. "Did you think about the position you're putting him in by doing this? My poor baby, I can't even imagine how he feels."

"He already knows." My blood feels like it's boiling. I know I need to calm down. This much stress isn't good for me, or the baby, but my mom's lack of support and three decades of baggage are a lot to manage. So I burst like a dam.

"And newsflash, Mom: Ryan is not *your* baby! He was *mine*. *I* carried him in my belly. *I* gave birth to him. He's *my* son. And I know you like to live in a world that revolves around you and all the fantastic things you did for him and how you're the reason he's so goddamn successful, but I think you're forgetting who it was who drove him to all of his hockey practices as a kid. I'm the one who woke up at five on Saturday mornings and took him to ice time. I went to all of his games. I was there every step of the way, too." I drive home the point by stabbing the counter with my finger.

"In fact, he took his first steps with me, *not you*, because you had book club with your friends. But I never told you because I didn't want you to be upset that you missed it, even though I missed a million of his firsts and you told me about every single damn one! So you can cut the shit and the *poor Ryan, poor you* garbage. I don't need you to tell me about all the things that can go wrong. I'm more than fucking aware." I know there's going to be fallout after this, but she needs to see this isn't about Ryan.

My dad bursts into the house, followed by Gerald. "What in tarnation is going on here?"

"Go ahead, Hanna, tell your father what you've done." My mother tips her chin up and looks down her nose at me.

"And rob you of the satisfaction? How could I?" I sneer.

She keeps her glare locked on me. "Hanna's pregnant. Again."

"Holy shitballs!" Gerald says. "For real? Like you're knocked up? With a baby?"

"Gerald." My dad raises a hand to stop him and gives me a bright, somewhat naïve smile. "Is this true, Hanna Banana? Are we finally gonna be grandparents like we always wanted?"

Leave it to my dad to try to turn it around when my mom and I are in the middle of a fight.

I'm exhausted from more than a quarter century of placating. "I already made you grandparents. Three decades ago." I push out of the chair and head for the door. But I only make it a couple of steps before the world turns black.

MY PARENTS TAKE me to urgent care, and I message Paxton to meet us there, because I honestly can't handle any more of my mother's lectures or her tendency to steamroll and undermine my decisions. Especially since my blood pressure is a lot higher than they like.

Urgent care ends up calling Dr. Tumbler, and I'm put on blood pressure medication right away. And I have an appointment with her the following day.

The whole thing scares the crap out of me. I'm very glad Paxton is staying the night, because the alternative is staying at my parents', and that's where I went the last time I had complications. Gordon had been out of town for work, and I hadn't wanted to stay in my house alone while I dealt with the loss.

"Your mother is damn lucky I was too worried about you to rip into her." Paxton grips the steering wheel. She's trying to keep it together, but I think she's as rattled as I am.

"I knew the Jake part was going to be a thing, but I didn't expect her to react quite so...badly." It was a shock, one I obviously didn't need.

"No offense, I love you, and I can also appreciate your mother, because I know her heart is usually in the right place, but she needs to get a damn fucking clue. You're a self-sufficient adult. She had no right to say any of the stuff she did."

"I know." I scrub a hand over my face. "I should have let Jake come with me when I told them. Or maybe it would have been worse. I don't know."

We pull into my driveway. "I can't see Jake letting any of that shit fly. And honestly, Hanna, you've been holding onto all of this for a long time. The only thing your mother should have been was supportive. And she wasn't. Not at all." She inhales a deep breath through her nose and exhales a huff. "I need to calm down. Me being this fired up can't be good for you."

"Thank you for being such a good friend and being on my side."

She reaches across the center console and squeezes my hand. "I'm always going to be here for you, Han. You know that."

"I do." In all the years we've been friends, she's never let me down. This kind of friendship is rare, and I love her dearly.

She helps me inside, and I don't fight her on the mother-bird hovering.

Once I'm settled on the couch, she makes me a tea and pulls a box of cookies out of the cupboard. I didn't have dinner, and I had a hard time stomaching lunch, so I blamed my fainting on low blood sugar. Which wasn't a lie. But the raised blood pressure was, and continues to be, an issue.

"I think I have to tell work I'm pregnant," I announce.

Paxton takes the cushion at the other end of the couch. "I know you wanted to wait a little longer, but it might be a good idea. Do you think you should try to reduce your hours? Lower your stress levels?"

"I can't reduce my hours. Not when I'm being considered for that promotion." And I need this one thing to hold onto, in case the worst happens.

Pax sips her tea, then lowers her mug. "Can I say something?"

"Of course. Your blunt honesty is my favorite thing about you."

She snorts. "You should probably wait until after I say what I'm going to say before you commit to that statement." She sets her mug onto the coffee table. "Do you still want this promotion?"

"I've worked so hard for this, and it comes with a pretty substantial raise, the kind that I'm going to need with a baby on the way," I tell her.

"Okay. I understand not wanting to walk away from that, and I know how hard you've worked. But maybe you need to reevaluate where this falls on the priority list."

"I don't want to give it up just because I'm pregnant." And after tonight, I'm reasonably shaken about how the next few months are going to play out.

"I get that. But, provided things go well—" She motions to the very small bump starting to make itself known under my shirt. "Do you really want a job where you take on more responsibility when you'll have an infant to care for?"

"Say everything goes smoothly, a better salary means I'll be able to put more money away for his education." And I'll have a better pension. All things that seem important for safeguarding the future. I rub my belly, thinking about what JJ might look like, be like, in the years to come. Will he have his dad's size? Will he be athletic? Artistic? Will he be soft and kind like King and Jake? Will he be determined like me?

"If you were doing this alone, I'd say that makes sense. But you also need to take into consideration that he's going to have a father who will very much be in the picture, and who makes millions of dollars a year. He's one of the highest paid GMs in the league. I think it's safe to say you don't need to worry too much about socking away money for his education."

"Maybe not, but I don't want the financial side of things to fall solely on Jake. And what if I'm raising him here, on my own? I'll need to be able to support myself, even if he's helping support JJ."

"We're going to come back to that point in a minute." Paxton crosses her legs and props her elbows on her knees. "First, let me ask you this: are you really willing to only take three months off after you have this baby since that's what your company will give you?"

I keep dunking my tea bag into the cup. It's chamomile. I need caffeine like I need a hole in the head. I've thought about this a lot over the past few weeks. Thought about it and pushed it to the back of my mind because I had other things that needed my attention more. "No. Three months isn't enough."

She nods, clearly agreeing with me. "How much time do you think will be enough?"

"I don't know." I can see where she's going with this. This is what I've been avoiding these past few weeks, not letting myself see all the ramifications this pregnancy will have. Now I understand why Jake was concerned by all the changes our lives will go through and why it took him a while to wrap his head around it. I skipped that step, wanting to focus on a healthy pregnancy. "I want to be there for all the things I missed with Ryan." First smile, rolling over, sitting up, crawling, and first word.

She closes her eyes and tips her head back for a second, taking a deep breath. When she meets my gaze again, she gives me a sad smile. "Okay, Han, we have three decades of friendship, and I'm not going to start bullshitting you now. I know if I've been thinking about this, there's no way you haven't." She reaches out and takes my hand. "You didn't get to be a mom the first time around. Even if Jake wasn't in the picture, three months will never be enough for you. Hell, you'd sell your house and move into an apartment if it meant you could spend the next two years raising this baby full-time. Even when you and Gordon were together, you planned to take at least the first six months. It might be time to reassess. Maybe you don't need the promotion. Not right now, anyway. Maybe you put it off for a few years, or indefinitely."

"But I'm on my own." I swallow down the anxiety that comes with this discussion. All things I know I need to deal with but haven't yet.

"But you don't have to be," she says gently.

"Jake and I just started dating. We're not even close to the merging-our-lives stage."

"And you probably won't be if you stay here and he stays in Seattle. But what is that going to look like in the long term? He raised Queenie on his own. How happy do you think he'll be trying to part-time parent from across the country? How happy will you be?"

I drag my hand down my face. These are the things that keep me up at night. The thoughts I keep pushing aside because I don't want to face the truth. Maybe I'm more like my mother than I realized. "Not very."

"I think maybe the promotion is masking the bigger issue, which is you really looking at the whole picture. I know what you're scared of, Hanna, and I'm not saying you need to make this decision tomorrow, or that you should, but you need to consider what the future looks like after this baby is born. So you're going into this with eyes wide open."

"I'm afraid to start planning beyond doctor's appointments because of what happened the last time," I tell her.

"I know. And I empathize completely. Your fears are legitimate. But you can't keep doing that when the decisions you make now will affect your future. You're past the first trimester hurdle, which is a big deal. I know there are more genetic tests coming up, and those are scary, too. But I think you need to figure out the point where you feel safe, and then you need to start making decisions with Jake, as a team."

"Maybe after the amniocentesis and the second trimester blood tests?" It's framed more as a question than a statement.

"If that's what it takes to make you feel safe, okay. But you and I both know you were half in love with him for months, so I'm not sure putting it on hold for a few more weeks really makes sense."

"I guess I want some kind of control over some part of this, and Tennessee and the people here are currently the only consistent, stable thing I have to hold onto."

"It's hard when you're at the mercy of your own body. But setting up roadblocks is only going to make your relationship with Jake that much more of a challenge." She props her cheek on her fist and sighs. "I haven't forgotten how sad you were after the wedding. Maybe you didn't want to admit you were heartbroken, but I could see it."

"I wanted to do the right thing."

"Ryan is an adult. And sure, this might be hard for him to come to terms with, but what if you and Jake are right for each other? You'll never know if you've got one foot in and one foot out. From what I've seen, he's the type of man who would sideline himself because he doesn't want to take this baby away from you. He already knows what you've been through with Ryan. He's seen how hard it's been. And so have I. Hell, it's why you ended up in Tennessee in the first place." Her voice is soft and it cracks at the end.

"My whole life is here," I say meekly. It's really the only thing I have left to hold onto. And she's right. Jake will one hundred percent step back, even if he doesn't want to. For me. And doesn't that tell me everything I need to know?

"None of us are going anywhere. And your past might be here, but I think you and I both know your future is waiting for you in Seattle. You'll never know if it's supposed to work out by staying here."

CHAPTER TWENTY

Big Steps

Hanna

THE NEXT DAY I call Jake—on video chat—and tell him what happened, including the trip to urgent care and how things went with my parents. Before I can tell him that I'm considering making the move to Seattle, he gently suggests that we need to talk about our future living situation.

His concern is clear on his face and in his voice. "Can I fly out so we can talk about this in person?"

"If you think you need to, but I agree that it's something we need to discuss."

"I've been looking into options close to Tennessee, but there aren't any GM positions that aren't still a flight away, which defeats the purpose. I'm willing to take a lower-level position if I have to, though," he says.

"Oh, wow." I'm not sure why I'm surprised to hear this. "I figured I'd move to Seattle."

"I don't want you to be the one giving up everything. It was selfish to assume you'd want to move here."

"It doesn't make a lot of sense for you to take a lower-level position, though. And you've already given up one career, I don't think it's fair that you'd have to give up another one."

He's quiet for a few seconds before he says, "Let me book

a flight. I can take a couple of days off and we can figure it out together. This is a big decision, and I don't want it all to fall on you. And honestly, I need to see you. In three dimensions. So I know you're okay. I don't love that you're this far away and I can't be there when you need me."

HE ARRIVES THAT evening, and the second he's in the door I find myself wrapped up in his arms. I don't expect him to be as emotional as he is. Or the searing kiss he lays on me that makes my knees weak.

"That felt like the longest flight I've ever been on." He cups my face in his hands. "If I need to, I'll take a leave of absence from the league."

"Can you do that? Is that best for the team?" I can't see an abrupt change in upper management being easy.

"It's not about what's best for the team, Hanna. It's about what's best for us. I don't think I can live in a state of anxiety like this for the foreseeable future." His honesty is shocking, and frankly sobering.

So we sit down and talk it out. What the pros and cons are if he takes a leave of absence, or moves to another team, versus me moving to Seattle.

"My firm has a branch in Seattle, and I could apply for a transfer?"

"What about your promotion? Would that carry over?" Jake is sitting on the other end of the couch, my feet in his lap.

"It really depends on if they're looking for a branch manager or not." I trace the heart at my throat. "I looked into it when Ryan first found out he was my son, thinking it might be a good move for our relationship."

"I didn't realize that."

"I didn't tell him. And then he started dating Queenie. I didn't think it made sense for me to move there when his career can be so fluid and he was starting a new relationship." I hadn't wanted to interfere, and we'd seemed to have found a new balance.

"Do you want to talk to your boss, see what's possible?" Jake asks.

"I think it's a good idea. Maybe we can start setting things up? Regardless, me moving to Seattle makes the most sense." After my discussion with Paxton, I realized I was holding onto staying here and the idea of the promotion as a layer of protection. A *just in case something bad happens at least I'll have this.* But I don't want to live my life and make decisions *in case* something bad happens. Bad things happen all the time and I cannot live in fear. And I want to be closer to Jake so we can work on our relationship, and I want to be closer to Ryan and Queenie, even if it means leaving Tennessee.

"Even if the promotion isn't on the table in Seattle?"

I prop my cheek on my fist. "Honestly, Pax and I talked about this last night, and I think the promotion needs to be put on hold regardless. I'm not saying I won't want to revisit it in the future, but I need to focus on what's important, and this baby takes priority over everything."

"What about your support network here? I don't want to take that away from you when you'll need it the most."

It's clear Jake has been thinking this through, trying to see it from all sides. And it gives me confidence that the choice I'm making is the right one. "I'm trading one support network for another. I'll have you, and Ryan and Queenie, and the other wives to rely on. My parents can come visit whenever they want, and so can Pax." Although leaving her behind will be hard.

And so it's decided. I'm going to meet with my boss, and once I'm past the twenty-week mark, the plan is for me to move to Seattle.

It turns out I need the five weeks to get everything set up. I meet with my boss, and after two meetings, we agree that instead of me transferring to the Seattle office, I'll work remotely, because she doesn't want to let me go or transfer the accounts I've been managing for a lot of years. When needed, I can go into the Seattle office.

My entire life has shifted course, and my personal and professional goals have changed along with it.

While I could move in with Jake, I want to give our relationship more room to grow, without the pressure of living together. Instead, I rent a small house that's less than five minutes from Jake.

And when I reach twenty weeks, I'm that much closer to being able to breathe a little easier, knowing in just four weeks I'll have reached the point the baby can survive if he's born earlier than expected. The second round of tests, including the amniocentesis, come back negative for chromosomal abnormalities, and my blood pressure is under control again. My doctor has referred me to a maternal fetal medicine doctor in Seattle, so I know I'll be well taken care for the remainder of my pregnancy.

Everything seems to be falling into place.

Apart from how my parents are handling this move.

To say they aren't happy about me going to Seattle would be a huge understatement but staying in Tennessee isn't what's best for the baby or me, and it's definitely not what's best for Jake. My mother keeps trying to find reasons for me to stay, fretting more than usual. As frustrated as I am, I don't want to leave with things unsettled between us.

The week before I'm scheduled to move, I invite her over so we can have a come-to-Jesus talk and I can explain why this is what's best. Usually I'd make the twenty-minute trip to their place, but I want this to happen on my turf, not hers.

She stands on the front porch, holding a Tupperware container of my favorite cookies, looking nervous and uncertain.

"Come on in, you'll have to excuse the mess."

"Oh! Are you doing this all yourself? I would have come to help if I'd known." She surveys the endless piles of boxes lining the walls. They're carefully labeled and organized based on room.

"I hired movers who also do most of the packing," I explain and take the Tupperware from her. The truck is scheduled to be here tomorrow to pick everything up, and I'm staying with Pax for a few days before I head to Seattle.

"Isn't that expensive?"

"It's a reasonable expense considering the short timeline and my current circumstances." I pat my belly. I'm past the it-looks-like-I'm-bloated stage. There's an obvious bump now that can't be hidden, even with loose shirts and leggings.

"Of course. That's a good idea. If you need any help, though, you know I'm here. I should have made you a casserole or something. I'm sure cooking is a challenge with most of your kitchen packed up."

"Jake's been sending me prepared meals, so I'm pretty good foodwise, but I'll never say no to your chocolate chip oatmeal cookies."

"He's not sending you the ones from the grocery freezer section, is he? Those are loaded with salt." My mother has never, ever bought prepared meals from the freezer section.

"No, Mom. He's been ordering them from a food prep service called Chef's Own. You can either prepare the meals entirely ahead of time or they send you the ingredients and you put them together on your own. He's been having them prepared for me, though, to make it easy."

"Oh. Well. That's very thoughtful of him."

"He is thoughtful like that." I motion toward the sliding door. "I just made a pot of tea. Can I pour you a cup and we can sit on the back deck? It's the least cluttered space in the house right now."

"That would be nice."

I pour us both a steaming mug and Mom brings the cookies outside.

She looks nervous, probably because she's worried I'm going to lay into her again.

The thing about looking at your childhood through an adult lens is that you can see all the sides of the situations you were in, but they're tainted by the emotions and perception of those events based on the age when they happened.

When I was a teenager, I was inexperienced and scared. I wanted to keep Ryan in my life, so my parents made a sacrifice right along with me. They gave up their friends and their careers and moved us to a new state so we could have a fresh start. It wasn't a perfect scenario, and I'll never truly know my mother's motivations, but they did what they believed was right. I don't know that they truly thought through the ramifications, or considered the potential fallout, but we all made it out the other side in one piece. And Ryan was loved and cared for, which was what I'd wanted, most of all.

And I couldn't fault them for that. I could not like some of their decisions, I could do my best never to repeat it with my own child, but burying my parents in guilt and blame wasn't going to make any of it better.

"I didn't realize how angry you were at me about the way Ryan was raised." She fidgets with her napkin, having trouble focusing on anything else.

"I'm not angry at you, Mom. I know you did what you thought was right. At the time, it seemed right to me, too. And I appreciate everything you and Dad did for Ryan and me."

"I don't want you to resent me for it. I wanted what was best for you. For our family. For Ryan's future," she tells me, for what has to be the millionth time.

Our relationship will always be complicated. There's no way around that. "I know that, too."

"Knowing and believing are two different things." Her voice is soft and her eyes are too-full glasses, ready to spill over.

"I believe you had all of our best interests in mind. And I also know you had to give up a lot in order to make it work. We all did. Especially me. I don't think I understood how much that affected me until Ryan got married, and then I got pregnant." I'm only doing more damage to our relationship if I can't tell her the truth. "The part that was always the hardest for me was the fact you would never acknowledge that Ryan is truly *my son* and your *grandson*. I could pretend to be his sister all I wanted, but in my heart I knew who I really was, and I was never allowed to own that. The lying didn't just hurt Ryan, it hurt me, too."

"Oh, sweetheart." She keeps twisting the napkin in her hands, turning it into confetti. "I made an even bigger mess when I tried to clean up the first one, didn't I?"

"Your heart was in the right place, but things are so much different now." It's hard to see my mom looking so devastated, but we both need this, or things will never change. "He and I need a chance to figure out this new us, without worrying we're hurting your feelings. Especially now that I have another baby on the way."

"Is that why you're moving to Seattle then? For Ryan? I'm worried about this baby and about you being so far from home. And how this is all going to work out. Your life and your family are here. In Tennessee."

"Part of my life is here. But a very big part of it is in Seattle. And I need to make some compromises, because Jake has to stay in Seattle for his job."

"But he could manage a different team. He could move to Tennessee instead."

"We looked into that as an option, and it wasn't the best choice. General managers don't usually move around like the players do. And he's already had to sacrifice one career so he could be a present father to Queenie. I won't ask him to do that again."

"What if Ryan gets traded? What will happen then?"

"He still has a few years left on his contract. And he's one of the top goalies in the league, so if he wants to stay put, I'm sure he'll be able to. Ryan is definitely one of the reasons I'm moving, but it's more than that."

"You need to get away from me?" Her voice is so small. It makes me want to hug her and shake her at the same time.

"No, Mom. It's not to get away from you. This is about what's best for the baby, Jake, and me. This situation isn't ideal, and I realize that. I'm not perfect, and I make mistakes. Maybe it would have been better and easier for everyone if Jake and I hadn't acted on our attraction for each other, but we did. And there are consequences for that. Ones we didn't expect. But he is a good man and a great dad, and I can't rob him of the opportunity to be a father to our child because of an awkward family dynamic or because I'm too scared to try to make it work."

"I didn't think about it that way."

"Neither did I at first. At least not until Paxton pointed it out."

"She's a good friend, isn't she?"

"She is. And I'm going to miss the hell out of her. And you. But I need to do this. I need to give Jake a chance to be a parent so our son can grow up knowing he has a mother and a father who love him."

Mom squeezes my hand. "Your selflessness has always amazed me. You're going to be a wonderful mother. You were amazing with Ryan, even if you didn't get to bear the title the way you deserved to."

I pull her into a tight hug and let the tears fall. I could blame it on hormones, but it's more than that. It's hearing those words and realizing, maybe for the first time in my life, that one of my biggest fears has always been not being good enough to be a mom. That my parents stepped in because they didn't think I'd ever be capable of doing it on my own.

CHAPTER TWENTY-ONE

This New Start

Hanna

PAXTON DRIVES ME to the airport the following Friday morning. Saying goodbye is hard. There are tears. A lot of them.

"Now I have a reason to use my vacation time for things other than staycations. I'll come out and see you in a couple of weeks, once you're settled in, okay?" She hugs me again for the tenth time.

She suggested coming with me to help me move in, but I'd rather have real time with her once I'm unpacked, so we decided to wait.

The moving truck is scheduled to arrive in Seattle this morning, and Jake is supervising the movers. They're not only bringing all the boxes and furniture to my new two-bedroom house, they're also unpacking for me. The only rooms they've been asked to hold off on are my bedroom and the bathroom. The bed and dresser can be set up, but I'll unpack all of my clothes and other important bedroom items.

I could have easily stayed in Jake's pool house, where Queenie used to live before she moved in with Ryan, but I felt it would be an easier transition for all of us if I got my own place first. That way we could have some time to date—if that's what you call me passing out by nine while we watch Netflix—as we settle into our new normal.

I'd like to get my feet under me first. I've spent most of my life in small-town Tennessee, so I need time to get used to my new digs and a new city.

I land in Seattle in the early afternoon. It's hard not to get all swoony the second I spot Jake at the airport, waiting for me. He's wearing jeans and a t-shirt. The shirt looks like something Queenie might have bought for him. The sleeves are tight around his biceps and it reads *BEER AND HOCKEY ARE MY JAM* across his broad chest. A wide smile forms when he sees me, and his long legs eat up the distance between us. He pulls me into a tight hug and kisses his way across my cheek to my lips. He keeps it chaste, though, since we're in a public place.

"You look beautiful as always. Let me take your bag. How was your flight?" He takes my suitcase and settles his palm on my lower back as we head for the exit.

"The flight was lovely. Thank you for upgrading my seat." I booked economy, but when I got to the airport, I'd been moved to first class.

"I have a ridiculous number of air miles. It's not a big deal. Do you need the restroom before we get in the car?"

"Oh. Yes. That's probably a good idea." I don't remember the incessant need to pee being this bad with Ryan. Or the ridiculous thirst. It's not ideal or convenient.

Jake waits for me outside the women's restroom, and then we're on our way to my house.

"I hope you don't mind, but King and Queenie stopped by the house to help with some of the unpacking. I thought we could order takeout and have a meal together before they leave, but I understand if you're tired and want some time on your own."

"That sounds perfect, actually." I haven't seen Ryan in a few weeks, and although we talk regularly, it still feels like there's a new distance between us that I'd like to work on bridging.

The kitchen and living room are all set up by the time I get there, the art and photos hung on the walls, instantly transforming it into my new home. Even my bedroom is mostly set up, apart from the boxes of clothes and other things no one needs to see but me.

The baby's room is untouched, but there are paint swatches taped to the wall. "I know we have lots of time, but I would love to help you paint this room when you're ready. And, of course, we'll do the one in my dad's house too, but he's already set on a hockey theme, so I thought maybe we could do something fun and artsy here." Queenie slips her arm through mine and rests her cheek on my shoulder. "But we can wait on that. I'm just so excited you decided to make the move. I know it must have been a tough decision, but I think you're going to love living here. The art scene is great, and I can introduce you to everyone at the art therapy clinic when you're ready."

"That sounds perfect. What do you think about an appetizer and mocktail party with the girls next week sometime?"

"The girls would love that! I bet your messages must have blown up as soon as you landed with all the chatter in our group text." Queenie's eyes sparkle with her excitement.

"It's great to feel like I already have a girl gang here. I can't wait to get Paxton out to meet everyone."

"Does she like hockey?" Queenie asks.

"I don't think she's opposed to hockey players."

Queenie laughs. "They are pretty yummy, aren't they?"

While Ryan and Jake finish hanging photos, Queenie and I organize my books and trinkets on the shelves that have been assembled. Ryan smartly told them to leave those boxes, knowing I would want to set them up myself and that however they were organized, there was a good chance I would end up rearranging them. He knows how I am about my books. I organize them by genre, author, and sometimes, if I'm feeling particularly outrageous, by color.

While we're organizing shelves, our group chat lights up on our phones ,so Queenie puts them on video chat.

"How's the move going?" Stevie asks as Bishop walks by in the background wearing nothing but a pair of boxers with a print I'm glad I can't identify.

"It's great. Queenie and I were talking about having an appetizer night here when I'm all settled."

"Oh! That would be fun. I can't wait to see the place. Give us a virtual tour!" Lainey exclaims.

"As long as the apps are dairy free, I'm in," Violet adds.

We show them around the house, and Stevie invites me to join the girls on a spa day next week. I love that I'm already included in the group.

We end the video chat when the pizza arrives and take a break from unpacking.

Ryan has been pretty quiet, and while he's never been one to dominate the conversation, he usually gives more than one-word answers, which isn't the case as we take a seat at the dining room table and dig in.

"Do you have another ultrasound coming up?" Queenie asks.

"It's in a few weeks. I have an appointment with my new doctor here, and I'll get the specifics then." I had one at twenty weeks and everything looked fine, but my doctor wanted to schedule another one for the beginning of my third trimester.

"If it's during one of the away games, I can always come with you," Queenie offers.

"I'll try to make sure it's not, but I'd absolutely love the company if it is," I tell her.

"I'll stay back if the team is supposed to be out of town," Jake says.

Ryan pauses with his glass of milk halfway to his mouth. "You always travel with the team."

"This year is going to be different." Jake brushes my hair over my shoulder and Ryan follows the action, then refocuses on his pizza.

"Right. Yeah. Of course. That makes sense."

Queenie tries valiantly to keep the conversation going, but it's like pulling teeth with Ryan. Once we've finished eating, he excuses himself to take a call, and then tells Queenie they need to head out.

His hug feels…stiff and not full of the usual warmth I'm used to from him.

Queenie pulls me in for a tight hug and pushes up on her tiptoes, whispering, "He's working through some things. I'll talk to him."

When they leave, I feel the emotion bubbling up. Today has been intense, between the flight, my whole life being moved, and Ryan's less than warm reception, I feel defeated and uncertain.

Jake doesn't say anything, just wraps me up in his arms. "I thought things were better with King."

"So did I. I wish I knew what to say or do, but everything is so strained with him. And while I love how excited Queenie is, it shines a bright light on how not-excited Ryan is. He handled finding out I was his biological mother better than he's handling this. The worst thing he did was go to a bar and try to get wasted. Then he got over it and moved on. But with this…I don't know. He hasn't been himself since I told him I'm pregnant." I flinch at the sharp pang in my stomach.

"Are you okay?" He covers my belly with his palm. "Come sit down. Should I call the doctor? Maybe we need to go to urgent care?"

It passes as quickly as it came. "I'm fine. It was probably all the cheese on the pizza. I love it, but my body sometimes doesn't appreciate it."

Jake leads me over to the couch anyway and gets me a glass of water before he joins me. "Do you wonder if maybe Ryan isn't as over finding out you're his biological mother as you thought?"

"I think he would probably like to be over it, but it wouldn't be unreasonable to believe this pregnancy is bringing up feelings and emotions we might not have realized were there, just like the wedding did for me. Every time I try to broach the subject, he brushes it off and says he's fine."

"And you don't think he is." Jake slips his hand under my hair, and I get a whiff of his cologne. He always smells so good, and the way his thumb smooths up and down the back of my neck makes my toes curl. It's a welcome distraction from the emotional turmoil.

"Based on what I've seen so far, no. We're usually so open with each other. I wish he'd talk to me." I lean into his touch.

"Maybe now that you're here and closer, you'll be able to have those discussions that weren't possible with you living halfway across the country. King is always very aware of what other people are feeling, and I'm sure he doesn't want to upset you, but I think in keeping whatever is bothering him bottled up, it's doing more damage than good."

"Maybe he and I should have a lunch date this week. We can have a heart-to-heart."

"That's a good idea." He presses his lips to my temple.

He does that often, and I've come to crave it.

He leans back and smiles, his expression both hot and tender. "Can I tell you how glad I am that you're here?"

"I'm glad, too. And thank you for being so incredibly supportive. I know I've been nothing but emotional, and you're probably pretty tired of tears and hormones."

"You're human and you're making big changes in your life. If you weren't emotional, I'd have a lot more questions. I know this wasn't an easy decision to make, and that leaving your family and everything familiar isn't a small thing, so whatever I can do to help make this transition easier for you, just tell me."

"Do you think you can stay here tonight? With me?" It shouldn't be a big thing, but I'm nervous asking, and a kaleidoscope of butterflies lets loose in my stomach. Or maybe it's JJ moving around in there.

"Of course I'll stay." He brings my hand to his lips and kisses my knuckles. "Is there anything else I can do for you, Hanna?"

"Maybe you could give me a hand in the bedroom."

"Unpacking?"

I shake my head no.

A slow, knowing smile tugs at the corner of his mouth. "You need some connection and stress relief?" His fingers trail up my arm, causing a wave of goosebumps to break across my skin. "Or are you just looking to cash in on some snuggles?"

I can see the hopefulness mixed with heat in his gaze.

"Can I be greedy and say all three?"

That smile grows wider, and with it, the promise of a perfect distraction. "Absolutely. Anything for you, Hanna. You know that."

CHAPTER TWENTY-TWO

The Things That Keep Me Up at Night

Jake

IT DOESN'T TAKE long for Hanna to settle into life in Seattle. It's made that much easier by Queenie's enthusiasm and the way the hockey wives fold her into their group. I also sit down with King so we can talk things out. We decide it's best for him to answer to Alex when it comes to the team, and that I can understand the difficult place this puts him in. He seems receptive, and I have to trust that he'll tell me if things aren't okay.

Over the next month, Hanna and I split most of our time between her place and mine, and more often than not, a sleepover ensues.

At this point, I have a small section in the closet at her place for those mornings when I have to go straight to work, and she has the same at mine. Although, she's working remotely these days, so she only ever really needs to get dressed from the waist up. She's taken to stealing my grey sweats and letting the waistband sit under her bump. Once all her Zoom meetings are done for the day, she trades her blouses for t-shirts. Half the time those are mine, too.

I don't know what it is about seeing her dressed in my clothes, but I can't deny, or hide, how much of a turn-on it is. The parts below the waist find her particularly appealing.

It's a Saturday afternoon, and I'm working on the schedule for next week while Hanna tackles a few emails. "Are you sure you're okay with the guys coming over for poker night? I can cancel if you want."

Hanna doesn't look up from her laptop, which is perched on the lap pad, her legs stretched out and propped up on the coffee table with a pillow. As usual, she's wearing a pair of my sweats and a shirt that reads *LOADING* on it. Queenie bought her the shirt. "You don't need to cancel. Besides, Queenie's picking me up in an hour, and we're heading to Lainey's for movies and mocktails."

I flip my pen between my fingers. "Are you going to come back here tonight?"

She stops typing and looks up at me over the rim of her blue light glasses. "I figured I'd go back to my place. Why?"

"Just wondering. You know, you're always welcome to come back here if you don't want to miss out on my legendary spooning skills."

She grins. "That's a kind and generous offer, Jake, but my night will probably end a lot earlier than yours, so I think the safer bet is to stay in my own bed."

"If you change your mind, the invitation is always open."

Hanna sets her laptop on the table beside her and stretches, exposing a couple inches of rounded belly. "I'm thinking about taking a cat nap so I'm not passing out on the girls before nine. Are you interested in joining me?"

"Definitely." I roll my chair back and round the desk, extending a hand and helping her out of the chair. She's twenty-four weeks now, which means she feels like she can relax a little. Her fears and worries are real and understandable. For me, it's been much different than the first time I went through this.

Kimmie had never been excited about the baby—she'd cried over stretch marks. She'd been emotional and angry a lot of the time. I'd spent the majority of her pregnancy reassuring her that once Queenie was born she'd feel better. That it would get easier when she had her body back.

But with Hanna, it's clear she's in love with this baby, and it makes it easy for me to fall in love in the same way. We're both all about JJ, and it's such a shift from what I experienced last time around. Reaching the point where the baby has a chance of surviving even if Hanna goes into labor early feels like a weight has been lifted and gives us both the room we need to breathe and be excited together.

Obviously, we want him to stay put for as long as possible. All the test results have come back clear, including the amniocentesis and neural tube defects. We have another ultrasound scheduled for early next week, between exhibition games. Every time I see our baby bouncing around inside her belly, I'm reminded of how real this is going to get in a few more months. I'm a hybrid of nervous, realistic, and excited.

As for my relationship with Hanna, my goal is to make her as comfortable as possible at my place, so by the time the baby finally arrives, she'll be ready to give up her house and move in here. Based on the number of sleepovers we have every week, I'm going to say I'm well on my way to making that happen.

QUEENIE PICKS HANNA up at five, and the guys are supposed to start arriving at six. I head out to the pool house where the food and poker table have been set up. That way the smell of wings, burps, and beer isn't the predominant and unpleasant odor in the house, should Hanna change her mind about coming back here tonight.

A group of us gets together once a month for a card night. I stay up way too late, drink too much beer, and usually sleep until noon the next day. It's been a thing since I moved to Seattle and took the GM position.

In that group are some of my buddies who work in NHL upper management, Bill, the team physician, and Alex. Occasionally,

Rook joins us, and tonight happens to be one of those nights. He's also bringing along Bishop, who's decided to grace us with his presence. Bishop has never attended poker night before, so this should be interesting, if nothing else.

Alex, Rook, and Bishop show up first, which isn't unexpected. Alex brings a bottle of scotch, and he cracks it open while I pull lowball glasses from the cupboard.

Rook holds out his hand to stop me from pouring three fingers into the third glass. "You mind if I make myself a coffee first? Otherwise I'm going to be passed out before the game even starts."

Bishop makes a noise that sounds like a snort and a scoff. "Nice opening line, dude. If you spend the night bitching about how much your wife wants to fondle your crown jewels, I'm switching your body wash for Nair."

Alex laughs. "This sounds like a story I want to hear."

Rook gives Bishop the side-eye. "Lainey's ovulating, so I'm basically her personal joystick for the next few days."

"Rough life." Alex snickers into his glass.

"He's trying to lowkey brag about all the sex he's having." Bishop rolls his eyes.

"I'm not bragging, asshole. I'm more than happy to take care of my wife's needs, but she's a little hardcore right now about it because it took more than half a decade to give Kody a sister and she's determined to make sure Aspen isn't out of diapers before we have the next one."

"Makes sense to me," Alex says.

"Same." Rook nods. "But being married to a woman with three master's degrees and a PhD, one of them in mammal reproduction, means she can get a little intense about the timing. I took care of her before bed, and she went and set her alarm for three in the morning because that was apparently the optimal time. Which is fine. But Kody was up at five wanting to shoot the puck around and then Aspen was up half an hour later."

"Kody's already on the practice schedule." I don't bother to hide my grin.

"That kid was born to play hockey," Bishop agrees. "He's got a mean slap shot. I gave him a regular puck last week and he nearly broke my damn kneecap with it."

"That's why we only give him the soft pucks." Rook puts one of the pods into the coffee machine. "Normally, I'd just send him back to his room, but the last time I did that he managed to put a hole in the drywall because he used the outdoor pucks instead of the indoor ones."

"Must have been a hell of a shot," Alex says with a laugh.

"Right? He nicked the bar and it ricocheted. I thought it was funny, but Kody got upset because the hole was in the Alaska mural and it went right through a bear or a moose. He felt bad, and I had to reassure him that he didn't actually hurt an animal. Anyway, I'm figuring it's easier now when we're already used to the sleep deprivation. So I'm really hoping it doesn't take another half a decade to knock my wife up again."

"Half a decade doesn't seem like much compared to this guy's quarter of a century." Bishop thumbs over his shoulder at me, half-hiding his smile behind his beer.

"Couldn't resist, huh?" I arch a brow.

"You're gonna have a teenager when you're sixty. Better hope that kid likes the oldies," Bishop deadpans.

Alex makes a face. "I never even thought about that."

"Me either," Rook says.

"Anyway." Alex turns back to Rook. "Back to your stressful life having to deal with your wife's sexual demands. Maybe you should take Lainey away for a weekend or something."

Rook dumps half a bag of sugar into his coffee. "She's been talking about this museum in North Dakota she wants to check out. Maybe I should take her there. Lainey's mom is always happy to watch the baby, but with Kody's hockey schedule it can be a lot."

"Kody can come stay with us for the weekend," Alex offers. "You know he's always welcome at our place."

"At least until he's a teenager," Bishop adds his two cents. "Then you'll need to keep him away from your daughter."

"Oh, come on, they're kids." Rook raises a brow.

"Until they're teenagers and then boom. Hormones." Bishop motions to his junk.

Rook ignores him and stirs his coffee. "Anyway, hopefully I can plan it for next month. As long as games don't conflict with the ovulation cycle or whatever."

"I basically looked at Violet and she was pregnant, so I can't say I know what you're going through, but we're always here if you need to complain about how hard it is to have sex on demand." He makes a circle motion with his finger, including Bishop and me in the we.

"Uh, no, man, you can't complain to me about this. If Stevie wants to set an alarm for three in the morning to wake the beast, I'm gonna let her, every damn time."

Rook slurps his coffee and gives Bishop the evil eye over the rim. "I'm not complaining. I'm just saying, setting an alarm for three in the morning is not the best for a good night's sleep, especially when we already have a baby who wakes up in the middle of the night for feedings."

"This is not a conversation I ever thought I'd be having in my kitchen." I sip my scotch.

"You're basically a bystander. And man, having to get up at ass o'clock in the morning for diaper changes and feedings at your age is going to suck." Rook chuckles.

"I'm in my forties, not filing for my old age pension."

Rook gives me a look. "When was the last time you got less than six hours of sleep?"

"Probably last week." Although I can't be sure of that. Hanna goes to bed pretty early these days, and I usually join her, regardless of what time it is.

"Well, enjoy it while it lasts, because once that baby is born, you can kiss those six hours goodbye. I wonder how King is going to deal with it when he and Queenie start having kids? That guy is a solid seven and always has been."

"He'll survive. They should probably think about getting a dog, though, as training. Knowing King, he'll have it crate and night trained in like three weeks. I've never met anyone as regimented as he is." Alex rolls his glass between his hands. "That'd be pretty damn crazy, wouldn't it? If you and Hanna have a kid and King and Queenie ended up having one, too?"

"They just got married." I take another gulp of my scotch. Although the thought has definitely crossed my mind, considering the number of times Queenie has talked about wanting to start a family recently. I can't say it would be the worst thing if she and King decided to start their own family, even if the level of strange is high.

"You're not even married and you're having a baby," Alex points out.

"I'm aware, thanks." I give him the hairy eyeball.

"You know we all kind of called this a while ago." Rook takes another slurp of coffee.

"Called what?"

"This thing with you and Hanna. I mean, I'll be honest, I never really picked up on it, but Lainey sure as hell did."

"Oh hell no, if anyone called this, it's me." Bishop points to his chest and then holds his arms wide. "I'm like a goddamn oracle."

"What do you mean, you called this? I think we all called Hanna and Jake hooking up." Alex crosses his arms, like this is suddenly some kind of competition. "Vi kept talking about how it would be so wild, because if you two get married then Queenie and King would be stepsiblings."

"Yeah, well, I caught these two coming out of a bedroom all cozy, cozy at the wedding, and then again in one of the private rooms at Queenie's birthday party," Bishop says. "I thought it was messed up enough that you two were getting all fresh with each other and that you'd make them stepsiblings, but now they're sharing a half-brother, too. That makes *your* kid *their* kid's uncle. Think about that for a second." He puts his fingers at both temples and makes the "mind blown" hand gesture.

Silence follows. The kind that's heavy and a little awkward.

"On the upside, if King and Queenie end up having a kid

sooner rather than later, you can raise them together," Rook says.

Alex rubs his chin. "That would be—"

"Fucked up?" Bishop supplies.

"Kinda cool, really, if you ask me," Alex comes to my defense. "Age is just a number, man. And kids keep you young. At heart anyway. Look at my dad's relationship with Robbie. Doesn't matter that he's over sixty and loves Led Zeppelin and The Grateful Dead. Robbie treats him like some kind of genius overlord. He loves hanging out with my dad. I actually think he believes his Gram Pot is a wizard, Harry Potter style, you know? Anyway, what I mean is, you can be sixty and still cool to a teenager. And as unconventional as it may be, you're still young, and lots of people start families in their forties. And you'll have tons of support. Except maybe for this guy." Alex thumbs over at Bishop. "I wouldn't trust him to take care of my goldfish, let alone my kids."

"I have a cat," Bishop points out.

"Dicken lives with your brother," Rook says.

"We have shared custody."

"I hadn't really thought about that. I mean, I've thought a lot about the energy demands of toddlers, but not what it would be like to be able to raise a kid alongside my daughter," I muse.

"Plus, you have the benefit of experience, and none of the financial or career worries. Once you get past the unconventional family situation, I think it has the potential to be a really cool experience, for all of you," Alex adds.

I decide to take the opportunity for what it is. If anyone knows how King is dealing, beyond what I'm seeing, it's Bishop. Not that I expect him to say anything to me, but the digs have to mean something. "I don't think King is particularly excited about this whole thing, let alone the idea of Hanna and me together as a couple." I rub the back of my neck.

"I thought things were better there," Alex says.

"I think it's a lot to handle for him. I'm basically his boss and his father-in-law. And now Hanna and I are having a kid together. It's a bit of a mindfuck, I'm sure. Mostly I'm worried about how it's going to affect Hanna. Anyway, I'm sure it'll be fine." I don't want to put Bishop or Rook in a difficult position where they feel like they have to tell me what's going on with King behind his back.

"Maybe you need to sit down with him and talk it through," Rook suggests.

"I did. He seemed okay, but I'm not sure if he's giving me lip service," I reply.

"Think about what he's been through over the past couple of years. Finds out his sister is his mom, gets married to the GM's daughter. Now his momster is pregnant with his father-in-law's kid. He's good at toeing all the lines, better than most, but it's a lot of hats to try to wear successfully. Maybe cut the guy some slack," Bishop says.

It seems like maybe I need to sit down with King again and give him an opportunity to air his grievances with me without worrying about there being repercussions—professionally or on any other level.

The doorbell rings, ending that slightly uncomfortable conversation. When the rest of the guys show up, we head out to the pool house and settle in for a night of cards. Both Alex and Rook have their phones facedown on the table. It used to irk me, but now I understand why they do it. Bishop keeps his face up. An image of Stevie flipping him off appears every time it flashes with a message.

I've never been someone's husband. After Kimmie walked away, the idea of bringing another woman into mine and Queenie's lives who might potentially abandon us again seemed unfathomable. And irresponsible. The only women whose welfare I've been concerned about have been Queenie and my own mother. I shifted my focus to being the best dad I could so she wouldn't feel like she was missing out by not having her mom around. But now I have Hanna and our baby to think about. And I find I think about them often. To the point I'm not fully focused on the poker game. I wonder how she's doing with the girls. If she's tired. If she's having fun, and if I can still convince her to come back here tonight so when I wake up in the morning she's next to me and not a short drive away.

At nine-thirty, my phone pings with a message. We're in the middle of an intense hand, so I don't look at it right away. But fifteen seconds later, Rook's phone pings and Bishop's goes off next, followed by Alex's. Every time he gets a message, the refrain from a song plays. It's "Every Breath You Take." I have to believe it was his wife who did that. Alex jokes about how hard he pursued her when they first started dating.

Rook turns his phone face up, and Alex does, too. Before I can follow suit, mine rings.

It's Queenie.

I hit the answer button. "Hey honey, what's up, is everything okay?"

"Hey. Hi. Um, I don't want you to panic—" Queenie's voice wavers.

"Fuck," Alex says.

"Oh, shit," Rook mutters and pushes his chair back from the table.

"What's wrong? What happened?" I take in the panicked expressions on Rook's, Bishop's, and Alex's faces.

"Hanna fainted in the bathroom. She threw up and she's cramping now. We're taking her to the hospital. Can you meet us there?" Queenie asks.

"We're leaving right now." It's a flurry of action, Rook holding up his keys, and the rest of the guys pushing away from the table. "Are you with Hanna? Can I talk to her?" I ask.

"I am. She's pretty upset right now, but I'm giving her the phone. It's on speaker."

I take mine off speaker and bring it to my ear, reminding myself that I have to stay calm, for Hanna's sake. "Hey, sweetness, I'm sorry I'm not with you right now, but I'm on my way to the hospital, too."

She makes a sound that isn't a word.

"I know you're scared, but let's see what the doctors say, okay? You've been doing so well so far, and the doctors have been pleased with how everything is progressing, so let's not borrow trouble before we need to." My stomach twists and knots, my own anxiety making it hard to keep my voice steady.

"I just want everything to be okay," she whispers, her voice cracking.

"I know. Me, too, Hanna." And I mean it. More than I ever thought possible, I want them both to be okay, because the alternative isn't something I want to face. Or even consider.

The twenty-minute trip to the hospital feels like it takes an eternity. I stay on the phone with Hanna until she gets there— only minutes before us. And in the short span of time that we're disconnected, I feel like I'm losing my mind.

Rook drops me off at the emergency room doors and Alex comes inside with me, likely to keep me from bulldozing my way through the place in search of Hanna.

He claps a hand on my shoulder as we wait at the front desk for someone to tell us where to go. I feel like I'm on the verge of hyperventilating. "Vi had spotting with the twins. They put her on bed rest, and everything turned out fine."

I want to take the reassurance for what it is, but his wife is a decade younger than Hanna. And Hanna has miscarried before. The risks are much higher, the chances that something can go wrong that much more likely.

Violet comes rushing down the hall. "Oh, thank baby Jesus you're here. They've taken Hanna in for an ultrasound, but they know to expect you. She really needs you with her right now." She jumps up and mashes her face against Alex's jaw, maybe to give him a face-punch-kiss, and then grabs my sleeve and almost trips over her feet as she pulls me down the hall.

I'm barely tracking anything as I'm led to the ultrasound clinic. Lainey and Stevie are hovering near the door. I tell the attendant who I am, and I'm guided down the hall to one of the rooms. The attendant knocks and announces that I'm here. The door opens and Queenie steps out, eyes wide.

She gives me a huge, brief hug. "Hanna needs you. We're all here for you no matter what."

I kiss her on the cheek, an odd state of numbness falling over me as I slip into the room. I'm preparing for the worst. My brain in high gear, considering the potential outcome should Hanna lose the baby. I shut those thoughts down because they're not going to help me. I can lose my shit later, but Hanna needs my support.

Her face is pale, her cheeks tear-stained. But the second she sees me, she reaches out and half-tries to get up off the ultrasound table despite the fact the nurse is attempting to take her blood pressure.

I rush over to her and take her face in my palms. "I'm here. I've got you. We're gonna get through this together. All three of us." I hope like hell that's not a lie. The nurse gives up trying to take her blood pressure for a minute while I calm Hanna down, encouraging her to slow her panicked breathing.

Most of what she says is incoherent, which is unnerving, but she keeps telling me how much she wants this baby and she doesn't want to lose him.

I stay for every part of the exam they'll allow.

After three hours and a lot of tests, the doctor tell us that Hanna fainted as a result of her gestational hypertension and not eating enough before she went to visit the girls.

The doctor advises modified bed rest, and they keep her overnight to make sure Hanna's blood pressure isn't too high, and give her steroids to help mature the baby's lung, should she go into labor sooner than we'd like, or they're unable to keep her blood pressure under control. The doctors allow Queenie and King to come into the room, but everyone else has been sent home hours ago, with the promise of text updates.

Queenie and King are only allowed to stay for a few minutes. King whispers in Hanna's ear, his face a mask of worry as he hugs her and promises to come back in the morning.

Once they leave for home, I settle into the chair beside her bed and take her hand in mine. "You need to sleep."

"I know. You should go home and get some rest, too. You must be exhausted. And the team has practice in the afternoon."

"Alex will handle all of that. I'm not going home until you do." I lace our fingers together and bow my head, kissing the back of her hand.

"That chair is a terrible place to sleep."

"They'll bring me a cot if I ask." I brush a few stray hairs from her forehead. She looks spent, which makes sense since she's had one hell of a day. "Listen, I know we're still navigating this relationship and where it's going, but I don't love the idea of you being on your own in that house when you're supposed to be on bed rest and taking it easy. How would you feel about coming to stay with me? After the baby is born, we can reassess and see where things are?" I don't want to push her into a decision, but the thought of something like this happening and her being alone is untenable.

She's silent for a few seconds, maybe mulling it over. "I think that's probably a smart plan."

I exhale a relieved breath. "I know you don't need me to take care of you, but being able to ensure you're safe and okay on a daily basis is going to keep my blood pressure down."

She chuckles and brings our clasped hands to her belly, settling them there. "I definitely don't want you in the same boat as me." Her expression grows serious. "I was scared today, Jake."

"Me, too." I trace the contour of her face, the contact as much to console her as it is to ground me. "Let's try to keep your stress levels to a minimum for the next sixteen weeks, okay?"

"Okay."

"It's you and me, Hanna. We're in this together." I seal that promise with a kiss.

CHAPTER TWENTY-THREE

Selfless Love

Hanna

I'M RELEASED FROM the hospital the next morning, early enough that no one has had a chance to visit. Jake drives me back to my place and makes me lie down while he packs my essentials. It seems ridiculous to have this house sitting empty when I've only been living here for a handful of weeks, but I agree that living on my own is not in either of our best interests.

While I may have felt the need for independence when I first moved to Seattle, in the weeks since I've been here, I've realized that it had less to do with moving in with Jake and more to do with my fear of things changing too quickly, or the pressure it would put on our relationship. I didn't want to force closeness before I felt ready. Or become an inconvenience in his life.

Jake has proven to be patient and understanding, letting me lead, which probably doesn't come naturally to him. Having support doesn't mean I have to lose my independence. It just means I have people I can count on.

When he reaches the bottom drawer of my dresser, I sit up. "Oh, uh, you can leave that one for now."

"Are you sure? This looks like it's got all your comfy sweats in it?" He lifts the pair of grey sweatpants I stole from him when I first moved to Seattle and his eyebrows pop. "Oh, hey now." He gives me a sidelong glance. "Looks like I found your pleasure chest."

I feel my cheeks heating, but I shrug nonchalantly. "I'm a woman with needs."

"I'm familiar with those needs." His gaze moves over me in a hot sweep that I feel all the way from my toes to the top of my head.

"You can close that drawer and go about your business, Jake." I don't need to be thinking about the contents of that drawer and all the fun we could have.

"You sure you don't want me to pack any of this for you? Just in case your needs need taking care of by someone other than me?" He rubs his bottom lip.

I make a circle motion with my finger. "You need to stop this."

"Stop what? I'm trying to be proactive here, Hanna. And packing your pleasure chest seems like a smart thing to do."

"I need to ask my doctor about what's reasonable in that department."

Jake's brows pull together. "It's not like you're going to go without an orgasm for the next four months."

"It raises my heart rate, which raises my blood pressure."

He props a hip against my dresser and crosses his arms. "I can make sure they're more like a canoe ride on the lake instead of a rocket launch so we don't put you in the danger zone. But we can call your doctor and find out what the limitations are so we know what can and can't happen." He slides his phone out of his pocket.

"What are you doing?"

"Calling your doctor."

"Right now?"

"Yeah, Hanna, right now. No point in waiting until your next appointment if we can find out immediately." He lifts a finger. "Hi, Jake Masterson here. I'm Hanna Kingston's partner. I was hoping I'd be able to ask Dr. Deloris a couple of questions regarding Hanna's bed rest, so I know what is and isn't okay for her and the baby. Yup, I can definitely wait."

"I can't believe you! Give me the phone." I hold my hand out.

"Only if you put it on speaker so I can hear the answers."

I roll my eyes. "Fine. Give it."

He passes me the phone after he puts it on speaker.

Three minutes and a red face later, I'm given the go-ahead to have sex. Just not the swinging from the rafters kind. And I should try to keep my heart rate under one-twenty.

Jake finishes packing up the drawer with all my fun items— they get their own bag—and we drive back to his place.

He sets me up in the living room on the couch. Then he unpacks all my clothes and puts them away for me. I'm pretty sure I'm allowed to put clothes away, but he's determined I relax as much as possible.

"I don't expect you to do nothing for the next four months, but I think you need to be very gentle with yourself for the next few days at the very least." Jake takes a seat beside me on the couch.

"I can do that."

"King and Queenie were asking if they could stop by. Is that okay with you?"

"Of course." I'm sure I scared the crap out of Queenie last night. I know the whole thing scared me.

He nods once and his fingers drum on the back of the couch.

I tip my head to the side. "What's up? You look like you want to say something."

"I know your relationship with King is different, but I can't lie and say I'm not worried about the amount of stress his visit could cause. I can't put myself in his shoes, and I'm trying my best to understand and not overstep, but you and the baby are going to be my top priority. Always."

"Which means what exactly?"

"Can you promise me that if anything is making you upset, you'll tell me?" He chews on the inside of his lip. "What if he stresses you out to the point where you end up back at the hospital?"

"This is a hard position for both of you to be in, isn't it? You're his boss, his father-in-law, and now you have this new role in his life and mine. Ryan would never do anything to hurt me."

"Not intentionally, no."

"I appreciate your concern, Jake. And I will try to stay as level as possible. But I can deal with my son. He has a right to feel whatever he feels, and I'm not going to tell him he can't because it might stress me out. What you're asking isn't fair. I need you to have faith in both of us." This is probably the most challenging part of this situation. Because I have these two very strong, very important men who I care deeply about, and they're both struggling to manage the roles they've taken on.

I know better than anyone how that feels.

"Okay. Backing off."

I laugh and he presses his lips to my temple.

The doorbell rings and he gets up to answer it.

Ryan and Queenie appear a minute later, arms laden down with food and flowers. I didn't really get to talk to Ryan last night, apart from him telling me he was glad I was okay.

Queenie bends down and hugs me gently. "How are you feeling?"

"Better, thanks. Thank you so much for being there for me last night."

"I'm just glad I could be." She rises and gives Jake a bright smile. "Dad, can you help me in the kitchen? I brought all the makings for an awesome charcuterie board."

Jake looks from me to Ryan, who's hanging back, thumbs tucked into his pockets.

Jake plants a kiss on my cheek and murmurs, "We'll give you two some time."

Queenie threads her arm through his and they disappear into the kitchen.

"You gave us quite the scare last night." Ryan pokes at the chip in his front tooth with his tongue.

"It definitely wasn't my favorite day." I pat the cushion beside mine.

He sits down and wraps his arm around my shoulder. "I'm so sorry, Han. I know I haven't been as supportive as I should, and I feel awful knowing I've been causing you stress."

"You're not the reason I ended up with gestational hypertension."

"No, but the way I've been acting sure hasn't been helpful, and I'm sorry for that. I want you to know this has nothing to do with you and Jake being together. Or the fact you're having a baby. He's a great guy, and he cares a lot about you, more than I realized maybe." He takes my hand in his. "You know, it wasn't even a shock that you two ended up together. I mean, Queenie's been rooting for it from day one."

"She has?"

Ryan grins and shakes his head. "Oh yeah. She basically called it from the first time you two met. She said you had the *zing*. I guess it's the same way with her and me. You know when you just connect with someone on a deeper level without even trying? You and Jake have that. It makes sense. You have similar histories and understand what it means to have to give something up in order to do what's best for the people you love. Which is what has been the hardest for me to come to terms with, I think."

"Because I had to give you up in a way when you were a baby?" This is the conversation we've needed to have for a long while, or maybe he needed the time to come to terms with it and figure things out.

"Queenie and I have been talking about it a lot lately. It's not that I don't want you to have this, because I do. You deserve to be a mom, and you're going to be awesome at it. I mean, you basically raised me without me knowing it. And that's the part that's been the hardest for me to deal with." He swallows thickly, taking a moment to compose himself.

"I see it, Han, all the things you gave up for me. Not going away to college, not going out with friends on weekends so we could watch movies together. Always being the one to get me from school, take me to hockey practice. I noticed all of it. Even when I was a teenager, and I figured I was just really lucky to have an older sister who was so involved in my life."

"I didn't want to miss any of the big moments." There were so many times I'd wanted to come out and tell him. But I hadn't wanted to be selfish.

"I think part of me always knew. There were these little things you'd do. Like you always wrote me notes from the Tooth Fairy. You were there for everything. You taught me how to swim, to skate, you played street hockey with me. And you never got to hold the title you earned. Because you did, earn it, I mean. You were always there, for everything, exactly like a mom." His expression is pained. "It's been messing with my head because I'm going to watch you be the mom to this baby that you weren't able to be for me, not openly. I've been really selfish and only thinking about how it affects me, and I'm sorry for that."

Hearing him say all of this, while painful and difficult, is in a lot of ways exactly what I needed to hear. I think we've both been trying to navigate this on our own. And Ryan never wants to cause people pain, emotional or otherwise.

"You don't have to be sorry, Ryan. I know how tough all of this is. For both of us." I squeeze his hand. "And it's okay if sometimes it's hard for you. I just want you to tell me when it is, so we can deal with it together. I feel all the same things you do. I lost it on Mom hardcore and I'd like to say it was because of the hormones, but that would be a huge load of BS. And you can't even really get mad at me because I'm pregnant and you'll feel guilty."

"I felt awful about the way I reacted when you first told us. I'd been prepared for you to tell Queenie and me you were dating or something, and then you dropped the baby bomb and…well… all the stuff I'd thought I'd dealt with slapped me right in the face." He sighs. "Queenie set me up with one of her therapist friends last week, and it's been good to have a sounding board. I don't know how you'd feel about talking to someone together, but maybe it's something you would consider? Just so we can work on keeping the communication in our relationship open, and then Queenie doesn't have to get on me about keeping things bottled up until I explode." His cheeks turn pink, and I have to wonder what that's about. Or maybe I don't want to know.

"If talking to someone together will help you and me, then that's what we'll do."

He wraps me up in a gentle hug. The kind that tells me without words that we're in a much better place. "I love you, Momster."

"I love you, too, Ry-ry. You'll always be my baby, even when you have your own."

CHAPTER TWENTY-FOUR

Home Sweet Home

Hanna

I EXPECT THERE to be an adjustment period when I move into Jake's place, even though we've been spending several nights a week at each other's places. Apart from getting used to each other's routines and habits, it's fairly seamless.

Jake is an easy guy to live with. He's tidy, organized, and the only thing I can really complain about is the fact he often leaves his socks in very random places around the house. Apparently, he gets hot easily, and when that happens, his socks come off.

I've taken to tossing them on his recliner, which hasn't been getting much use these days since he's migrated to the couch so he can sit with me in the evenings.

He hands me a bowl of ambrosia salad—something my mom used to make when I was a kid, and I perfected by the time I was a teenager because I loved it so much. And just like when I was pregnant with Ryan, I can't seem to get enough of it. I'm very grateful my dairy aversion has let up in the final trimester of my pregnancy.

Jake drops down on the couch beside me, and, as expected, props his foot on the coffee table and shucks off his socks, dropping them onto the floor.

I spear a chunk of pineapple and chase a mini-marshmallow

around the bowl. "I have an idea."

"If it includes leaving a laundry basket in every room for my socks, I'm game."

I roll my eyes and grin, but give him the side-eye. "You know, if you really want to cool down faster, you could always take your shirt off instead of your socks."

"You just want to ogle my dad bod." He runs his hand over his abs. He's gained a few pounds along with me, possibly because I've been a fiend for chocolate pudding and all things chocolate, period. I've gone down to part-time at work, and I've been on modified bed rest since my visit to the hospital. It means I've had a lot of spare time, and I've spent quite a bit of it making easy, but delicious food. While sitting down, of course.

But while my belly is swollen, his is still mostly a four-pack.

"Well, duh." I pop a mandarin slice into my mouth. "Of course I want to ogle you."

He gives me a smirk that makes everything below the waist clench. My hormones are ridiculous right now. But I'm as big as a house, and sex is off the table until the baby is born. Not because I don't want to have it, but because my doctor is concerned an orgasm is going to raise my blood pressure too much. I'm scheduled for an induction at thirty-eight weeks. But that's still a week away.

"But then my shirts would be all over the place, too."

"Your socks aren't all over the place, they're right there. You probably have enough to do a sock load." I motion to his lounger with the fork before I close my lips around it.

"Well, shit. I mean shoot." His fingers find the hem of my shirt, and he lifts it until about six inches of my belly is exposed. He leans over and presses his lips to my skin and whispers, "Sorry, little man. I didn't mean to swear."

As if he can hear his dad talking to him, a fist or an elbow moves across my belly. I've been having Braxton Hicks contractions on and off for the past week. Ryan was two weeks early, and being older means there's a greater likelihood that this little guy is going to make an appearance before the due date, too.

I set my bowl aside so I can run my fingers through Jake's hair while he coos at my stomach. He's been amazing these past months, and what started as a mutual attraction has shifted. Especially since we had the scare and I moved in here. That's what it took for me to finally come to terms with the fact that baby or no baby, we had something special. And it would be a lot easier on all of us if we gave our relationship the chance it deserved to evolve during the final months of my pregnancy.

He's become my confidant, my biggest supporter, and my best friend. He's thoughtful, kind, and compassionate. He's driven, intense, and take-charge in his work life. He's an incredible, attentive lover and partner. And I can't wait to raise this child with him, because I already know what a phenomenal father he is.

THE NEXT NIGHT there's a game in Seattle. I sometimes attend them with the girls, but with me being so far along, it's tough to sit in one of those seats for three hours. And I constantly have to pee, so I'll have to wait until after the baby arrives before I can go again.

Tonight, Queenie is keeping me company. She arrives as Jake is heading out the door.

"I'll have my phone on me the entire time. Call if you need anything." He puts his hand on my belly but directs the comment at Queenie.

I smooth my hands over the lapels of his suit jacket and adjust his tie. "We'll be fine. Go do your job."

"My job is to make sure you and JJ are comfortable before anything else." He presses a lingering kiss to my lips.

"We're good. And I have Queenie. I'll see you in a few hours."

I send him out the door, and Queenie and I settle in to watch the game.

"How are you feeling? Can I get you anything?" Queenie's sitting at the other end of the couch, hand stitching felt animals for the mobile she's making for the baby.

"I'm good." I shift around, trying to get comfortable, but my lower back has been aching all day. Probably because I snuck in a quick vacuum when Jake went out to pick up more fruit for me. It's basically all I've been eating the past few days.

"Are you sure? You keep grimacing. Do you want me to move the laundry from the lounger and you can sit there?"

"Those are your dad's dirty socks."

Queenie's nose wrinkles. "You're not serious."

"Oh, I totally am." I rub my belly when it feels like JJ is doing somersaults. "He's moving, want to feel?"

"Oh! Yes!" Queenie slides across the couch, and I take her hand, placing it over my belly as JJ does another spin in his cramped quarters. "He's really moving around in there, isn't he?"

"This is his most active time of day." I pat my belly. "Not long now, little man." I cringe at the sharp pain that shoots across my stomach.

"Are you okay?"

"I'm fine. Lots of Braxton Hicks lately. And I've been eating a ton of fruit, so that's been a thing."

I manage to make it to the end of the first period before I have to waddle to the bathroom. I don't even get the door closed before a gush of warmth makes me pause. For a second I think I've peed my pants, until I realize I haven't.

"Oh crap." I watch as the grey sweats darken at the crotch.

When I gave birth to Ryan, it all happened so fast. Faster than I thought possible. I had a midwife, and we'd planned a home birth. Something that wasn't as common as it is these days. My parents had wanted to limit the number of people who knew I was pregnant. He'd been in breech, and it had taken time to get him turned around. It hadn't been comfortable, and I hadn't had an epidural, but within four hours of my first contraction, I'd been holding him in my arms.

"Queenie! Can I get a hand?"

I can hear her running down the hall. The bathroom door flies open as the first contraction hits. It's mild, but I grab the edge of the vanity to steady myself.

"Oh my gosh. Is it time?" Her wide eyes shift to my wet sweats. "It's time!"

I nod. "It's time."

She flails and takes a step toward me. "Do you need to sit down? I need to get the bag. We have to go to the hospital. I need to call my dad."

I raise a hand and smile. "Take a breath, Queenie. The baby isn't coming in the next five minutes."

"Right. Okay. Sorry. I'm supposed to be your support, not the other way around."

"Well, to be fair, I've done this before and you haven't."

She inhales deeply and exhales a slow breath, collecting herself. "What do you need me to do first?"

"Can you bring me my phone and then start the car?"

"Yes. Absolutely." She rushes down the hall and reappears a handful of seconds later with my phone in her hand.

"My bag is sitting on top of the bed in the spare room. Can you grab that for me, please?" I've slept in there maybe a handful of times since I've moved in. Mostly when I'm uncomfortable and thrashing around like an angry walrus in the middle of the night and don't want to keep Jake up. Even on those nights, I usually spend an hour in the spare room and go back to our bed when I inevitably have to make another trip to the bathroom.

"Yup. Should I grab you a fresh pair of pants?"

"I can do that in a minute."

I sit on the closed toilet seat and remember I haven't used the bathroom yet. Which I'll need to do before we leave for the hospital. But first I need to call Jake.

He messaged less than a minute ago, asking how I'm doing.

I accidentally hit the FaceTime button, but it's too late to turn back now.

His handsome face appears in the small screen, a furrow

already decorating his brow. "Hey, babe, everything okay?"

A calm settles over me, so different than the last time I did this. I have a partner, someone who will stand by my side at every turn and who is going to love this child with his whole heart, just like I am. "Everything is fine."

His gaze shifts to my surroundings. "Are you sure?"

"Positive, but you should make your way to the hospital because I'm pretty sure we're having a baby in the next few hours."

"I'm sorry, what did you say? I can't hear a damn thing." It's noisy in the arena. I can tell he's walking based on the way the phone moves around and then suddenly it's quiet and dark. A second later there's light.

"Are you in a supply closet?"

He looks around. "Seems that way."

"Okay! I have your bag. There aren't any pants in the dresser." Queenie's grin tells me she found *the drawer*.

"Your bag? What's going on? Are you in labor? Is it time?" Jake's eyes are suddenly wide.

"It's time," I tell him.

"He's supposed to sit tight until next week." There's worry in his tone. It's understandable after everything we've been through during this pregnancy.

"I guess he has other plans." I rub my belly. "It's okay, Jake. He's going to be fine." My doctor assured me that we're safe now, and even if JJ does come earlier than we planned, I'm safe to deliver. I have to trust that we've made it this far, and that we can handle whatever is next.

Jake runs his fingers through his hair. "Should I come home and get you?"

"It's probably better if you meet us at the hospital." I cringe as another contraction hits. This one stronger than the last. "I don't know how fast this is going to go."

"Shit. Okay. I'm leaving now. I'll see you soon." He's in motion again, the phone jostling as he jogs.

"We're leaving now, too."

I'm about to end the call.

"Hanna?"

"Yeah."

"I…" He closes his mouth and presses his lips together. "Drive safe, please."

"Of course. You, too."

I end the call, use the bathroom, and change into dry underwear and sweats. Queenie shoulders my bag and I slip my feet into my shoes, pull on my jacket, and waddle to the door. She throws it open and we both stop short.

"You've got to be kidding me." Queenie's cheeks puff out.

"Since when was it calling for snow?" I ask.

"I didn't think it was." She takes my arm, and we cross the slick driveway. "Why does February always have to be so unpredictable?"

At least we have my SUV, which is new and has good tires.

Unfortunately, Seattle is not like the Midwest or the states near the Canadian border on the other side of the country, which are used to snowfalls. The drive to the hospital usually takes twenty minutes, but thanks to the inch of white stuff, we're crawling along at ten miles per hour. It blows my mind that a tiny bit of snow has the ability to paralyze an entire city.

And the contractions are getting closer together. And stronger. A lot stronger.

"How you doing over there?" Queenie is white-knuckling the steering wheel. She's also leaning forward in the seat, and the wipers are going eleven million miles a second.

The light fifty feet ahead turns yellow, and she eases her foot off the gas and applies the brake. The back tires skid for a moment before they find traction again. We both hold our breath sigh in relief when the car comes to a stop and doesn't manage to slide into the intersection like the one coming in the opposite direction.

It all happens in slow motion. The car shifts course and starts to head toward us. I can see the panic on the driver's face. It's a young man. Early twenties at best. He spins the wheel and fishtails.

Queenie and I brace for impact, and the back bumper skids toward us and nearly hits the front of the SUV but manages to miss us by mere inches.

Both Queenie and I breathe another sigh of relief.

Unfortunately, the car coming up the left lane can't see what's happening and the two collide. Thankfully, neither of them is going particularly fast on account of the bad weather, so it looks like a fender bender, but the entire intersection is blocked and we're currently boxed in on three sides.

"Shit. Crap. This is a mess! Are you okay?"

Queenie reaches for me as I plant one hand on the dash and grip the armrest, huffing through a groan as another massive contraction rolls through me. It's a full thirty seconds before this one passes.

"You should put your hazards on and park the SUV because I don't think we're going anywhere for a while. Then call 9-1-1. I'll call Jake and tell him where we are."

"Okay. I can do that." She shifts the SUV into park. Her phone is set in the cradle on the dash. We're still a good ten minutes from the hospital, and that's without an accident blocking the intersection or the snow. There are now five cars involved and a lot of people yelling at each other.

It takes me two tries to pick up my phone. Giving birth in my car is not ideal. Giving birth in an intersection where an accident has happened is even less ideal.

I call Jake, this time audio and no video.

"Hey, babe. It's taking me a lot longer to get to the hospital because of the snow. I'm on the freeway, but we're crawling along here. It looks like I'm still about twenty minutes out. Are you there yet? How are the roads?"

"What's your next exit?" I survey the scene and glance at the clock on the dash. I need to start timing these contractions.

"Is everything okay?"

"We're stuck at an intersection. Hold on. Contraction." I clench my teeth and focus on breathing as it hits.

"Hanna? What the heck is going on? Where are you?"

"Dad, there was an accident," Queenie says.

"You were in an accident?" I hear the panic in his voice.

"No. We're fine. There was an accident, but we weren't involved. It's blocking the intersection so we can't get around them. I don't know if I should try another route or not." Queenie looks to me, her uncertainty evident.

I shake my head. "No. Don't do that. I don't know if we're going to make it to the hospital before this baby arrives."

CHAPTER TWENTY-FIVE

Hang on, Baby, It's a Bumpy Ride

Jake

THERE IS NO way in hell I'm missing the birth of my son. I nearly missed it the first time around. That's not going to happen again. Queenie tells me what intersection they're at and I get off the freeway. I'm only ten minutes from where they are, but people are driving like idiots and I'm trying to be careful while also trying to get there before my son makes his appearance in the world.

I want to switch to video chat, but Hanna doesn't want my attention divided between her and the road. Which I understand, but still.

A handful of minutes later, I hear the telltale sound of sirens through the phone.

"Oh, thank God. The ambulance is here and so are the fire department and the police."

"I'm going to flag someone down and see if we can't get some help," Queenie declares.

"Good plan," Hanna pants through what I assume is another contraction. "I can't believe I'm not going to be able to have an epidural *again*." She groans loudly.

"I'm going to be there in a few minutes, okay? Do you think you can hold on that long?"

"I'm going to try my best, but it feels like this guy wants out in a big way."

I make it within a block of the accident, but barricades have been set up, preventing me from getting to Hanna by vehicle. I park like an asshole and run the rest of the way to her.

The EMTs are in the process of moving her from the SUV to the back of the ambulance when I reach the scene. "Hey! That's my girlfriend," I shout.

"Dad, oh, thank God you made it on time!" Queenie gives me a hug and then shoves me in the direction of the ambulance. "I'll meet you at the hospital."

An attendant gives me a hand up when Hanna tells them I'm the father and that she definitely wants me with her. And then we're off, heading toward the hospital, sirens blaring and lights flashing.

"I'm so glad you made it." She squeezes my hand, and her warm smile turns into a grimace, her grip tightening until it feels like my fingers are at risk of breaking.

"Wouldn't have missed it for the world." I kiss her sweaty forehead. "I'm here. I've got you."

"I really wanted a goddamn epidural this time," she says through gritted teeth.

"You've got this. Just breathe through it."

"Easy for you to say. You're not pushing a watermelon out of your vagina." She smiles for a second and then groans again.

"I'm sorry I did this to you." I let her use my hand as a stress toy.

"I'm not. There's no one else I can imagine having a baby with in a freak Seattle snowstorm."

By the time we make it to the hospital, the contractions are right on top of each other. One barely waning before another hits. The doctor is waiting at the doors for us, and we rush down the hall.

"You're a badass, Hanna," I tell her as she tries to pulverize my hand for the hundredth time. "A beautiful badass."

"I probably look like a hot mess."

"Just hot, minus the mess."

"You're such a liar, Jake, but I love you anyway."

She breathes her way through another contraction.

I don't know if she's even realized what she said. I wanted to tell her the same thing earlier, but I didn't want the first time I said those words to be over the phone.

"Not a liar at all, and I love you, too." I kiss the back of her hand and her gaze shoots to mine, eyes flaring a little.

She smiles for a moment, but it quickly contorts into something pained. "This baby is coming now," she tells the doctor.

We barely make it inside the delivery room before the pushing starts.

I stand by her side, telling her she's doing an awesome job. Based on the feral sounds she keeps making and the way she white-knuckles the bed rails with every contraction, giving birth is no walk in the park. I'm glad I'm here for the experience this time, instead of arriving at the tail end, when the hardest part was over. "I'll get you a peanut buster parfait right after I meet our son."

She laughs and then grunts. "Stop making me laugh! I'm trying to push a damn baby out."

"And you're doing a damn good job."

"How big is this freaking kid?" She bears down again. "Doc, you better do a good job stitching me up."

"I promise I'll make sure you're as good as new," her doctor assures her.

"You better or I'm giving you a bad Yelp review," she gripes, but she's smiling. At least until she has to push again. "Come on, kid, let's get this done. I have a peanut buster parfait with my name on it waiting for me at the end of this. Your dad said so," she grits, then turns to me. "Thanks for making me hungry."

"I'll even spoon-feed it to you."

"You're such a romantic."

"Hey." The doctor snaps her fingers. "I need you two to focus instead of flirting with each other."

Hanna shifts her attention back to the doctor.

"One more big push on the next contraction, okay?"

"Okay." She grips the bed rails.

I'd offer my hand, but I don't want to leave here in a cast.

As soon as the contraction hits, Hanna bears down.

"And the head is out! Give me another one."

Two more pushes later and some serious profanity directed at me, our son is born.

His little cry is music to my ears. They clean him up before they rest him on Hanna's chest. Her eyes fill with wonder and tears as she takes in his tiny, perfect face.

"Hey there, my beautiful boy. You came in like a storm, didn't you?" Her gaze lifts to mine as two tears track down her cheeks. "We did it."

I brush them away. "It was all you, babe. I just came along for the ride."

"Come here." She grabs my tie with her free hand.

I'm still dressed in a full suit. I bend to meet her lips. The kiss is soft and lingering. The disgruntled cry from her chest causes us both to smile and me to pull away.

"Hey there, little man, I'm glad you're finally here."

I carefully cradle him in my arms, marveling at how tiny he is and how much fuller my heart feels already.

CHAPTER TWENTY-SIX

Parenting, Round Two

Hanna

LESS THAN TWENTY-four hours after his birth, we take Jacob Storm Masterson home.

So much for nixing the weird names. But it seemed fitting that our son be named after the fact he came into this world in the middle of a snowstorm. In Seattle.

We decide that it makes the most sense for me to continue living at Jake's. He doesn't want to miss out on any part of being a parent and neither do I. Apart from the first few weeks with Ryan, I never had the chance to breastfeed, and this time I want to do it all if I can.

Co-parenting is a completely different experience. And Jake is a fully immersed dad. While we have the nursery set up, I move the bassinet into the bedroom so JJ can be close for the first little while. I've offered to sleep in the spare room, so Jake can get a solid night's rest, but he wants me next to him at night. And I want to be there.

I'm currently sitting on the couch, burping JJ post-feeding. He lets out a belch, and at the same time, another, less delicate sound comes out the back end. Jake, who's busy searching for lost socks under the lounger, turns my way, one eyebrow arched.

"Sounds like someone needs a diaper change."

"And possibly a bath." I move the breastfeeding pillow aside and pull myself up off the couch.

"I can help," Jake offers.

"I've got it. Carry on with the sock finding mission." On the upside, all of Jake's socks are black, grey, or striped, so if one happens to go missing, it's not a big deal.

"The socks can wait. I'd like to help." Jake slips around me, kissing me on the cheek as he rushes down the hall to the nursery.

By the time I get there, he has the wipes out.

"I haven't changed a diaper yet. And it's been a while, so I figure it's time to get my hands dirty." He wiggles his fingers and his eyebrows at the same time.

I gently set JJ onto the changing table and Jake starts unfastening his onesie. I step back and let him have at it, pulling out the zinc cream and a facecloth.

Jake makes a face as he gently pulls JJ's legs free of the footed onesie. "Looks like we've got an explosion."

"The kind that requires a bath or thorough wipe down?" I ask.

"Nah, no bath required, just sprang a leak on the right side." He removes the onesie completely and sets it aside. Then he takes JJ's tiny feet between the fingers of his right hand and holds out his left, palm up. "Wipe, please."

I grin and tug one free from the dispenser. It has a warmer and everything. Jake cleans up the leak on the outside of the diaper before he carefully peels the adhesive back on the diaper, cooing and talking to JJ the entire time.

"Look at you, you little stinker, making a big old mess right out of the gate. Is this a sign of things to come?"

"I'm going to wet a couple of washcloths." If it's leaking out the side of the diaper, it could be a pretty substantial mess.

"Sure thing." Jake's attention is focused on JJ.

I drag my fingers along his broad back, disappearing into the bathroom. I turn on the hot water and wait until it's warm before I wet and wring out three washcloths and return to the bedroom. Jake's tongue peeks out as he wipes JJ's tiny bum and his backside, almost all the way to his shoulder blades. "Wow, buddy, that's some serious reach."

The diaper is rolled up and set to the side. My heart swells and other parts of my body start to tingle as I watch Jake being a dad.

I'm still sporting a tender vag since JJ was over nine pounds and I have stitches below the waist that are healing, so those tingles aren't something I can do anything with. Jake's gentleness is something I've experienced regularly, ever since I told him I was pregnant, but seeing him with our son, taking care of him... it makes me emotional. And it's impossible not to fall in love with both of them more and more every day. Knowing how hard it was for him with Queenie, and how much I missed out on with Ryan, makes us both appreciate JJ and each other that much more.

He lowers JJ's bum to the change pad and tosses yet another wipe onto the small mountain that's amassed along with the dirty diaper. JJ kicks his feet jerkily and makes a squawking sound.

"We gotta clean up the jewels now, buddy."

I cross the room, intending to hand him a washcloth to help with that and to cover JJ's business since he's doing a lot of flailing, but I don't make it in time.

Just as Jake turns back to JJ, he pees. And it gets Jake in the forearm. "Ah, shit!" Jake is quick, covering JJ's little firehose with the wipe he's holding, but it's too late.

I chuckle. "I guess both of you need a bath now, huh?"

JJ shrieks, likely not happy that he's wet.

"I can't believe that happened."

"Always point the firehose down, and always keep it covered when you can't." I wink and nudge Jake out of the way. "Why don't you get the bath set up and I'll finish here?"

Jake pulls his shirt over his head and wipes his forearm down. "I feel like a rookie all over again."

I settle a hand on his warm, bare chest. "It's been a while. And last time you weren't contending with firehoses, so it's okay to make rookie mistakes."

He motions to the crotch of his grey sweats. "Yeah, but I have a firehose. I know what happens when they're all loose and free."

I bite my lip. "You'll have plenty of opportunities to teach JJ all about firehose etiquette when he has a better command of his body."

Jake's eyes light up. "Oh, hell yeah! I can't wait to show him how to play sink the Cheerios." He takes one of JJ's big toes between his thumb and finger. "I have so many things I'm going to teach you."

"Please don't let one of those things be how to write his name in the snow with pee."

"I feel like there's a story to that."

"There is. And it involved Gerald." I roll my eyes and push him toward the bathroom. "Go run a bath."

He does as requested and disappears into the bathroom to run the hot water.

"You have the best daddy in the world, JJ." I finish cleaning him up and wrap him in a light blanket, thinking about how lucky I am and how sometimes life tosses us a curveball that ends up bringing a miracle along with it.

CHAPTER TWENTY-SEVEN

Forever Unfolding

Hanna

JAKE PROVES TO be not only a dedicated father, but also a true partner. Even though he gets up every day and goes to work, he also helps manage middle of the night diaper changes.

The first two weeks are a blur of feeding, changing diapers, and napping. I'd forgotten about the honeymoon phase. At first, JJ sleeps, like . . . well, a baby. A very happy, very content baby. I settle into a new groove. I can't believe I've lucked out and managed to have another easy baby, exactly like Ryan was.

Although, my mother had stepped in and taken over most of the middle of the night responsibilities where Ryan was concerned, since I was attending high school full-time a couple of weeks after he was born.

But all the same, JJ doesn't cry or fuss a lot. In fact, he seems like the perfect baby. Sweet, happy, and adorable.

And then, just as his middle name suggests, the winds change a little over a month after Jacob Storm comes into the world.

He becomes more alert, awake for longer periods of time. And he loves to be carried around. I try to use one of those baby carriers, so my hands are free, but it's like he knows that I'm not actually holding him, and he starts to fuss unless he's in my arms. His favorite thing to do is stare at my face. It's sweet, but it also means I can't get a whole heck of a lot done.

He also decides that three in the morning is a good time to be awake. And not just to feed or have his diaper changed. He legitimately wants to be entertained. This wasn't one of the things I had to contend with when Ryan was a baby. So it takes some real discipline on my part not to pick him up every single time he makes a noise.

Last night he was up three times. Once for a feeding, once for a diaper change, and once because he felt it was time to play, not sleep. At six-thirty, I give up on the idea of getting any more sleep and settle into Jake's lounger so I can breastfeed, hoping it will help calm him and allow me to get another twenty minutes of half-sleep. Which is better than no sleep.

I'm sure I look like something the cat dragged in. My hair is pulled up into a messy bun. I keep having to blow strands out of my face and my giant boob is hanging out of my shirt. JJ's hand rests protectively on the swell, his eyes closed, sucking contentedly.

"That's the life, right there." Jake is standing in the middle of the living room. He's wearing navy dress pants, a white button-down, and a tie that matches his eyes hangs loose around his neck.

I give him a sleepy smile. "Got some boob jealousy?"

He holds his fingers half an inch apart. "Maybe a little."

"The cleavage might look sweet, but being a feedbag doesn't scream sexy."

He crosses the room so he's standing next to me. "I'll agree to disagree on that. You're one hot mama."

I snort a laugh. "Liar, liar, pants on fire."

"I'm not lying, Hanna. There's something ridiculously sexy about seeing you mom like a boss." He strokes my cheek and tips his head to the side. "How are you doing? You were up a lot last night."

"I'm okay. Tired. Hoping JJ will want a big, long nap this afternoon."

"I'm sorry I can't stay home today."

Jake took the diaper change and I took the other two middle of the night disturbances, but the broken sleep isn't as easy to manage as it was when I was younger. Even the frequent get-up-to-pee in the middle of the night during the last trimester have nothing on this. And I can see the fatigue on Jake's face. I feel bad that he has to go to work and manage a team while I get to spend my entire day with our son. I can be a total zombie, but he has to be productive and effective. He's still sexy, even though he looks like he could use at least three more hours of sleep.

"You don't need to apologize. Playoffs are right around the corner. Queenie's supposed to stop by this afternoon, and she offered to watch JJ for a couple of hours later in the week so I can do a grocery run."

"What day is that? Maybe we can work it so we can go together."

"Like a date?" I ask.

"Mm. Like a date. Which we'll have to go on one of these days." Jake's eyebrows pull together, as though he's trying to figure out how to make that work.

We skipped over that whole part of the relationship process, going from secret weekends together, to suddenly contending with a later-in-life pregnancy fraught with worries and potential complications.

"We should try scheduling that. In six months to a year from now, we'll probably be able to swing it." It's sort of a joke, sort of not.

"We have built-in babysitters coming out the wazoo. Queenie's offered a million times to take JJ for a few hours. And when your parents come down to visit next time, we can go on a real date. The kind where I take you out for dinner. Wine you and dine you."

"I haven't had a glass of wine in nearly a year, so we should go easy on that part."

My parents came to visit a few days after JJ was born and stayed with Ryan. It was a little awkward, especially with the way my mom always wants to give advice on how to do things the *right way*. I bit my tongue and let Jake politely put her in her place. But it was nice to have them visit and for my mom to tell me I'm a good mother. The best part of the visit—which was also the most emotional—was when she asked if she could take a picture of me with both of my sons and told me she knew I would be a great mother to JJ because I'd been a wonderful mother to Ryan, even if he hadn't known at the time.

"Noted. We'll go light on the drinks so you don't fall asleep on me before we get a chance to make out post-date." He waggles his brows.

"That may have to take place in the back seat of the car if my parents are staying here." In the post birth-haze phase, there hasn't been much of an opportunity for snuggling or connection. I miss it. I miss Jake, even though we're in the same house, under the same roof, sleeping beside each other every night.

"Or." He holds up a finger and his eyes light up. "We could go back to your house since the lease doesn't run out for a few more months."

"Oooh. Now that's an idea." And one I hadn't thought of.

Jake's phone buzzes with a message. "Let's put a pin in this conversation for now, but we are definitely going to talk about it later tonight." He checks his phone. "I should be home around five. I ordered a bunch of those meals for us that have all the ingredients. We can choose whatever looks good to you and we can make it together, sound good?"

"Sure. Sounds great."

He grabs his suit jacket and heads for the door. Thirty seconds later, he returns because he forgot his keys and his tablet on the kitchen counter. And his travel mug of coffee.

A FEW DAYS later, Queenie and Ryan come over to watch JJ while Jake and I go grocery shopping.

Since JJ was born, I haven't been away from him for more

than a few minutes. Unless you count sleeping, which I do not.

"I fed him before you came, so he should be good for at least a couple of hours, but if he gets fussy, there's a bottle of breastmilk in the fridge. It just needs to be put in a warmer for a couple of minutes." I show Queenie where everything is in the kitchen, and then take her to the nursery where the crib and diaper changing station are set up. We turned the top of the dresser in Jake's bedroom into a second one, since the bassinet is in there, but over the past week, we've been transitioning JJ to his own room.

"We'll be fine," Queenie assures me. "You two enjoy grocery shopping and we'll see you in a couple of hours."

"Okay. Just text if you need anything. Or you have questions. We'll both have our phones."

"King is a baby whisperer. You have nothing to worry about. And this is good practice for us." Queenie hands me my purse and pushes me toward the front door, where Jake is waiting for me.

Ryan is holding JJ. Jake kisses him on the forehead—JJ, not Ryan—and I do the same. And then they're shoving us out the door, telling us not to rush back.

"Should we stop and get coffees before we do the whole shopping thing?" Jake asks.

"Oooh, that sounds great! I'd love a latte." And I could definitely use the shot of caffeine.

We make a stop at one of my favorite coffee places. They don't have a drive-thru, so we go inside to order. Jake slings his arm over my shoulders as we walk across the parking lot back to the car. He pulls me into his side, his lips finding my temple. "Is it weird that I miss having JJ with us right now, even though I've also been dying for some alone time with you that isn't filled with folding tiny pairs of socks and facecloths?"

I chuckle and sip my latte. "Not weird at all. I feel exactly the same way."

"Queenie said she would love to be able to do this for us once a week if we're interested. She said it's good training for her and

King."

"It's kind of crazy that grocery shopping is now considered alone time, isn't it?" I tip my chin up and smile at him. "And I don't think it'll be long before Ryan and Queenie are announcing their own baby."

"I agree, on all fronts. Once Queenie has her master's under her belt, I think she'll be jumping on the baby train."

"So letting them babysit is in everyone's best interests."

"As often as they want." He grins and unlocks the car door, holding it open for me.

My phone beeps with a message from Queenie. I check it, expecting that maybe we'll have to go home a lot sooner than planned. But instead, it's a video of Ryan holding JJ.

"Little bro, you and me, we have the best momster, and your dad's pretty cool, even though he's my boss." He smirks a little, clearly unaware that Queenie is filming him at this point. "You're gonna be so loved, buddy. And if you start giving Mom a hard time in your teens, I'm going to be there to make sure you know how good you've got it. I'm going to try to be a great big brother to you, and I'm trying to convince Queenie we should give you a nephew to hang out with, too, sooner rather than later."

"How do you feel about seeing Hanna be a mom?" Queenie asks.

"It makes me appreciate even more the relationship we had when I was growing up. She's awesome. And now I get it. Why she needed this. Why she needed you." He tickles JJ's toes. "She deserves to be able to love in the way only moms do. In the way I couldn't recognize she loved me my entire life, until now." He sniffs and Queenie ends the video.

My eyes fill with tears, and Jake hands me a tissue, putting his arm around me so we can watch it again.

"Feels good to hear that, doesn't it?" He kisses my temple.

"So good," I whisper.

"We have great kids, don't we?" he says softly.

"The best, really."

Our gazes meet and lock. He leans in and presses his lips to mine. It's chaste at first, sweet even. Then his hand comes up to cup my cheek, and all the emotions I was feeling a few seconds ago shift. We tip our heads and part our lips. He tastes like coffee and butterscotch.

Eventually, he pulls back, tongue sweeping along his bottom lip. "I have an idea."

"I like ideas."

"Your house is only five minutes from here."

"You are absolutely correct." I can already see exactly where he's going with this.

"And it's empty." Jake's gaze moves over my face in a slow caress I feel everywhere.

"Very empty." I'm healed below the waist, and we're close enough to six-weeks post birth for sex to be okay. "We should go there."

He nods slowly. "We should."

"But we should stop at a CVS first and get condoms."

"Smart idea. And I'm going to go ahead and schedule a vasectomy once the season has ended, because as much as I love JJ, I think I'm good with two surprise babies in one lifetime."

We both chuckle. Jake stops at the next CVS we spot and I rush in, buy a box of condoms, and then we're on our way to the house. I'm lucky I have my keys on me since I haven't been to check on the place since before JJ was born.

It's quiet, and the air is stale. But the bed still has sheets and a comforter, and it's all we need.

We undress each other slowly and climb onto the bed. It's been weeks since we've been able to get lost in each other like this, connect in the way only intimacy allows. Jake drags his fingers slowly from my hip, over my stomach, and between my breasts, all the way to my collarbone before he reverses the circuit, skimming along the swell of my breast.

When he brushes my nipple, I gasp. "Gentle, they're sensitive."

"Tell me if it's too much or not enough." He kisses along my neck to the edge of my jaw, fingers drifting back down to tease between my thighs. But I'm needy, and desperate, and I've had enough of this slow and soft.

I settle my hand on his chest and push until he's on his back and I can straddle his hips. His hands roam my curves with familiarity, and his gaze turns hot as I wrap my hand around his erection and stroke slowly, thumb sweeping over the head, spreading wetness.

Jake tears the condom open and rolls it down his length, and I rise and take him inside. My eyes fall closed as I absorb the feeling of being connected to him this way again. Finally.

I lean down as I roll my hips, slow circles and a rhythmic back and forth.

"I missed this," Jake groans, holding my hips and helping me rock over him.

"Me, too. So much," I pant against his lips. "I missed you."

"I missed you, too. We need to do this way more often," Jake mumbles around my tongue.

We both laugh, and then the mood turns serious as he sits up so we're chest to chest, wrapping his arm around me. He stays deep, dragging me closer to the edge with every gentle thrust and roll of my hips, until I come. He's right behind me, finding his own release, sinking into the comfort of connection.

Afterward, we lie in bed, basking in the post-coital glow.

Jake drags his fingers up and down my arm. "It's kind of convenient to have a sex pad."

I bark out a laugh. "It is, but also not very economical. We could always sneak out to the pool house and get busy there the next time Ryan and Queenie babysit."

"Just drive around the corner and come in through the back gate?"

"Or we could drop JJ off at their place?"

"That seems logical. Does that mean you'd be willing to break the lease on this place and move in with me for good?" His fingertips make a figure eight pattern on my shoulder.

I press my hand to his chest, feeling his heart beat under my palm. His expression is soft and nervous. "Is that what you want?"

"I could tell you that it makes the most sense, that I want what's best for JJ, and that I think living with me will accomplish that, but honestly, it's not just about what's best for JJ anymore." He traces the edge of my jaw, thumb sweeping along the contour of my bottom lip. "I know our relationship hasn't been conventional, but we started as friends. We already had the foundation before we gave in to the attraction. Do I wish I had an opportunity to date you? Absolutely. But over the past six months, I've had a chance to fall in love with every side of you, Hanna. I think we can be great together, as more than just a couple. I think we could be an amazing family."

"I think so, too."

"So we'll break the lease? You'll move in for good?" he asks.

"I'll move in for good."

"That means we're one step closer to you being exactly where I want you. And where I want to be." His lips touch the back of my hand.

"Which is where, exactly?"

"Right here." He presses his hand over my heart.

"You're already there, Jake. You've been there for a long time."

"I'm glad to hear that, because I'm feeling pretty permanent about you, Hanna."

He kisses me, and I feel the promise of a forever unfolding.

CHAPTER TWENTY-EIGHT

The Heart of the Matter

Hanna

"I THINK I have everything." I turn to Paxton, who's carrying my baby bag. Last month, I went with JJ, Jake, and the team when they played Tennessee. I stayed for a few days and nervously flew back to Seattle on my own. The nerves had nothing to do with the flying part and everything to do with sitting in first class with a baby who very well might start crying at any moment. Thankfully, he was the picture of calm the entire flight home.

In return, I invited Paxton to Seattle to visit for the week. The pool house is a great place for guests. And, of course, my parents also flew out so they could see Ryan play in the finals and get in some time with their grandson. Things have gotten better with my mom over the past couple of months. I've learned that her love language is to be helpful to the point where she sort of steamrolls people and offers advice, whether or not it's wanted or needed. But the way she's started to acknowledge and talk about what a great mom I am to JJ and how good I was with Ryan when he was JJ's age has gone a long way to helping heal our relationship and my heart.

Paxton pats the bag. "I think we're probably good to go."

"I should grab one more extra bottle and a couple extra diapers, maybe?"

"You have three bottles and half a package of diapers already in here. And there's another bag in the car already. I think you're set, Han. It's a hockey game, not a weekend trip, and if it comes down to it, you can always sneak off to the offices and breastfeed there."

"Okay, right. I think I'm ready to go then."

She arches a brow and inclines her head toward the living room. "You're missing one thing."

JJ kicks his legs and flails his arms from his spot in the baby seat, making the rattle jingle. "Oh my gosh, where is my brain, and when do I get it back?"

Paxton shrugs. "Can't say that I'm much of an expert on the subject, but based on all my friends who've had kids, possibly a year from now, possibly never?"

I shoot her a glare. "Not funny."

"It's a decent trade-off, though, right? I mean, look at this bundle of cuteness. Boop." She bops JJ on the nose. "You are the most adorable baby in the history of the universe. I hope you're exactly like your mom when you're a teenager."

I poke her in the side. "Don't you dare wish that on me!"

"You were a great teenager. At least you were by the time I met you. And you and Jake are already kickass parents. The swoon on that man is serious. Do you think he'll wear the baby for a while at the game? Oh, and what about the coach? Alec?"

"It's Alex."

"Alec, Alex, whatever. Can you imagine the number of ovaries exploding with those two guys standing next to each other and Jake is holding a baby?"

"You are ridiculous about those two." I chuckle and follow her out to the car.

"At least I'm not alone. There's a whole group of women who ship their bromance. They even have an online group. It's a ridiculous level of dad hotness."

I buckle JJ into his car seat and make sure it's secure before I get behind the wheel of the SUV, and then we're off to the arena.

We park in the lot close to the offices, and we're let in by a security guard who takes us through the back entrance so we can avoid the crowds. This isn't JJ's first game. He's been to a bunch over the past couple of months. With proper ear protection, his pediatrician gave me the green light. But we've only been in the boxes so far.

We still have one reserved for tonight, but we also have the opportunity to sit closer to the ice. JJ's a few weeks out from being able to face forward in his carrier, but by the time next season starts, he'll be able to watch the games.

Lainey is up in the box. She's pregnant again, and just starting to show, which means she got her wish and she'll have two kids in diapers in the coming months. It seemed the weekend getaway Rook took her on over the holidays was exactly what she needed. Aspen is passed out in her stroller and her son Kody is sitting in one of the seats at the front of the box, closer to the ice, with the other slightly older kids. Violet's twins are glued to her side, her daughter Lavender holding onto her sweater while Queenie crouches beside her and offers her a bag, probably full of art supplies based on the way Lavender's eyes light up.

Paxton has been to visit enough times that she's become one of the girls.

My parents are sitting on the ice tonight, along with Violet and Alex's family. Their parents are a hoot, and while my mom tends to run more on the conservative side, I find that she loosens up a lot around those women. Especially when they ply her with wine.

We settle in to watch the game, chatting amongst ourselves, enjoying each other's company.

At the end of the first period, Seattle is down one goal. I can see Ryan on the ice, talking to Bishop and Alex. Jake comes up to check on JJ and me.

"You think I can take our little man down to the ice for a bit?" he asks.

"Sure. You can bring him back up if he gets fussy, or I can come down to you?"

"Either works for me, as long as you're okay with it."

"Absolutely."

He shrugs out of his suit jacket and I pass JJ to Queenie and help Jake get the carrier on and adjust it to fit him, rather than me. Then we carefully put JJ in the carrier, making sure the ear protection is in place, and Jake shrugs back into his suit jacket.

"Okay, this is totally a photo op." Queenie and the rest of the girls take a thousand pictures in less than five seconds.

"I'll see you in a bit. Have fun with the girls." Jake drops a quick kiss on my lips and disappears out the door.

Lainey, Paxton, and Violet have their heads together. "Oh, this is just too much. It almost makes me want Alex to go through with having his vasectomy reversed," Violet says.

"Wait. What?" Lainey puts one hand over her belly and the other comes up to her mouth. "You want to have another baby?"

Violet raises her hand. "I said almost. Four kids are enough for me. I love them all, but the twins nearly broke my vagina on the way out. And my brother has six freaking kids. And you all keep popping out the babies." She motions to the group of women and pats Lainey's tiny bump. "And I know the two of you are up soon." She points to Queenie and Stevie. "So I'm going to auntie it up and be happy that I can pass the babies back when they start crying."

"That's fair. I keep telling Shippy we should get a dog so he can get used to the idea of kids, since they're like training wheels for wanna-be parents, but he's worried that Dicken won't adjust well."

"Isn't Dicken his brother's cat?"

"Yeah." Stevie wraps her teal hair around her finger. "It's not his best argument since Dicken doesn't even live with us anymore."

"I think Bishop would make a great dad," Lainey says.

"Does he want kids?" Violet asks.

"Shippy wants whatever I want. He'd let me adopt a freaking walrus if I said I wanted one. The issue with the dog and the kids is that Shippy isn't the best at sharing. And kids mean he's not the top priority anymore. He's also worried about the impact on our sex life."

"Well, the last worry is a legit one. It sure does have an impact on the sexy times. Or at least the frequency and the location." Violet nods solemnly.

"Mom, I can hear you, and there are already enough reasons for me to need therapy without this being one of them!" Robbie yells over his shoulder.

"I guess it's a good thing your dad has a great medical plan then, isn't it?"

He turns his head slowly, gives her the side-eye, while muttering "*indeed*" before turning back to his book.

"That kid's sense of humor is drier than beef jerky." She looks to me. "Anyway, I have to say, you are honestly the most badass mother I have ever met. Most of the time I'm in bed by ten because the four of them suck all the energy out of me." She thumbs over her shoulder. She could direct traffic with all the hand gestures. She makes a face and drops her voice. "Actually, it's just Maverick who does that. He's a pure hybrid of his dad and my mother. I'm terrified of what's going to happen when he's a teenager."

"He seems like a pretty good kid." I glance over to where he and Kody are sitting, watching the game.

"He is. A little impulsive and probably too smart for his own good, but definitely a good kid. It's great that he has Kody around. He's a real rule follower, kind of like King."

"That's just his personality. He always loved the rules. Still does." Whenever he takes JJ, he follows the naptime routine like it's the law.

"Except when it comes to Queenie." Violet smirks.

"If it wasn't for Queenie, I wouldn't have any of this." I motion to the group of women I've come to love like a family, especially since I made the decision to move to Seattle.

Queenie slips between the girls and wraps an arm around my waist. "I'm so grateful that you and King came into our lives."

"Me, too, Queenie. Me, too."

The sound of cheers coming from the jumbotron has us all

turning to see what's going on. I expect we've been so immersed in our conversation that we've missed the beginning of the second period. But that's not it at all.

On the screen is Jake. He's gotten rid of the carrier and he's holding baby JJ in his arms, and beside him is Ryan.

I can see the family resemblance.

Pieces of myself, of Jake, of Ryan.

JJ may have come along when we least expected him, but he's certainly going to know what it's like to be part of a big, amazing family who loves him with our whole heart.

EPILOGUE

Strangely Perfect, Perfectly Strange

Jake

"DA-EE! CAN I show Scout how to play hockey? Pee-se!" JJ pulls on the hem of my shorts, looking up at me with his wide, dark eyes. His hair is the same color as Hanna's and has the same unruly waves. It appears as though we never brush it, and there's a flip at the front that makes him look like he's part of an aspiring toddler boy band.

I crouch down so I'm at eye level with my son. There's some kind of orange residue around his mouth. Probably from a Popsicle. I pat my pockets, but I don't have a tissue on me. "You've got something on your face," I tell him.

I'm about to try to wipe it away with my thumb, but he twists his head away. "Mommy will get it for me. She more gentle than you."

I chuckle. He's not wrong about that. Hanna is a gentle soul. And that softness and warmth make her an incredible, patient mother.

"You can give it a try, but he might not be able to get the hang of it. Tell the boys to use the foam pucks and make sure Scout gets the red plastic stick, okay?"

"Okay. Thanks, Da-ee." He runs full tilt to where Queenie is sitting with my grandson, Scout, at her side, eating what I'm guessing is probably his seventeenth Arrowroot biscuit. That kid always has food in his mouth and he's forever holding a sippy cup of milk. He seems to be a lot like his dad in that respect.

Alex, Ryan, and I watch as JJ skids to a stop in front of Queenie and Hanna. "You want me to tell the boys to switch out the plastic pucks?" Ryan asks.

I shake my head. "Nah, they know the drill."

And they do. Because we spend a lot of time together. It's the best kind of built-in family.

And even better is the fact JJ gets to grow up with his nephew Scout. Is the dynamic a bit strange? Definitely. But it's only brought me closer to my daughter and my son-in-law, and nothing in the world beats that kind of love. JJ keeps me young in ways I didn't expect, and I feel like the second time around I'm better prepared to handle raising a child. It helps that I have a partner who loves our son with the same intensity I do.

Hanna beckons JJ closer and takes his chin between her finger and thumb. Then she reaches into her purse and pulls out a wipe, clearing away whatever that orange business is on our son's face. When she's done, she plants a kiss on his puckered lips, then showers him with kisses and he giggles, burying his face in her side.

Eventually, he must ask about hockey, because both Queenie and Hanna look over where the older boys are shooting the puck around.

Queenie nods and JJ takes Scout's pudgy hand in his, leading him to the edge of the rubberized hockey rink.

Kody and Maverick stop passing the puck as soon as they approach and they set up the "little kid" net, showing them how to shoot and aim. Maverick works hard at the sport, and Kody is the kind of natural that takes your breath away.

He's almost flawless.

I can't wait to watch him grow into his talent, and I'm almost sad that I'll be retired by the time he's ready to start his professional career. JJ could go either way. He's equally as athletic as he is artistic. I'm excited to see him grow into his own person.

I turn my attention back to Hanna. She and Queenie have a unique relationship. They're like sisters, but at the same time, she's very much become someone Queenie goes to when she needs a mother figure.

JJ may have been an accident, but without him, I don't think I'd have realized what my life had been missing. A partner. A confidant. Someone to parent with, not around.

The last four years have been amazing. Exhausting, but amazing.

Having a child in your forties is no joke. The sleepless nights, the juggling work and family, and everything that life throws at you aren't always easy, but I wouldn't trade it for the world.

After JJ was born, Hanna and I had a long discussion about what she wanted. I knew what I wanted as far as our relationship went. I'd known for months. I'd gone out and bought the engagement ring two weeks after JJ was born. I didn't want to push too fast, worried I'd repeat the same mistakes as I had last time. But Hanna is a different woman. She's invested in our son and us, as a couple and a family.

Still, I don't ever want her to feel boxed in, so I let her set the speed. Two months after JJ was born, Hanna gave notice and broke her lease, aware she wasn't ever going to stay there and the only time it ever got used was when we went on one of our grocery shopping trips. Which we made a habit of visiting every week until the lease ran out. After that, she figured we could drop JJ off at King and Queenie's if we really needed to swing from the rafters. Which we've done a couple of times.

At the five-month mark, we had another discussion, this time about her return-to-work plan. It coincided with JJ learning how to roll over and his first teeth. The waking up in the middle of the night because his gums hurt was taking its toll on both of us. We knew it was temporary, though. So we powered through it. But we also knew there were more milestones coming, and we still had a handful of years before JJ was school age.

I want her to have the full motherhood experience, whatever

that looks like for her. I don't want her to have any regrets. And she is a phenomenal mother. Dedicated, patient, loving, and so, so gentle.

Six months after JJ was born, Hanna made the call to shift from her modified remote schedule with her accounting firm to working with Violet on a contract basis. It was the perfect solution and gave her the freedom she needed and the independence she loves. And the opportunity to work with one of my closest friends' wife was definitely a plus. She needs her own friend group and colleagues to talk shop with, and I'll support her in whatever way she needs me to.

Because she's not only the mother of our child, she's my partner in every way.

Seven months after JJ was born, I proposed.

She said yes.

We got married the following summer and JJ was our ring bearer.

Along with my daughter, Hanna and JJ are the best things to happen to me.

I thought I had everything I needed, until they came along.

And gave my heart a home.

ACKNOWLEDGEMENTS

When readers asked for Jake and Hanna's story, I knew I was going to get to do something I never had before. But then I realized what I needed most, and what Hanna needed the most, was to have the experience she wanted but never got when she was a teenager, and that meant I not only got to write characters my own age, but I was also writing a very complicated family dynamic and the challenges and potential complications that came with pregnancy later in life. It's a departure from my norm, and I'll be honest, I spent a lot of this book on the verge of tears, not because I was scared to write it, but because, as a mom, all of those fears and worries about parenting are so very relatable. And real.

I loved being back in this world. I loved giving Hanna and Jake their happily ever after. But more than that, I loved exploring Hanna's relationship with King, and how Jake and Hanna's histories and experiences allowed them to be empathetic, loving, and patient.

Kidlet, you're my favorite creation. I'm so glad I have you and your dad in my life. You teach me that love is boundless.

Pepper, thirteen years and a billion releases later, I'm still as grateful as I was the day I first busted into your messages and forced you to be my friend.

Kimberly, thank you for always being there to talk things through. You make me a better storyteller.

Sarah, you are magic, and I am so lucky to have you in my life and my world.

Hustlers, I couldn't ask for a better book family. You're my crew, and I love you.

Tijan, you're such an amazing human being. Thank you for sharing your friendship with me.

Sarah, Jenn, Hilary, Shan, Catherine, and my entire team at Social Butterfly, you're fabulous, and I couldn't do it without you.

Sarah and Gel, your incredible talent never ceases to amaze me. Thank you for sharing it with me. Lindsey, thank you for helping me make this a better story with your insight. Paige, thank you for your eagle eye and grammar skills. To my ARC review crew, thank you for ironing out the fine details with me, your support means the world. Julia and Amanda, thank you for catching all those little things and helping me polish this story.

Beavers, thank you for giving me a safe place to land, and for always being excited about what's next, especially this one, because I doubt it was what you expected, and you still showed up for it.

Deb, Tijan, Leigh, Kelly, Ruth, Kellie, Erika, Marty, Karen, Shalu, Melanie, Marnie, Julie, Krystin, Laurie, Angie, Angela, Jo, and Lou, your friendship, guidance, support, and insight keep me grounded. Thank you for being such wonderful and inspiring women in my life.

Readers, bloggers, and bookstagrammers, thank you for your love of books, of romance, and of happily ever afters. I'm lucky to have you in my corner.

OTHER TITLES BY HELENA HUNTING

New York Times Bestselling Author

HELENA HUNTING

NYT and USA Today bestselling author of PUCKED, Helena Hunting lives on the outskirts of Toronto with her incredibly tolerant family and two moderately intolerant cats. She writes contemporary romance ranging from new adult angst to romantic sports comedy.

Find more books by Helena Hunting
by visiting helenahunting.com